Something or Everything

Lily St. Michael

ISBN-13:9781699646748

Lily St. Michael's Website:
https://callalil1.wixsite.com/lstm

Dedication

"You know what's really powerfully sexy? A sense of humor. A taste for adventure. A healthy glow. Hips to grab onto. Openness. Confidence. Humility. Appetite. Intuition. Smart-ass comebacks. Presence. A quick wit. Dirty jokes told by an innocent-looking lady. A woman who realizes how beautiful she is." - Courtney E. Martin

For all of the women in my life - Friends, lovers, confidantes, sisters, and partners in crime. Especially those who have reminded me that my glass is half-full, that I need to keep moving forward and that life should be fun.

Be nice. Siempre en frente.

Chapter 1

It was the voice that did her in.

"A lemon drop martini with a sugar rim, please."

Maddie had noticed the woman as soon as she walked in because she was attractive and impeccably dressed, but it was definitely the voice that did her in. Maddie had almost shivered when she heard its distinctively deep and raspy quality. It was the type of voice that Maddie had heard referred to as "whiskey-soaked", but what she simply considered sexy as hell.

Maddie smiled as she realized that she couldn't remember the last time a woman had captured her attention in this way, and that might explain why she was presently celibate and had been for longer than she cared to admit. The celibacy was the consequence of never being able to reconcile her preference for women with the circumstances of her life.

Maddie had deliberately ignored her natural attraction to women for years and she had assumed that her sex drive had simply gone dormant from neglect. This woman had just blown that theory completely out of the water and that simple realization was enough to make Maddie feel slightly off balance. The instant and intense attraction she felt surprised her, as she had successfully hidden these feelings for longer than she could remember.

Maddie had found herself giving the woman a very long look as she walked in, something she had trained herself to never do, but she couldn't seem to help herself. The woman carried herself confidently and wore a beautifully tailored business suit that hinted at her full figure. The fabric was charcoal colored with a classic white vertical pinstripe. The jacket had black and white accents at the collar and pockets, and the skirt had a kick pleat at the back. The starched white blouse beneath was unbuttoned low enough to be tantalizing but the French cuffs with real cufflinks added a nice touch of masculinity. The glimpse of the red soles of her pumps identified the Louboutins gracing her feet and Maddie wondered if they were real or good knock-offs. Her shoulder-length, light brown hair was thick and straight, the cut and subtle blonde highlights suited to her lovely features perfectly, as was her light and understated make-up.

While taking her drink order, Maddie tried not to become completely distracted by her full lips, straight nose and clear, crystal blue eyes. When the woman smiled, small laugh lines crinkled at the corners of her eyes. She reminded Maddie of an old-fashioned movie star, especially with the Lauren Bacall voice.

The woman smiled as Maddie placed the lemon drop in front of her. "Thank you. By the way, I really love your earrings," she purred in that lovely, rich alto tone.

"Thanks," Maddie said, self-consciously reaching for one of her large silver teardrop earrings.

"They're beautiful but I don't think I could pull those off," the woman said.

Maddie shook her head. "Oh, I think you could pull anything off," she said flirtatiously before she could censor herself.

The woman's laughter was rich and deep. "That might be the best line I've ever heard."

Maddie smiled. "Not a line. Just my honest opinion."

"Well, thank you, Tracy."

Maddie looked down at the nametag pinned to her vest and laughed lightly. "Tracy's not my name. I'm required to wear a nametag when I work here, but I refuse to let any of these people know my real name." Maddie held her hand out and made sure that her grip was firm, her gaze direct. "I'm Maddie."

The woman shook her hand and smiled. "Hello, Maddie, I'm Julia."

It was still early in the evening so the lounge inside the elegant Boston hotel held a good number of patrons but was still reasonably quiet. Maddie went back to expertly dispensing another draft beer into a pilsner glass, automatically tipping it to minimize the foam forming at the top. She slid the full glass toward the young man in a wrinkled suit waiting for it and took his offered debit card as he began a stuttered request to buy her a drink after her shift. She schooled her features into a pleasant mask as she started to shake her head in polite refusal, the bogus excuse about already having a date automatic and instantly forgotten. She had grown accustomed to her fair share of unwanted attention while doing this particular job but still found it tedious.

Maddie watched her rejected suitor as he took his beer and sauntered over to try his luck with the sexy-voiced Julia. He was politely but firmly dismissed, much to Maddie's amusement. She knew he would be shot down, but she couldn't blame him for trying, especially with this woman. Even Maddie was having trouble keeping her gaze from repeatedly straying over to her. Julia met

Maddie's gaze and smiled at her, quickly winking at her in solidarity as Maddie smiled back.

Maddie tried to concentrate while she poured bourbon over rocks but when she glanced over again, Julia was slowly lifting the martini glass to her full lips, her throat moving as she swallowed. When Julia finished the generous sip, she slowly licked her full lips and Maddie felt her breath hitch at the tantalizing sight. Maddie lowered her gaze, reminding herself not to stare, wondering what in the world had come over her.

When Danny, the bar manager, arrived to relieve her for the last shift of the night, Maddie removed the required bow tie and fitted vest of her bartending uniform and sat at the opposite end of the bar. She unbuttoned the cuffs of her white uniform blouse and rolled up the sleeves, casually gazing over the clientele, once again lingering on Julia. Maddie couldn't remember the last time she had allowed herself the simple pleasure of looking at a woman with appreciation, and she could not seem to stop looking at this one.

"Someone caught your eye, Layna?" Danny's soft voice startled her. Since Danny knew her brother, he used the name her family called her. She answered to Layna reflexively, but she thought of herself as Maddie and always would.

Maddie smiled. "The lemon drop martini at the end of the bar."

Maddie did not often let her guard down in this way, accustomed to automatically concealing her appreciation for women, but she and Danny had worked together for years and he had always been observant, sympathetic and thankfully, discreet.

Danny returned her smile. "Ah, the always classy Ms. Sinclair. She's been in before. I remember her because she's a good tipper."

"Not because she's gorgeous?" Maddie teased him about his eye for the ladies.

"Well, yes, that too, and because she attracts a lot of attention whenever she's in here."

Maddie nodded. "She doesn't seem to want the attention, though. She's just having a drink...minding her own business."

Danny shrugged. "As usual for her, but you must know how it is, Layna, being very easy on the eyes yourself. I'm sure it's hard for you to have a drink alone in peace. She's not interested, but a real looker, so they keep trying."

Maddie shook her head. "I'm hardly in the same league," Maddie said as she tried not to stare as the very attractive Julia Sinclair crossed her legs.

Danny snorted. "Don't sell yourself short, Layna. You're like a daughter to me, but I got eyes. I can see how pretty you are."

"You need glasses, old man," Maddie teased him.

He flicked the bar rag at her playfully. "Why don't you stick around for a while tonight? Have a drink? Keep me company?"

Maddie usually refused his offers, but the object of her interest chose that moment to look up and meet her gaze, smiling at her softly. Maddie returned the smile and nodded at Danny. "I think I will, Danny. I don't need to get home tonight. Gabe is away for the weekend." She watched as Julia impatiently dismissed another hopeful suitor attempting to start a conversation with her. "Maybe I'll go keep the classy Ms. Sinclair company."

"You know I won't say a word to anyone," Danny said quietly, referring to her practice of keeping her personal life private. "And that'd be a pretty view for me." Danny wiggled his eyebrows playfully.

Maddie surprised herself as she slowly but confidently approached the seemingly unattainable Julia Sinclair, but her intention was simply to make a friendly offer to share a drink. Besides, what did she have to lose? She watched the woman's long fingers playing with her martini glass before she found herself caught by the intense blue gaze that suddenly met her own and studied her carefully. Standing this close to the woman, Maddie noticed light freckles sprinkled across her naturally creamy complexion.

"Excuse me, Julia." Maddie smiled at her. "I don't want to intrude, but maybe it would help to dissuade the bar rats if I sat with you for a few minutes and you could at least finish your martini in relative peace?"

Julia returned her smile easily, cocking her head. "And it's such a delicious martini. I'd love the company, but I'm not sure it will help. From what I've seen, I'd just have to fend them off of you instead of me."

Maddie decided that she couldn't get enough of the woman's raspy alto voice and she felt her face warming in a blush as she replied. "Well, thank you, but I used to waitress in some pretty sketchy places and I know how to discourage the most persistent Romeos."

"Well then, how can I refuse? You're a bodyguard, as well as the best-looking thing in here."

Maddie tried to gracefully slide onto the adjacent bar chair as she ran her gaze slowly and deliberately up and down Julia's form before she responded. "Thanks, but I beg to differ on that last one."

Julia smiled, her eyes crinkling at the corners, her bright blue gaze on Maddie. "Thank you. You're off duty now I take it? Please let me buy you a drink, Maddie."

"Thanks for offering, but I'm not angling for a free drink. Believe me, just your company will do nicely." Danny placed a margarita in front of her and Maddie smiled at him. "Danny, you are a prince, a mensch, meu querido." Maddie took a long sip of her drink. "Perfect, Danny, as always, thank you."

Danny bowed and smiled. "Anything for you, Layna."

Maddie held out a $20 bill to Danny, but the woman placed her hand gently over Maddie's. "Oh, no. It's Danny, isn't it? Please put the young lady's drink on my tab, please. Suite 4802."

Danny nodded. "Yes, ma'am, Ms. Sinclair." He winked at Maddie as he turned and left.

Maddie watched as she discretely slid some bills over the inside edge of the bar to tip Danny in cash and then turn to her. "I'm confused. Your nametag said 'Tracy' but you told me your name is Maddie, so why did he just call you Elena?"

"My name is Madalena Francisco."

"Mad-a-LAY-na?" Julia sounded out her name. "That's a beautiful name."

Maddie smiled. "Thanks. Danny actually called me Layna, short for Madalena, because he knows my brother and that's what my family calls me. I prefer Maddie." Maddie held up her glass. "It wasn't necessary, but thank you for the drink. So, are you staying here or just drinking here?"

"Both. I attended a conference here today and I knew I'd be too tired to fight the commuter traffic and drive home. How about you? Have you worked here long?"

Maddie shook her head. "On and off for many years but I don't actually work here anymore. I have a regular day job, but Danny

7

still calls me to cover shifts for extra cash on evenings and weekends when they're short-handed. I don't think I've ever actually had a drink here before."

"So you don't make a habit of rescuing bar patrons when you're off duty?"

Maddie smiled. "No. I've never done anything like this before in my life."

"Why me then? Do I look that helpless?" Julia asked as she took a generous sip of her martini.

Maddie gave Julia a pointed stare, her eyes widening. "We both know that's not even the slightest bit true. You seem much more than capable of handling yourself. I know what it's like to just want a drink at the end of a long day with no pressure or expectations."

"Well it's very much appreciated. It does get a bit much when they can't take a hint. I'm hoping they think I've gotten lucky with you." Julia whispered the last sentence.

Maddie's eyes widened at the unexpected compliment. "I think I would be the one getting lucky here," Maddie whispered back, beyond flattered.

Julia laughed lightly, the low register sounding sexy to Maddie's ears. "Okay, that might be the best line I've ever heard."

Maddie smiled as she shook her head. "Once again, not a line." Maddie heard Julia release an impatient sigh and noticed the young man in the wrinkled suit she had served beer to earlier sauntering over. He had already struck out with both of them but here he was again. Maddie gave him points for persistence.

He cleared his throat loudly. "Hey there, Stacy, I thought you said you had a date after your shift?" He was looking at Maddie.

Maddie winked at Julia. "Excuse me. Yes, I did...and here I am...on the date."

The young man frowned, looking bewildered and Maddie tried not to smile as she watched him scramble mentally, his eyes blinking rapidly. Obviously confused, he nonetheless forged ahead. "So, then...not a real date. Who's your friend?"

Before Maddie could reply, Julia leaned toward her, placing a gentle hand on her arm. "Would you allow me?" Julia whispered.

"Go for it," Maddie answered softly.

Maddie watched as Julia straightened her posture and turned to look directly at her clueless admirer. "Pardon me, young man, I'm not her friend. I am indeed her real date. So...thanks so much for stopping by and gracing us with your sparkling personality, but *Tracy* is busy...and quite taken."

The young man's frown deepened as he looked from Julia to Maddie and back to Julia. "You two can't...you're not..."

Maddie was surprised as Julia smiled and leaned closer to her, the scent of Julia's perfume wafting pleasantly under her nose. "Oh, we can and we do and..." Julia glanced around quickly, as if to ensure that they were alone. "...she's fucking amazing," Julia said, her voice lowering conspiratorially.

Maddie pressed her lips together, trying not to laugh out loud as she heard the young man audibly gasp behind her. She found herself leaning forward, resting her head against Julia's shoulder, shaking with silent laughter as Julia moved her hand to gently caress the back of her neck with the tips of her fingers in a blatantly proprietary gesture. Maddie knew they were simply play-acting, but she found that she enjoyed this woman's gentle caress. It had been too long since Maddie had felt the touch of another woman in this way and it felt good, albeit slightly forbidden.

9

"He's found a clue and he's gone," Julia whispered near her ear.

Maddie lifted her head and looked at Julia, smiling widely. "Well, that was impressive and it worked like a charm. Thank you."

"It was my pleasure. What a clueless ass. He couldn't even get your phony name right. Anyway, I'm sorry if I embarrassed you."

"What? No. Why would I be embarrassed?"

"Because I'm sure he's telling his merry band of drunken revelers over there that the only reason he keeps striking out is because we're lesbians. I couldn't care less, but you do have to work here," Julia said.

Maddie smiled at Julia's concern. "If that particular rumor spreads it'd only make my life here easier and I'd be flattered if they think I could actually get a woman like you."

Julia stared at her for a long beat, her gaze running slowly over her features. "Oh, trust me, sweetie, you could...easily. I'm the one who looks like a desperate cougar here, trying to pick up the young and beautiful bartender."

Julia's low, deliciously raspy voice calling her beautiful made Maddie shiver. "Just stop it," Maddie said. "You're not that much older than me."

Julia released a surprised laugh. "You are a very sweet girl."

Maddie leaned closer. "I'm afraid I'm neither one of those things...and you smell fabulous, by the way."

Julia smiled at the comment. "Why thank you. So do you."

"I'm not wearing perfume."

"No? You smell really nice. Like…lemons and vanilla."

The realization that this woman was attentive enough to recognize and note the subtle scents of her shampoo and body lotion made Maddie feel flattered and warm. She took a long drink from her own glass and noticed that Julia was spinning the stem of her empty martini glass with her fingers.

"So, Maddie, tell me, do you have time for more than a drink?" Julia asked quietly.

Maddie paused at the question. "I guess that depends." Maddie decided to go with the flow for once instead of worrying about anything at all, including her suspicion that Julia might actually return her interest. She looked at Julia closely, meeting and holding her gaze. "Are you…trying to pick me up?"

Julia smiled widely. "No…and not because you aren't deserving of that kind of effort because, trust me, sweetie, you most certainly are."

"Thank you." Maddie's pleasure at the compliment was tempered with a sharp stab of disappointment that Julia was not interested in her in the way she had hoped.

"I'm enjoying your company very much and I hate to eat alone, so…can I buy you dinner? On the slim chance that someone like you doesn't already have plans for the evening."

"Someone like me?" Maddie asked, not understanding the inference.

"Yes, sweetie, look at you. Someone as lovely as you…would have to have plans on a Friday night."

Maddie smiled. "You're sweet for saying that but I have no plans this evening. I wouldn't ordinarily be this free, but my son is spending the weekend with his father."

"You have a little one?" Julia asked.

Maddie laughed at the question. "Little? He's 16 and taller than me."

Julia's eyebrows rose in apparent surprise. "Did you have him when you were 10?"

"No, but I wasn't much older than he is now." Maddie shook her head, trying to shake the memories from that time in her life.

Julia's hand rested on her forearm. "The same thing happened to me...but I was a little older than you. I married her father, which I regret, but I never regretted having her."

Maddie covered Julia's hand with her own. "I feel the same way about my son."

Julia nodded, and then she frowned, looking as though she was working through something. "I just did some quick math in my head. I'm a good 10 years older than you."

Maddie squeezed Julia's hand and smiled as she slowly perused her features, deciding to say exactly what she was thinking. "Look at you...you can't possibly be."

"Charmer," Julia whispered. "So, how's the restaurant here in the hotel?"

"The Essex? I hear it's very good, but it's also very expensive."

"Sounds perfect."

"Here? No, we can't. I can't," Maddie said, her eyes widening in surprise at the suggestion. The Essex was so far above her price range she had never even considered dining there.

"It's my treat, please," Julia reassured her.

Maddie looked down at her uniform of black slacks and white buttoned shirt, suddenly feeling way out of Julia's league. "Thank you, really, but I'm not dressed for it."

Julia slid off the bar chair and gestured to Maddie to do the same and they stood facing each other. Julia looked her up and down and smiled. "May I?" Julia asked.

Maddie nodded, not sure what she had given Julia permission to do, but not wanting to discourage this woman's focused and flattering attention. Julia reached her hands past Maddie's shoulders and gently pulled off the tie holding her ponytail, loosening her hair gently with her fingers. Maddie vigorously shook her hair out, her natural waves falling loosely around her shoulders. Julia smiled widely at the transformation.

"Your hair is gorgeous. Do you have lipstick?" Julia asked.

Maddie reached into her pants pocket and pulled out her lipstick, applying it generously as Julia stepped back and pulled her own suit jacket off and down her arms, leaving her in just the skirt and crisp white blouse. She held it out to Maddie.

"Try this on. It'll be a little too big on you, but I think it will work with those slacks." Maddie looked at the beautiful designer jacket, hesitating. Julia shook the jacket at her. "Just do it."

Maddie slid the jacket on, still warm from Julia's body heat and smelling like her perfume. Julia smiled as she stepped forward to adjust the collar of Maddie's blouse under the jacket and then brought a thumb up to correct the line of lipstick along her bottom

13

lip. Julia looked her up and down slowly and Maddie almost shivered at the intimate gaze.

"Am I acceptable?" Maddie asked.

"You're more than acceptable. I'll have the best looking date in the restaurant," Julia said softly.

"You cannot be serious," Maddie said. "I will. Have you looked in the mirror lately?"

Julia cocked her head. "Sure I have. I'm...very well put together, but you, Maddie, you're beyond lovely."

Maddie smiled at the compliment, wondering if she had ever been so flattered in her entire life. "Wow. You're already the best date I've had in forever."

Julia wiggled her eyebrows playfully at her. "Wait until I wine and dine you."

Chapter 2

Julia smiled at Maddie as they walked toward the restaurant, thinking that she couldn't remember the last time she had met someone and instantly developed this kind of connection. Julia had certainly noticed Maddie earlier when she had ordered a martini from her because she was a natural beauty, especially when she smiled, displaying deep dimples in smooth olive toned skin. Her hair was dark and shiny, curling naturally at the ends. She wore large and distinctive silver earrings and little or no make-up and her eyes were dark and almond shaped. Julia had looked up several times while sitting at the bar to find that dark, curious gaze directed at her. Julia found the young woman to be personable and charming and just the kind of pleasant distraction that she needed after a long day.

Julia allowed Maddie to walk slightly ahead of her, holding a gentle hand against the small of her back to guide her as they strolled into the restaurant, being respectful but making it obvious to anyone looking that they were together. Julia suddenly knew how men felt when having an attractive woman on their arm. Julia confidently strode to the maître d' station and smiled widely, pouring on the charm to get a good table without a reservation. Julia realized that she was actually trying to impress Maddie.

Once seated, Julia noticed that Maddie seemed uncomfortable and realized she was probably feeling out of her element, the rich décor of wooden columns and leather upholstered seating rather pretentious. Julia tried to put her at ease, chatting to her about the menu and suggesting dishes they could share, as well as politely asking her permission before she ordered a bottle of wine for the two of them to share. Julia was pleasantly surprised to find that

Maddie had an adventurous palette, willing to try anything Julia suggested.

Julia smiled at Maddie as they were sharing a seafood sampler appetizer. "Thank you for doing this. I can't remember the last time I've done something this spontaneously."

Maddie shook her head. "Are you kidding? I've always wanted to eat here and you're really good company."

"I'm enjoying your company as well. So, what would you be doing tonight if you hadn't rescued me?" Julia asked.

"To be honest, I would be sitting at home in my sweats, probably eating a BLT and doing homework," Maddie replied. "I'm almost done with my degree."

"What kind of degree?"

"Business Management. I'm an Administrative Assistant at an advertising and public relations firm and a Bachelor's will bump up my salary and my title to Executive Assistant. It would also make me eligible for entry-level management positions." Maddie said. "I also do some freelance graphic design."

Julia realized she was staring and shook her head slightly. "You're an impressive woman, Madalena Francisco. You're a single mother...you work a full-time job and two part-time jobs...and you go to school?"

Maddie shrugged. "I just do what I have to do to make ends meet. Thankfully, my family has always helped with Gabriel, that's my son, and he spends time with his Dad and Stepmom regularly. They're very nice people, thank God."

"What do you do for fun?"

"My son likes hiking and the Red Sox so if it's his turn to choose, we do bleacher seats at Fenway or the Blue Hills reservation. I like art so if it's my turn to choose...it's usually a museum or art exhibit." Maddie smiled. "I know more about baseball than I ever imagined, but have become a fan and Gabe knows more about art than he ever imagined, but he's actually become interested in sculpture and wood carving."

"What kind of art do you like?" Julia asked, wanting to know more about this young woman. That was surprising since it had been a long time since she had had this kind of interest in anyone.

"Every kind really, the creative process fascinates me, but especially a group of artists known as the Hudson River painters. Sanford Gifford is my favorite."

"Hudson River are landscape painters, right?" Julia asked, grateful that she had recalled this random fact.

Maddie smiled at her widely. "You know art?"

"Not really. What is it about Gifford that you like?" Julia asked.

"I love the way he uses light in his landscapes. Beautiful and almost...spiritual. To me anyway."

"My youngest daughter loves to Google so we're going to be looking him up."

"How old are your daughters?"

Julia smiled. "Eleanor is 13...going on 30. Vivienne is 22."

"I can't believe you have a daughter that age and I love their names."

Julia was flattered by Maddie's compliment. "Thank you. So, what do you do...just for you?"

Maddie smiled. "I read. I love weird little art house films...I study Buddhism...do yoga...and I love beachcombing, even in bad weather."

"Wow. You're so much more than just a gorgeous face, aren't you? Buddhism, huh? Do you meditate?"

"Yes. Do you?"

"I try to. What do you read?" Julia asked quietly.

"I'm partial to historical biographies."

"Really? Me, too."

Maddie laughed lightly. "Are you kidding? What are you reading right now?"

"A biography of Jane Digby. I can't put it down. I'll let you have it when I'm done," Julia said, surprising herself with the offer. She realized that she wanted this encounter with Maddie to develop into something more and be repeated. Julia kept her gaze on Maddie for a long moment, wondering why she felt so drawn to this young woman.

"Thank you," Maddie said quietly. "Wow. I don't often meet someone...like-minded, I guess. I don't really fit in with the rest of my family. I think they consider me to be a bit of an odd duck."

"I don't think you're an odd duck at all. I think you're really interesting. You bring to mind the proverb 'still waters run deep'."

Maddie stared at her for a minute and Julia thought she looked a little surprised at her comments. She wondered about Maddie's family and if they had instilled the little glimpses of insecurity that she had revealed.

Maddie smiled. "Thank you. The last time I tried to share my interests with someone I had just met on a blind date, I had to explain...in detail...what all of them were, except for the beachcombing and that was because he thought I was using a metal detector for that."

Julia laughed lightly. "What kind of people are you dating?"

"The unsuitable kind. My family is always trying to fix me up with people who are completely wrong for me. If this was a blind date, I'd be thrilled since you have already surpassed any and all previous candidates," Maddie said.

Maddie's statement made Julia excited in a way she did not quite understand. "I'm glad because you certainly deserve the attention," Julia said, trying not to openly stare at Maddie, but failing miserably.

Maddie lowered her gaze. "So...what about you? What do you do...just for you?"

"I read and I walk. I like eating out and trying new things. But that's when I'm not helping my youngest daughter with her homework...or checking my e-mail or following up on any number of things I didn't get to at the office," Julia explained.

"What kind of office?"

"Real estate," Julia said.

"Are you an agent?"

"Broker. I have my own agency. Vivienne works for me."

"Commercial or residential?"

Julia liked that Maddie was not only interested, but she also asked intelligent questions. "Mainly residential."

"Here in the city?"

"Oh, no. On the south coast, the greater New Bedford area. I live in Fairhaven."

Maddie smiled widely. "You're kidding? I love Fairhaven. It's where Gabe's Dad and Stepmom live."

Julia smiled back, happy to know that Maddie might have an excuse to be in her area sometime in the future. "Really? The next time you're down that way again, please look me up. Butler Flats Realty. I'll give you a tour of the area and maybe we can do this again."

"I'd love to." Maddie started to say something else and then hesitated.

Julia cocked her head. "What were you going to say?"

Maddie shrugged. "Just being nosy. I was wondering...is there no one special in your life?"

Julia snorted. "No, not for a long time. After two divorces, I have finally learned my lesson. It's just easier being alone. Anyway...how about you? You're single?"

"Yes. I have no time to date really, with Gabriel, and work and school...and when I've had the opportunity..."

Julia reached over and touched her hand, encouraging her to continue. "What?"

Maddie's gaze met Julia's. "I'm torn between what my heart wants and what everyone else expects from me and I don't want to settle...so I simply...stopped trying."

Julia was surprised at her reaction to this young woman's confession, thinking that anyone would be lucky to be the object of her attention and affection. "You absolutely should not settle. You have a lot to offer someone, Maddie, and you should stay true to yourself. You're a real catch."

"What about you? Look at you. You're smart and beautiful and God, confident as hell," Maddie stated. "I'm not sure I've ever been this impressed with anyone before."

Julia felt her eyebrows lift in delighted surprise, as flattered as she could ever remember being. "Thank you, really, but confidence is simply having enough of an attitude to go after what you want. Unfortunately, I seem to have terrible luck with men."

Maddie laughed lightly as she tipped her wineglass at Julia. "Maybe you should try a woman."

Julia met and held Maddie's gaze for a long beat, the suggestive flirtation affecting her physically, her breath catching in her throat. She found her gaze settled on Maddie's mouth and she wondered what it would be like to kiss her. Maddie licked her lips and Julia felt herself swallow at the sexy gesture.

"Maybe I should," Julia finally whispered, shocked at her own reaction. Julia was trying to decide if Maddie was simply teasing her or was trying to convey a message, but Maddie shyly lowered her gaze and finished the glass of wine in her hand, the moment allowed to pass by the both of them.

After they shared a dessert, Julia signed for the meal and they walked out of the restaurant together. Maddie clutched at Julia's arm and leaned against her. "I can't thank you enough, Julia. The only thing better than the meal was the company and the meal was incredible."

Julia tugged on Maddie's sleeve, wanting to keep Maddie close, wanting the evening to continue. "I'm glad you enjoyed it. Would you like to continue this in my room? I've got a nice bottle of wine chilling."

Maddie stopped and looked at Julia. "Did you just ask me up to your room?"

Julia faltered for a brief moment, realizing that was exactly what she had just done and suddenly not wanting the offer to be interpreted as anything but exactly that.

"I...yes, I did." Maddie simply stared at her for a moment and Julia was afraid she had misinterpreted what seemed to be happening between them. "Have I offended you, Maddie?"

Maddie swallowed. "No. I'm flattered...and tempted...but not offended." Maddie smiled as she looked around with uncertainty. "Are you serious?"

Julia inhaled, taking in Maddie's warm gaze, her dimpled smile. "I'm not sure I've ever been more serious about anything in my entire life." Julia took her hand and gently pulled her into a small alcove, out of the path of passing hotel guests. "Look, we can go back to the bar and get a table if you'd be more comfortable, but I don't want to let you go just yet. I can't tell you how much I'm enjoying your company."

Maddie smiled. "Thank you for saying that." She inhaled deeply. "I would love to have a glass of wine in your room...and continue the conversation."

Julia felt both nervous and excited as she led them into the elevators, making sure to keep a polite distance from Maddie, wondering what the hell she was doing. Julia wondered if she had lost her mind or had simply had way too much to drink. She had never even considered asking anyone she had just met up to her room and certainly never considered it with a woman. Is that why this seemed so natural and so acceptable? Because Maddie was a woman?

Julia had always considered herself to be an open-minded and a "live and let live" kind of person. She had gay friends and gay colleagues and she had admired other women, certainly she had. She had actually thought about the possibility of being with another woman, had even discussed it with her friend Deborah, who was a lesbian, but this, right now, with Maddie, felt entirely different from any of those things.

When Maddie suddenly smiled at Julia she decided that she had definitely not lost her mind or had too much to drink, but she knew that she wanted Maddie. She had realized since dinner that she wanted to know what it would be like to kiss Maddie, but Julia was stunned to realize that she wanted to know even more than that.

Chapter 3

Maddie followed Julia into the small hotel suite, almost overwhelmed by her increasing attraction to Julia and the even more overwhelming fear of possibly giving into that attraction. She hadn't even contemplated the possibility of being with a woman in so many years that she wondered what it was about Julia that had her ready to break what had been the one absolute hard and fast rule of her life. She inhaled deeply, taking in the rich décor of Julia's suite. The woodwork was painted white, the wallpaper was textured and striped, and the plush mauve colored carpeting extended past the open French doors into the adjacent bedroom. She felt completely out of her depth, in this posh hotel room, and with this woman, who seemed to have bewitched her.

"I've never been in one of the rooms here," Maddie said quietly.

Julia smiled. "No? Well, please make yourself comfortable."

Maddie felt Julia's gentle hand on her back guiding her to the living area of the small suite. By the time Julia had opened and poured the wine, they had both kicked off their shoes and had curled up near each other on the small sofa in the room's living area. Neither one found a need to fill the extended silence with idle chatter so they sipped wine and watched each other quietly for a few minutes, both lost in each other, as well as in their own thoughts.

Julia smiled at her. "Maddie, I've never done this before...met someone and felt an instant connection. Being with you is so strangely comfortable, almost as if I already know you, as if you know me."

Maddie watched Julia carefully, deciding the only course of action was to be completely honest. "I feel the same way. I know this is going to sound crazy but earlier, in the bar, when you said you weren't trying to pick me up...I was actually disappointed."

Julia smiled at her. "Were you? God, I'm not sure I've ever been more flattered." Julia rubbed her forehead, looking nervous. "I'm a little out of my element here. I have never invited anyone to my hotel room before and I've never...been with a woman, but I cannot deny what I'm feeling for you."

They stared at each other for a long moment. Maddie took in Julia's deep blue eyes, her full lips and she swallowed as Julia reached out to her. Julia slowly ran the back of her fingers lightly against her face before her thumb brushed softly along her lower lip. Maddie released a small gasp as Julia leaned forward and boldly pressed her lips ever so gently against her own. Maddie parted her own lips slightly to kiss Julia back. Maddie felt faint as they kissed softly, chastely, for a long moment.

They slowly pulled apart and Julia stared at Maddie, reaching out to grasp Maddie's hand. "Are you okay?" Julia asked her and Maddie nodded mutely, staring, stunned at how much she wanted to lose herself in this woman.

Julia leaned forward, licking her lips. "Can I do that again?"

Maddie responded by simply closing the remaining distance between them, brushing their lips together again, this contact lingering. They pulled apart slightly before their lips found each other's again and again, each contact slightly longer than the last. It had been so long that Maddie had forgotten how wonderfully sensual it was to kiss a woman, to feel plush lips, soft skin and to inhale a distinctly feminine scent. Julia kissed her slowly and gently, deliberately planting kiss after kiss until Maddie was returning the favor, the both of them simply getting accustomed to the feel and the texture and the taste of each other.

Maddie discovered that everything about kissing Julia was intensely erotic. The softness, the slow exploration, the small sounds that Julia made, all of it affected her. Maddie heard Julia moan softly as she softly licked the inside of her lower lip. Maddie clutched at the back of Julia's neck, pulling her in and opening her mouth to her. Maddie became lost in the marvel of kissing Julia. Her tongue was wet and smooth and slid against her own slowly, gently, for long intense moments until they slowed the contact, gradually pulling away.

Julia was breathing deeply. "Wow."

Maddie stared at Julia. "I had forgotten...how good...being with a woman feels."

"You've been with a woman before?" Julia asked, sounding surprised.

"Yes, but not...it wasn't." Maddie inhaled deeply, trying to gather her thoughts. "It was a very long time ago and it didn't compare to this. You've never?"

"No." Julia shook her head. "Although, at this moment I can't imagine why the hell not." Julia caressed the side of Maddie's face with the backs of her fingers. "I can't get over how soft you are."

Julia cupped the back of her head and pulled her forward, their mouths pressing together. Maddie heard herself moan as the kiss deepened, their tongues tangling, their breathing turning ragged as it became impossibly more intense and erotic.

Maddie could not hold a clear thought in her head as her mouth was deliciously plundered, as her nipples became painfully stiff and as warm torrents of arousal gently flowed from between her legs. It was so incredibly good that she let Julia snake a hand under her shirt, caressing the skin at her waist as Julia slowly lowered her onto her back. Julia's leg pressed between her own as she lay over Maddie and continued to kiss her deeply. Maddie could not remember if she had ever been so completely and thoroughly aroused in her entire life. Every ounce of her body was vibrating in need and being pulled into the vortex of her desire for Julia, but a small part of her brain balked as old fears and guilt surfaced.

Maddie moved a gentle hand to Julia's shoulder and that was enough for Julia to slow the kiss and pull her mouth away. She caressed Maddie's bottom lip with her thumb. "You okay?"

Maddie nodded. "I...could we slow down?"

"Of course." Julia immediately pulled away and sat back. "I'm sorry."

Maddie sat up and reached for Julia, grasping one of her hands. "No, don't be sorry. I'm right here with you, but thank you...for not being...for not pushing. You're sweet." Maddie sat closer to Julia and ran a hand through her own hair. "I'm just a little freaked out. I do want this to happen. I just don't understand why it's happening now...with you. Why I can't seem to resist you when I've been basically celibate for such a long time."

"How long?" Julia asked with a small smile.

"You wouldn't believe me if I told you. I was involved with a woman a very long time ago...well, a girl really, named Sara. We were so young."

"And what happened?"

Maddie shook her head against the onslaught of bittersweet memories. "We loved each other, but I was raised in a strict Catholic family where being gay was simply not an option. The

29

guilt, the fear of being discovered by my parents was overwhelming. I ended it with her and tried to be...normal but when I found myself pregnant, it only added to the warped tangle of Catholic beliefs about sin and punishment in my head."

Julia leaned forward and placed a soft, sweet kiss to Maddie's forehead. "I'm so sorry you had to go through that. What about since then?"

"For a very long time I have simply...taken care of my own needs." Maddie felt herself blushing.

Julia smiled, squeezing one of Maddie's hands. "Don't be embarrassed. I take care of my own needs as well. So...you haven't been with a woman since then?"

"No. I've struggled quite a bit with these feelings and tried to suppress them. I've tried to date men, but it's just never felt right." Maddie shrugged. "I haven't even seriously thought about being with a woman again...and the opportunity has just never presented itself."

Julia smiled widely, holding her hand out to Maddie. "Hello, I'm Opportunity. Pleased to meet you."

Maddie laughed lightly at Julia's playfulness. "Opportunity has never looked so good or been so tempting."

Julia smiled. "I'm glad that you think so, but I don't want you to do anything if it's going to make you feel anything less than good."

Maddie rubbed her forehead. "I need to be who I am. I'm an adult and the less my parents...my family knows about my personal life, the better. Love shouldn't be conditional," Maddie said.

"No, it shouldn't. How upset would your family be by this?"

"I think everyone would get over it, but my mother...she wouldn't. I can't even imagine what she might do." Maddie shook her head. "It doesn't matter...it won't stop me from being with you, if that's what you want."

Julia inhaled deeply. "It is what I want, as much as that surprises me. I'm incredibly attracted to you, Maddie and I already feel...a level of intimacy with you that frankly, scares me a little."
"I know." Maddie lowered her gaze, suddenly shy.

"Don't look away," Julia whispered to her. Maddie returned her gaze to Julia and Julia licked her lips, swallowing deeply. "I want you...if you want me."

Maddie leaned in and kissed Julia lightly, their lips pursing and pulling gently, almost playfully and Maddie loved that Julia simply let her have control and set the pace. Julia moaned when Maddie opened her mouth and slid her tongue teasingly against Julia's, cupping her face gently as they kissed slowly. When they separated, Maddie saw Julia staring at her mouth before Julia's thumb brushed her lips gently.

"You are so very beautiful and charming and smart and if this is as far as this goes, I won't hold it against you." Julia's slow whisper was a sweet and sexy rasp.

The open look of desire on Julia's face, coupled with her sweet offer of an easy out, pushed Maddie into doing what she knew she wanted to do. She stood up, slipped off Julia's borrowed suit jacket and carefully draped it over the arm of the sofa.

Julia nodded. "It's okay. I understand. I really do. It's alright if you can't do this but you don't have to leave just yet."

Maddie realized that Julia thought she was returning the jacket on her way out. "I don't think you do understand," Maddie said as she started to unbutton her shirt slowly, from the bottom up, a small smile on her face.

Julia gasped. "Maddie, are you sure?" She was staring at Maddie's fingers as they slowly climbed up, button by button.

Maddie nodded as she released the last button. "Yes. I feel very safe with you."

Julia licked her lips. "You are, sweetie. I promise."

Maddie wondered where the courage was coming from for her to hold her hand out to Julia and pull her up as she walked backward, leading her slowly through the French doors to the bedroom. They stopped near the edge of the bed and Maddie pulled Julia to her in a loose embrace. They stared at each other.

"I haven't…been with anyone…in a really long time," Maddie admitted to her.

Julia simply stared at her for a moment. "It's been quite a while for me too. I hope you know that I've never…done this, after just meeting someone. I just don't do this."

"I know," Maddie assured her. "Me either."

"Trust me?" Julia whispered.

Maddie realized that she did trust Julia. "I do. No regrets," she whispered back.

33

Chapter 4

Julia felt Maddie shudder as she slipped her hands beneath her open shirt, caressing the bare skin at her back. She placed small sweet kisses against Maddie's forehead. Julia's senses were on overload by having this young woman in her arms. Maddie's skin felt soft and warm against her hands, her natural scent was clean and fresh and her soft gasps filled Julia with equal parts arousal and affection. This was like nothing she had ever experienced before. She was accustomed to the aggressive impatience of men, not this gentle and sensual exploration.

Maddie's lips were full, plush, and incredibly soft when brushed against her own, even when they opened and pressed, becoming insistent. Maddie's tongue was an absolute revelation. It slowly ran along her lips, seeking permission as well as teasing before entering her mouth slowly and smoothly. Maddie's tongue stroked against her own gently, teasing for long moments before pulling back slightly and allowing Julia to take complete control of the kiss. No man had ever completely conceded control of a kiss to her and it was exciting.

Julia savored this chance, taking her pleasure, sensually gliding her tongue in before she intensified the kiss, Maddie following her lead. They kissed each other deeply, passionately and Julia found herself pulling Maddie closer, wanting more of her, more of this wonderful and sensuous give and take.

Julia knew that she could be a passionate person, had certainly felt great passion in her life, but no experience in her past had prepared her for how she felt at the hands of this young woman. Julia found herself wondering how it could be possible that she had never seriously considered being with another woman when kissing Maddie felt so completely natural. Julia allowed herself to surrender to the feeling and kiss Maddie with wild abandon. Julia thought that it was the most sensual and singularly arousing thing she had ever experienced.

Julia watched as Maddie brought a hand up to the buttons on her blouse and began to pop them open, parting the blouse, swallowing as she openly stared at Julia's bra-encased breasts.

"May I touch you?" Maddie whispered to her.

Julia inhaled sharply at the breathless request. None of the men she had been with had ever asked her permission, their sense of entitlement taking over long before they had gotten this far. No one had ever been this solicitous of her feelings before.

"You're a little too good to be true," Julia whispered back.

"Is that a yes?" Maddie asked, smiling.

"God, yes. Touch me," Julia whispered.

Maddie brushed light fingers over her cleavage and Julia was suddenly insecure about her body. She had never been particularly nervous about what men would think about her body because men were easy, but this was not a man. This was another woman and Julia found herself worried about how this young, beautiful and slender creature would view her slightly older and heavier body. She was suddenly grateful for the dim lighting in the bedroom.

Before Julia could dwell on that negative thought, she felt Maddie's touch become more confident as she slowly ran the back of her hand against the satin cups of her bra. She felt Maddie reach for her hardening nipples through the fabric of her bra, squeezing them with her fingers. Julia heard herself moan as she pushed her breasts out, the contact just enough to entice and tease.

Julia watched as Maddie paused to carefully remove the mother of pearl cufflinks from her blouse, carefully placing them on the nightstand before she slipped the blouse off. Julia returned the favor and effortlessly slipped Maddie's uniform shirt down her arms. Julia shivered as Maddie placed a small chaste kiss to her cleavage, leaving her lips there for a moment as she reached around and unhooked her bra. Julia felt goose bumps rise on her skin as Maddie very slowly pulled the bra off her shoulders and down her arms.

Julia held her breath as Maddie stilled, seemingly amazed by the sight of her breasts, before she shyly cupped one of them, testing its weight and fullness. Julia felt her nipples get tight and hard, Maddie's intense gaze feeling like a caress.

"Please," Julia whispered, aghast at the need she could hear in her voice.

Julia closed her eyes as Maddie brought both her hands up to her breasts. The first touch of Maddie's fingers against her bare nipples was so intense that it caused Julia to bite her lip and shudder deeply. When she opened her eyes, she found Maddie watching her carefully.

Maddie slowly lowered her head and placed a soft kiss where her fingers had been and Julia gasped at the sensation of her nipple being gently taken into Maddie's mouth. Julia was surprised by the absolute tenderness of this woman's caresses, the gentle intent of it all, the deftness of her hands so different from the often-clumsy gropes of men. Julia was overwhelmed by this intensity of desire after feeling almost none for so long. She was stunned by the care and consideration shown to her by a virtual stranger, amazed by her own physical and emotional reactions to the encounter thus far. She wrapped her hand around the back of Maddie's head, holding her in place as she allowed the cascade of sensations and emotions to wash over her.

In the midst of all this, Julia realized that she wanted to touch this young woman as much as she was enjoying being touched by her. Julia loosened her grip on Maddie's head and her nipple was slowly released as Julia reached for the front closure of Maddie's bra, popping it open and reaching for the bared breasts immediately. Julia softly stroked the brown nipples, so different from her own, and laid kisses along the sides of the impossibly soft breasts as she felt the nipples harden against her fingers.

Julia surprised herself when she bent to take Maddie's nipple eagerly into her mouth, but she was stunned when she found that she could not get enough of sucking it. She was beyond proud of herself at Maddie's response of gasps and soft moans at her efforts. Julia paid close attention to those responses, adjusting her touch to bring Maddie the most pleasure. Julia sucked a nipple more deeply into her mouth and Maddie moaned loudly.

Julia reluctantly paused. "Too much?"

"God, no, never enough," Maddie whispered.

Julia returned her mouth to Maddie's breasts, lavishing them with the kind of attention she had always wanted paid to her own but had rarely received. Maddie seemed to appreciate her efforts, arching into the contact and holding Julia's head exactly where she wanted it.

Julia loved that nothing was rushed, that they stopped to kiss leisurely between caresses, Maddie's tongue stoking a constant simmering heat against her own. Julia was amazed at the ease of it

37

all. It was give as much as take. It was desire and arousal enhanced by reverence and care. Julia wondered if she had ever felt this particular kind of intimacy with any man.

While they kissed Julia felt Maddie's hands caress her ass through her skirt, squeezing it gently. Julia thought she had experienced intense desire in her life, but when Maddie's hands started to slide up her thigh, raising her skirt up, she realized that she never really had a clue. She gasped when Maddie's hands found the bare skin of her thighs at the top of her stockings, gently tugging on a garter.

Maddie smiled against Julia's mouth. "Oh my goodness. Real stockings?"

Julia bit her lip and nodded as she reached a hand down to assist Maddie unhooking them from the garter, but Maddie shook her head as she removed Julia's hand and gently eased her back to sit on the bed, crouching in front of her.

"Please let me do this." Maddie slowly and easily unhooked the stockings, placing soft kisses against her thighs. "Julia, you're like a beautifully wrapped gift with pretty paper...with ribbons...bows...it's so gorgeous, but you can't wait to unwrap it because you know there's something even better...more beautiful underneath the wrapping."

Julia lost her breath at Maddie's sweet and romantic words and she had to inhale deeply as Maddie carefully raised first one leg, then the other, as she removed her stockings. Julia watched Maddie drape them delicately on the footboard of the bed, the way a woman would. Maddie rose slowly and pulled Julia up and into a deep kiss. Julia returned it with enthusiasm, this young woman putting her completely at ease while still ramping up her desire.

In between kisses and caresses, they slowly removed any remaining articles of clothing and when Maddie pulled the last tiny bit of satin and lace down her legs, she pushed Julia back onto the bed. Julia pulled Maddie over her and they were skin to skin for the first time. Feeling Maddie sliding against her, holding her with her entire body was impossibly soft and more sensual than anything Julia had ever known. They held each other closely for long moments, simply absorbing the experience.

"The way you make me feel is almost too much for me to take in...to process," Julia whispered.

Maddie nodded as she pulled away to look at Julia. "Yes, that's what I feel, too." Maddie smiled, her gaze moving slowly over Julia's face and breasts. "Do you have any idea how truly beautiful you are, Julia?"

Julia sighed, thinking that she had not felt beautiful in years when Maddie's fingers found the small, raised scar over the depression just under her nipple. Julia froze and inhaled deeply as she brought her hand to her breast protectively.

Maddie immediately stilled her hand, her fingers becoming still. "What is it? Did I hurt you?" Maddie asked.

"No. No. I just...God, don't look at it," Julia said, her voice breaking.

Maddie caressed the scar tissue lightly. "Shhhh. It's okay...it's just a scar. Trust me, you're a stunningly beautiful woman...you're actually more than beautiful...you're absolutely luscious."

Julia stifled a relieved sob as Maddie gently removed her hand and bent her head to place an open-mouthed kiss near the scar. Julia inhaled deeply and Maddie placed another kiss directly on the scar, lingering there until Julia took another breath, the tension in her body easing. Maddie placed a third kiss between Julia's breasts while cupping them and lightly thumbing the nipples, easing every one of Julia's insecurities.

Maddie whispered against the scar. "Tell me what happened to you, honey."

Julia sighed. "I had breast cancer and they removed a small mass and a good bit of the surrounding tissue, hence the unsightly dent."

Maddie lifted her head and looked at her. "Everything is good now? Tell me you're okay."

"Yes, I'm perfectly fine."

Maddie smiled, running her gaze up and down Julia's torso. "Yes, you most certainly are."

Julia laughed lightly. "God, Maddie, you make me feel that way."

Maddie pulled her close. "Everything about you is beautiful...inside and out." Maddie gently kissed the scar. "You have the kind of body that I've always been so attracted to."

Julia swallowed, slight apprehension setting in. "I'm almost afraid to ask what kind of body that is."

Maddie smiled. "Full-bodied and curvy...soft and luscious. You really are gorgeous."

Julia watched as Maddie lowered her head to her breasts and kissed each nipple in turn before she pulled one into her mouth, sucking gently. Julia moaned in pleasure as Maddie pulled her close, sucking the nipple deeply before moving to the other one, ramping up her desire. Julia arched into the contact for long moments until she decided that she wanted to touch Maddie.

"Can it be my turn?" Julia asked.

Maddie looked surprised and then she smiled. "Anytime."

Julia wrapped Maddie in a firm embrace as she deftly and playfully rolled them over. She licked her lips as she looked down at Maddie. "I want you so much. Would you let me–?"

"Yes," Maddie answered, interrupting Julia.

"Can I–?"

"Yes," Maddie said, once again cutting Julia's question short.

Julia smiled. "Maddie, sweetie, you don't even know what I want to do."

Maddie smiled, panting lightly. "It doesn't matter what you want to do. The answer for you, Julia, is yes, to anything you want."

In her excitement at having been given free rein, Julia surged over Maddie, wanting to touch everywhere, try everything and make Maddie feel as beautiful as she made her feel. Julia heard Maddie moan as she plundered her mouth with a firmly questing tongue. She felt aroused and powerful and the feeling was unfamiliar, but deeply exciting. Julia squeezed Maddie's breast as she moved down to suck a nipple deeply into her mouth. Julia was almost aggressive in her caresses, moving her hands and mouth over the soft terrain of Maddie's body causing her to arch and moan in response.

Julia felt thrilled when Maddie muffled a scream with the back of her own hand when Julia's fingers ventured boldly through the soft patch of dark hair between her legs. Julia slowly ran her fingers into the warm and overflowing wetness and Maddie bucked, bending a knee to open herself further to Julia's touch.

41

Julia grasped the hair at the back of her neck. "Look at me...please, Maddie," Julia whispered.

Maddie's eyes fluttered open as Julia continued to stroke her folds gently and slowly before circling her clit teasingly. Maddie gasped and closed her eyes for a beat or two at the intimate touch, opening her eyes to fix her gaze on Julia. Julia slowed her touch.

"Is this okay? I've never..."

"So good...don't stop."

Maddie's passionate and breathless plea emboldened Julia, still slightly insecure due to her inexperience, and she coated her fingers in Maddie's wetness, circling her clit before dipping a finger near Maddie's opening, rubbing there. Maddie bucked at the teasing touch and Julia savored being able to watch Maddie's reaction to her intimate touch. Julia decided that she wanted more.

"Can I be...inside you?" Julia whispered.

"God, yes." Maddie spoke directly against Julia's slightly parted lips.

Julia had never before felt this unique combination of power and eagerness to please and she drew upon both emotions as she entered Maddie's mouth with her tongue at the same moment she entered Maddie's tight wet channel with two of her fingers. Julia moaned into the open-mouthed kiss, simply from the absolute wonder of actually being inside Maddie.

Julia had the sense of having been granted access to a sacred place and she felt honored at the privilege. She pulled Maddie closer, pushed deeper inside her, moving instinctively, her momentary insecurity at this unfamiliar act forgotten as her desire to bring Maddie pleasure took over. Julia had never felt anything quite like this before. Her fingers were surrounded by warm tight wetness, Maddie's inner muscles squeezing against them, as if encouraging Julia to keep them inside her. Julia enjoyed the glorious warm feel of Maddie against her fingers, the subtle wet sounds of her acceptance into Maddie filling her ears and the rich scent of Maddie's arousal wafting under her nose. Maddie clutched at her neck and Julia let herself be led back to Maddie's mouth. They kissed deeply as they moved together, entwined and connected, naturally in sync.

"Yes...God...please..." Maddie panted out in the same cadence as Julia's thrusts inside her.

Julia increased her efforts slightly, increasing the speed and force of her thrusts to meet Maddie's tempo, and this went on for long glorious minutes as Maddie's hips jerked in time. Julia took great pleasure in watching Maddie's response, her body moving in sync to Julia's steady plunging, her breasts swaying, her entire being striving for release.

Maddie pulled at Julia's neck and Julia kissed her, Maddie's mouth opening to her wetly as she moaned into it, her hips like pistons against Julia's fingers. Julia instinctively brought her thumb up to rub against Maddie's clit, causing Maddie to pull away from Julia's mouth as her heavy pants increased to sharp gasps and then to almost breathless shouts.

Julia watched with a sense of wonder as she pushed Maddie steadily and purposefully over the edge into an orgasm. Maddie arched up, her mouth open, her eyes squeezed tight as she cried out and bucked through a long shuddering climax, one hand clutching Julia's shoulder and one clutching the sheet as her vaginal walls squeezed against Julia's fingers. Julia thought it was gloriously beautiful and she could not tear her gaze away as Maddie continued to convulse in the pleasure that Julia had given her.

Chapter 5

Maddie slowly came back to herself, trying to slow her own breathing as she licked her dry lips after the earth-shattering orgasm that Julia had brought her to. She honestly didn't even know she was capable of having an orgasm that intense. She felt Julia cradling her tenderly and she felt small kisses on the side of her face.

"I have never seen anything as beautiful, never felt anything as beautiful as you...coming...for me," Julia whispered near her ear.

Maddie shuddered in response to Julia's tender words and became aware that Julia's fingers were still nestled deep inside her and she wanted Julia to keep them there. Maddie bit her lip to keep from crying, suddenly overcome with a myriad of unfamiliar emotions.

"Stay inside me." Maddie failed as her voice broke.

Julia pulled her closer. "It's okay, sweetie, I will. I'll stay forever if you want me to."

Maddie shuddered at the words, her physical responses as out of control as her emotions. Maddie felt tears fill her eyes as her inner walls contracted involuntarily against Julia's fingers in aftershock.

She heard Julia gasp. "Oh, that feels unbelievable...you're so beautiful...so sexy."

Maddie was not sure what Julia was doing with her fingers, but it felt incredible and Maddie bucked sharply into the sensation, wanting to orgasm again even though she had not quite recovered from the first one. The overwhelming need for more, for Julia to keep touching her frightened her and she could not stop the tears that spilled onto her cheek. She felt Julia become completely still against her.

"Oh sweetie, what is it?" Julia asked her.

"It's too good, it's too much," Maddie managed to whisper.

"No, it's not. You deserve to feel this good." Julia's voice was quiet but firm. Maddie felt Julia place small tender kisses against her face and lips. "It's okay, I promise...please let me," Julia pleaded quietly.

In response, Maddie simply spread her legs wider in invitation and she felt Julia push inside her deeper and harder. It felt as good as anything Maddie had ever felt in her entire life and she felt her hips bucking sharply and steadily and she knew she was losing any control she had left.

"Sweetie, tell me it's okay...tell me you want this." Julia's voice in her ear was clear and firm.

Maddie had never before felt this out of control, this desperate for someone else's touch, but all she could think about, all she could feel, all she wanted was Julia, on top of her, inside her, making her feel sexy and beautiful and so very good. She wanted Julia to take her, she wanted to lose control to Julia, to feel more of this wild abandon.

"Please, Jule, do it...fuck me harder."

Maddie was surprised at her own profane request, but it seemed to inject Julia with energy and she did as Maddie asked and everything seemed to ramp up, the speed, the pressure, the sensations and Maddie begged.

"Yes, oh God, right there, Jule, right there..."

Maddie clutched tightly to the woman making her feel things that she was sure she had never felt before, things that she was afraid to feel as she surrendered herself to Julia. The screaming, blinding orgasm that hit her was the most intense one of her life and she shouted out her satisfaction, and her denial.

Julia watched as Maddie recovered from the intense orgasm and slowly returned to herself for long moments before she pushed herself up on her elbow. Maddie opened her eyes and easily met her gaze before she pulled her down into an open-mouthed kiss, pressing a firm hand against her ass. Julia moaned into the aggressive caress and then moaned louder as she slid her center firmly up and down against Maddie's firm thigh, copious amounts of her own wet, warm arousal spreading easily between them. Their mouths melded together and they kissed deeply and intensely.

Julia pulled her mouth away to inhale and Maddie took the opportunity to bend her head and take one of Julia's nipples into her mouth. Julia released a primal sound as Maddie sucked her breast deeply into her mouth, as if she wanted to devour it. Julia bucked, already beyond aroused by making love to Maddie, but wanting Maddie to take her time because Julia wanted to savor every sensation and every emotion this woman was making her feel.

When Julia felt Maddie release her nipple, she opened her eyes and their gazes met before Julia lowered her forehead, resting it against Maddie's as she continued to slide her wet center against Maddie's thigh. Maddie rolled her over slowly, her thigh still pressed deliciously against Julia's clit. When Julia felt Maddie snake her hand down to her center, she slowed her movements and spread her legs wide, allowing Maddie easier access to where she desperately needed her.

Julia inhaled sharply as Maddie slowly glided her fingers through her hot wet folds, finding her hard and swollen clit unerringly. Julia could not believe how good it felt, Maddie's fingers circling her clit gently, then firmly, as if she knew exactly what Julia needed.

"Oh sweetie...so good," Julia whispered as Maddie caressed her, teased her and the sensations were so overwhelming that Julia lost herself for long moments.

"Tell me what you want." Maddie's voice brought her back.

Julia gripped the back of Maddie's neck and pulled her down, their lips brushing softly. "You...this...more."

Maddie coated her fingers thoroughly in Julia's wet folds and moved down to her opening, dipping in and out teasingly. "Do you want me...inside you?" Maddie asked.

"God...yes," Julia managed on a broken sob.

Julia felt Maddie slip inside her and she moaned, trying not to jerk wildly because the idea, as well as the sensation, of Maddie being inside her thrilled her beyond comprehension. When Maddie pulled out slowly and returned with more, stretching her open deliciously, Julia pushed back, forcefully impaling herself onto Maddie's fingers because it felt so damn good.

Julia managed to open her eyes, meeting and holding Maddie's gaze. "Fuck..."

Julia wanted to watch Maddie as she thrust inside her, the look of amazement on her face almost as good as the feel of her firm fingers thrusting inside her so she tried to hold Maddie's gaze, but she could not and her eyes rolled up and closed against the ecstasy. Julia could not believe how incredible it felt to have Maddie inside her, filling her more than she would have imagined and she could not help but buck her hips up wildly to meet them, again and again and again.

The fucking itself would have been exquisite, but then Maddie slowed her thrusts and did something with her fingers. Julia felt them shift inside and then the already intense sensations exploded into unimaginable pleasure. Julia arched her head back and lost complete control and awareness as she bucked and moaned into the glorious fucking.

Julia felt the pleasant and unmistakable stirring of an impending orgasm low in her belly. The sensation gained momentum and hurtled up, a deep, pleasant, warm burning, intensifying and spreading through her. Julia inhaled deep, ragged breaths, jerking her hips almost wildly until she heard herself shout and felt her entire being clench in pleasure, the intense orgasm tearing through her, wave after wave crashing over her for long intense moments.

When Julia finally started to come back to herself, she realized that Maddie was holding her, whispering things in her ear. "Tão linda...God, so beautiful...querida mulher."

Julia inhaled deep breaths of air into her lungs as aftershocks rumbled through her, Maddie's fingers still nestled inside her. "That was...you are...incredible," she finally managed to pant out.

When she finally opened her eyes, Maddie smiled down at her and Julia nearly lost her breath at the sight. Maddie leaned over and softly kissed Julia's closest nipple, and Julia's desire, just gratified in the most absolute way, immediately returned and that was a surprise to her. At the back of Julia's mind had been the faint nagging notion that this encounter was simply a long overdue itch that needed to be scratched, but she was now certain that it was much more than that. She wanted Maddie more than she had ever wanted anyone.

Julia arched up as Maddie gently sucked her neck and slid against her, her wet center still pulsing against Maddie's fingers, seeking more pleasure. Julia moved against Maddie's soft warm form, arching against her and the still welcome intrusion.

"God, I can feel you throbbing," Maddie whispered. "Do you want me again?"

"God, yes," Julia heard herself say.

Maddie could not believe how badly she wanted to touch Julia again, wanted to make her come apart again. Touching Julia had brought it all back, how glorious a woman's body was, how responsive, and Maddie found herself enjoying things she had not allowed herself to think about for many years. When Julia said she wanted her again, Maddie could not stop herself from giving in to the intense need to fill Julia, pulling out almost completely and pushing back inside her with three fingers, the tighter penetration stretching Julia open as Maddie filled her. Maddie wanted to hear Julia's deep and sexy moan again and she was not disappointed.

Maddie felt Julia firmly clutch at her forearm, keeping her deep inside and Maddie tried to go deeper still. Julia held onto Maddie's arm and rolled toward her, slightly onto her side, the angle bringing her clit slamming against Maddie's thumb with every wild buck of her hips. Julia moaned out and jerked in pleasure and Maddie was convinced that she had never seen or heard anything sexier in her entire life.

"Fuck...don't stop." Julia's voice was low and rough, the raspy quality making Maddie shiver.

Maddie inhaled a deep breath, her senses heightening as Julia bucked against her hand in a hard and steady rhythm. She heard Julia's breathy moans, smelled the intoxicating scent of Julia's arousal, watched Julia move against her as her full breasts swayed in time, felt her fingers getting sucked inside this sensuous and beautiful creature.

"You're so beautiful, querida, so sexy," Maddie whispered near Julia's ear.

Julia whimpered and Maddie increased the efforts of her strong and sure fingers. Maddie realized that Julia was starting to fall over the edge because the hold that Julia had on her forearm suddenly tightened. Maddie watched as Julia became absolutely still for a moment, her face caught in a mask of beautiful passion before she crashed into an orgasm of epic proportion. Julia's hips jerked wildly, a shout torn from her throat as she convulsed beautifully in wave after wave for endless moments, her hand gripping Maddie's forearm tightly.

Maddie gently sifted through Julia's hair with her fingers, kissing her forehead and whispering to Julia as she recovered. "You feel so good...you smell so good...I love holding you...touching you."

Maddie held onto Julia, her need to continuously run her hands and lips across the landscape of Julia's body just another thing she did not want to dwell upon. The experience of being with this beautiful woman was as surprising as it was frightening. It was not something that she had done lightly and she did not regret it, but she suspected there would be consequences, both emotional and otherwise, for her actions. As confused as she was, Maddie knew that she wanted whatever this was to continue and that was the most frightening thing of all. Maddie could not stop touching her

51

beautiful companion as she watched her sleep so she simply cuddled in beside her and let herself drift off as well.

Chapter 6

Julia had been overcome with sensation and emotion, the intense orgasm washing through her as Maddie touched her in places long dormant and, she had thought, no longer responsive. She allowed herself to remain in Maddie's arms, letting Maddie hold her and caress her, the need for this young woman's touch both compelling and mystifying. Julia had no point of reference for what she was feeling, the difference between being with Maddie and all others before her simply immeasurable. She had never before felt so satiated, so content in someone's arms before and she wanted to savor it. She decided she would wait to contemplate her feelings and a course of action at a later time. She wanted nothing more than to enjoy the safe and tender feeling of Maddie holding her and she let the young woman lull her to sleep.

Julia woke much later with Maddie's hand cupping her breast, a soft thumb strumming her nipple and she pulled Maddie closer, nuzzling into Maddie's neck. Only half-awake, Julia was finding it hard to believe that she was lying naked with this beautiful creature, that she felt as comfortable and as sexy as she had ever felt.

Julia arched into the contact. "Maddie...I thought you were a beautiful dream," she whispered.

"No, I'm real. I didn't mean to wake you."

"What did you mean to do?" Julia asked.

"I just can't stop touching you," Maddie said.

"I don't want you to stop."

Julia found Maddie's mouth with her own, kissing her deeply and their mutual desire flared to life as the kiss continued and intensified, hands roaming freely. Julia reluctantly pulled her mouth away and raised herself to her knees with the intention of moving over Maddie, but never got the chance as Maddie rose to her knees to meet her, pressing their fronts together deliciously. Julia circled Maddie's shoulders, pulling her close and Maddie sucked on her neck as she clutched Julia's ass. Julia slid her knee between Maddie's and lowered her mouth to Maddie's breast.

Julia was amazed at how quickly her desire had spiked, how her center had flooded with warm wetness, how badly she wanted Maddie to touch her and how badly she wanted to touch Maddie. Julia slid a hand between Maddie's legs and loved the gasp her touch elicited. Maddie snaked an arm around her waist, binding them together, and brought her hand to Julia's center. They both stilled and brought their foreheads together. Maddie slowly slid her fingers through Julia's wet folds as Julia slid her fingers through Maddie's.

Maddie licked her lips. "Go...inside..."

Julia gently rubbed her nose against Maddie's. "You, too...slowly, baby."

"Together," Maddie whispered.

"Yes," Julia agreed.

Maddie slid two fingers slowly into Julia, and the sensation was so incredible that Julia had to concentrate to be able to reciprocate, pushing inside Maddie. They both gasped, and then stilled, panting, their foreheads still pressed together. After a long moment, Julia slid out of Maddie slightly and Maddie followed her lead, doing the same. Julia waited a beat and then pushed back in and Maddie countered with her own thrust and then again until they found a mutual tempo, fucking each other slowly, steadily and deeply. Julia was not sure that she had ever felt anything quite like this sexually intimate dance of give and take.

Julia could smell the scent of her own arousal mixed with Maddie's, could hear her gasping breaths matching Maddie's own. Actions and sensations seem to mirror and it was as if she could feel what she was doing to Maddie every time Maddie slid into her. She kissed Maddie's neck, wanting to have another sensation, another point of contact.

Julia tightened her hold on Maddie, pushing into her harder, trying to meet her thrust for thrust as they climbed together. As Maddie started to orgasm, Julia clutched her harder.

"Oh God…Jule…Oh God," Maddie panted out in a sexy refrain.

Julia hung onto Maddie, absorbing each of the younger woman's moans, each sharp jerk as she helped her ride it out until Julia suddenly felt her own orgasm start. It sounded and felt like an echo as Maddie moaned and bucked and Julia followed suit, over and over again until she exploded, clutching to Maddie, jerking and shuddering for endless moments. After the shudders finally slowed, they gently eased out of each other and slid to the bed together, their hands still holding onto each other, still caressing each other.

"Tu es tão bonita… tão bom…Eu acho que te amo…" Maddie whispered to her quietly.

"Is that Portuguese?" Julia asked, watching her in the dim light.

Maddie's eyes widened. "You...? Uhmm...yes. I'm sorry."

Julia saw the panic in Maddie's eyes and suspected that Maddie had revealed too much. "For what...exactly?"

Maddie lowered her gaze. "For the ridiculously romantic things I just said."

Julia smiled. "I like ridiculously romantic things. I recognize the language, but don't understand that much so why don't you just tell me in English?"

Maddie swallowed deeply before she looked at her. "I said that you're so very beautiful...and make me feel so good."

"You're the beautiful one and you make me feel beyond good."

Julia placed small kisses along Maddie's face and neck and Maddie wrapped herself around Julia tightly. They cuddled together as though they had done the same thing every night for years, warm and comfortable as they drifted to back to sleep.

Maddie woke early and watched Julia sleep for long moments, still a little shocked at herself, at her own behavior, at what had happened between them. Her emotions were in freefall, everything from joy to panic rocking her. She wanted to wake Julia and make love to her again as much as she wanted to quietly gather up her clothing, dress and sneak out of the hotel room. She sighed and rubbed her forehead as she slipped from the bed, unable to think clearly with Julia so near.

Maddie went into the bathroom and saw herself in the mirror. She looked so different, almost sexy, that she almost didn't recognize herself. She took a long shower, allowing the soothing hot water to calm her nerves a bit. She used the mouthwash she found, wrapped herself in a large luxurious towel and came back into the bedroom.

She smiled at the sight of Julia, a pillow gripped firmly under her head and she wandered over to watch the sleeping beauty, gazing at her for long moments. Julia was lying on her side, the sheet only partially covering her, allowing Maddie a view of her upper torso, dappled sunlight from the large window dancing across her skin and hair. Maddie looked her fill, trying to take in every detail to add to the memories of the night before. Maddie inhaled a deep breath and realized she was trembling.

"Are you okay?" Maddie was startled by the sexy, gravelly, sleep-filled voice coming from the bed.

Julia was blinking slowly and Maddie tried not to gasp at the intense blue color of her eyes, so much more brilliant in the morning light. "Yes...no...I'm not...how can you be so beautiful?"

Julia slid herself up onto her elbow, watching Maddie carefully. "I was just thinking the same thing about you."

Maddie looked away and fidgeted with the towel. "I took a shower. I hope that's okay."

"Of course it is. Can I get you some coffee...or order you some breakfast?"

Maddie shook her head, swallowing as she tried to gather the courage to do what she knew she needed to do. "No, thank you. I have to go, but I didn't...I wasn't sure. I never...I don't do this so I'm not sure of the etiquette."

"Well...since I don't do this sort of thing either." Julia's gravelly voice was soft, but strained and she looked away from Maddie, the hurt feelings clearly evident on her face.

Maddie closed the small distance to the bed and sat near Julia. "I didn't mean to imply...Julia, I wanted to talk to you, but I didn't want to wake you. I'm sorry if I've said or done anything to hurt you."

Maddie averted her gaze from Julia because she knew that no matter what she said, she was going to hurt Julia.

Julia watched Maddie fidget with the towel wrapped around her. Julia did not want to think that Maddie was trying to sneak out without saying good-bye. She wouldn't have taken a shower if that were her intention, would she? Julia did not know what to think, except that she wanted Maddie back in the bed with her. Julia did not want to lose the connection that she had made with this beautiful young woman.

"When can I see you again?" Julia whispered.

Maddie gently cupped the side of her face. "Thank you...for...everything that happened between us last night...for dinner...for treating me with kindness and respect...for making me laugh and making me feel beautiful and sexy...for making love to me like no one ever has..." Maddie's voice faltered and broke.

Maddie's words were heartfelt and beautiful, but they broke Julia's heart as understanding and cold dread set in. "You're saying good-bye to me, aren't you?"

Julia watched Maddie avert her gaze. "I think I have to. My life right now...I don't know if I can do this— "

Julia stopped Maddie's words with a finger to her lips, not wanting to hear any more. "You don't have to explain anything to me, sweetie. I didn't expect this, any of it...meeting you...feeling like this."

"I'm sorry," Maddie whispered.

Julia lowered her head in defeat. "Please don't say that…don't be sorry." Julia tried to stifle her soft sob.

She felt Maddie reach for her, pull her close, the embrace feeling desperate. Julia turned her head and pressed her mouth to Maddie's roughly and Maddie responded immediately, opening her mouth and plunging her tongue against Julia's.

The kiss was wild and desperate as they clutched at each other, hands gripping heads and shoulders and waists, tongues dancing and plunging, their breathing deep and ragged until someone moaned. Julia felt the kiss gradually slow, their hands easing to caress instead of clutch, their tongues soothing instead of arousing. When Julia reached up to cup her face, she felt Maddie's tears and her own tears started. They kissed tenderly, crying, until Maddie pulled away, sliding off the bed as she clutched the bath towel to herself. She slowly gathered up her scattered clothing and walked silently into the bathroom, closing the door quietly behind her.

Julia tried to pull herself together, wrapping herself in a sheet and wiping her eyes with the edge of it. When Maddie came out of the bathroom she handed her a business card, careful not to touch her and she saw that Maddie was trying very hard not to cry.

Julia cleared her throat. "This is my business card. I wrote my personal cell number on the back. I would very much like to see you again, but I won't hold it against you. I also want you to know that this meant something…you, Maddie…mean something to me. So even if you can't do…this again…it wasn't just about the sex. I still would like to see you…talk to you…we don't have to do…this."

Julia watched as Maddie tried to smile, a few stray tears slipping over her lower lashes. "I'm not sure I could ever be near you again, Julia, and not want you with everything that I am."

Julia nodded, knowing that she felt the same way. "I...okay but please...if you ever need me...if you just want to talk...no strings...if you ever need anything...call me day or night."

Maddie's eyes were wide and wet and she nodded as she took the card from Julia, clutching it in her hand as she picked up her purse and slowly walked to the door. Julia wanted to scream, to block her escape, anything to keep Maddie here with her, but she simply stepped forward.

"Maddie, sweetie, please, at least text me...to let me know...that you're okay."

Maddie didn't respond, she simply clutched her purse as she opened the door and walked out of Julia's hotel room, out of her life. The door clicked shut behind her and Julia clutched her chest as she slowly sank to the floor, the pain there greater than when they had cut her open to remove part of her breast. It felt as though she might never recover from it.

Chapter 7

Julia tried to keep her business persona firmly in place as the casual Friday morning staff meeting was winding down, several of her real estate agents talking amongst themselves as they slowly walked out of the conference room of the small storefront office that she kept in the center of town. Her daughter, Vivienne, was one of the agents and she stopped at the door, glancing in her direction. Julia politely asked her to shut the door to the conference room, waving her phone as if she needed to make a call. Julia had no call to make, but simply wanted to be alone. The door clicked quietly behind her and she inhaled deeply and willed herself not to cry as she looked out the large windows of the conference room that overlooked the harbor.

Julia thought she would feel better by now. She had been completely lost since Maddie had left her in her hotel room nearly three weeks before. She knew that people had noticed she was not quite herself, and Vivienne most certainly had, asking about her mother's mood more than once or twice. She had been trying to act as though nothing was wrong, but she knew it wasn't working.

Julia inhaled deeply again as she watched the moored boats bobbing gently in the harbor. As she had done too many times, Julia allowed her thoughts to stray to Maddie and the time they had spent together. She pictured Maddie's dimpled smile, her warm brown eyes, her soft laugh and the way she looked and sounded when Julia brought her to an orgasm. Julia's insides seized as the memories washed over her, the joy, the eroticism, and the anguish as Maddie walked away from her in the morning.

Julia had not heard a word from Maddie in the nearly three weeks that had passed since then and she wasn't really surprised. Julia was a great believer in keeping her expectations within reason so she would not be constantly disappointed, but it hadn't worked this time and disappointment was only one of the emotions she was currently dealing with. A combination of shame and regret settled in her gut every time she recalled pleading for Maddie to let her know that she was okay. Julia automatically glanced down at her phone to check for a message from Maddie and finding none for the thousandth time, brushed away the millionth stray tear from her face and sighed.

Julia had spoken to no one of her encounter with Maddie in Boston, but she had thought about her almost constantly since then and it still hurt. It hurt more than she could bear some days and it made Julia angry, at herself, at the universe, and at Maddie. She was angry because she had been perfectly content with her life before she had met Maddie and now she was anything but content. There were moments when the entire encounter seemed like a dream to her, a happy and erotic dream. She decided she needed some perspective or simply someone to talk to about all of this.

Julia quickly scrolled through the list of contacts on her phone and stopped on a name she had not called in a few months. Deborah Stone. Julia smiled. Why hadn't she thought of talking to Deb until now? Maybe because of that nagging shame and regret when she remembered pleading at Maddie to, at the very least, let her know she was okay.

Julia had met Deborah in a cancer support group when she had been going through treatment. Deb was brash, black, and gay and it became quickly apparent that she and Julia didn't fit in with the rest of the group. They agreed to become each other's support instead, continuing to meet and talk regularly, just the two of them, and they had become close friends.

That evening, Julia walked into the small but lively bistro that Deb had suggested, jazz playing softly in the background, the eclectic crowd enjoying quiet conversation. She found Deb waiting for her at a small table with a shot of what Julia assumed was tequila and a beer in front of her, and a martini waiting for Julia at the spot across from her. They embraced warmly and as soon as Julia sat down Deb leaned forward and reached for Julia's hand.

"Please tell me you're not sick, Julia," Deb implored.

Julia squeezed her hand back. "I'm not sick."

Deb exhaled in apparent relief and nodded. "Okay. Good." She released Julia's hand and smiled, picking up her shot glass and swallowing her tequila smoothly. "So, what's going on?" Deb asked before she took a long slow sip of beer.

"Thanks for this," Julia said before she drank deeply from her martini glass. "Well, I need your expert opinion on a hypothetical situation."

Deb smiled. "Okay. Shoot." Deb took another small sip of her beer.

Julia gathered her thoughts. "So...let's say you unexpectedly meet a woman and she's funny and charming and beautiful and after you have drinks and talk for hours, you spend the night with her...and it's incredible...the sex...the connection...everything."

Deb looked more amused than confused. "Okay?"

"In the morning, you ask to see her again, but she says she can't. She's...in the closet. You give her your number anyway because you realize, after one night, that you're falling for her. A few weeks go by and you don't hear from her. What would you do?"

Deb smiled. "Are you messing with me, Julia?"

Julia took a long slow sip of her martini, trying to keep her expression neutral. "No, I'm as serious as a heart attack. I need your honest opinion on what you would do."

Deb sipped her beer thoughtfully for a moment. "Okay. I would probably do nothing."

"Nothing? Why?"

"Because she was either telling the truth and will never be able to be with me openly...or she was lying and it was just a one-night stand for her all along."

The truth of Deb's words hit Julia hard and she swallowed deeply, trying not to cry. "Yeah, that's what I think, too," she whispered.

"So, who had incredible sex with this beautiful woman?" Deb asked quietly.

"I had incredible sex with her," Julia said, blinking as her eyes filled with hot, insistent tears as she quickly wiped them away.

Deb was well aware of Julia's romantic history and knew that history did not include any women. She reached for Julia's hand. "Julia, hon, talk to me. How did that happen, exactly?"

Julia slowly recounted meeting Maddie, the drinks and dinner and what happened afterward while Deb sat quietly, attentively listening.

"Why now and why this particular woman?" Deb asked her.

Julia shrugged. "I can't explain it, Deb. I noticed her right away, thought she was gorgeous, and when she talked to me, I found her to be charming and funny." Julia impatiently wiped away a stray tear. "And she made me feel smart and...beautiful."

Deb leaned forward. "Hey, you know you're smart and you have to know how attractive you are. Hon...you're hot."

Julia smiled. "Deb, I know how to work with I've got...my hair, my make-up and how to dress, but she...Maddie thought what I had to say was important and interesting and that's what made me attractive to her, not the...package I come in." Julia bit her lip. "This woman, she said she was impressed by me."

"Did neither one of your husbands, make you feel...valued?" Deb asked.

Julia shrugged. "Not like this, and when we were together, her focus was not on her needs because, let's face it...with a man, it almost always comes back to him and what gets him off."
"I'll take your word for that," Deb said with a smile.

Julia smiled back. "Maddie seemed to need to make me feel good, but for my pleasure...not for her own gratification and I found that I was completely invested in her pleasure, too."

"I think that's one of the best things about being with a woman." Deb's voice was low and quiet. "Making her feel good and beautiful, watching her get off at my hands."

Julia blew a breath through pursed lips and averted her gaze. "Well, if that was the case for Maddie, she enjoyed herself...a lot."

Deb laughed quietly. "How many times did she enjoy herself?"

Julia breathed past a brief moment of shyness. "Several...many times. And I more than enjoyed it, too. I fucking reveled in it. It was incredible." Julia's voice hitched as she tried to subdue a sob. "She was incredible...smart, gorgeous and young. We had a lot of things in common. We talked all night about art, books, our kids and I was...completely taken with her."

Deborah watched Julia for a long moment. "I think I know you pretty well. I've seen you sick and scared, but I'm not sure I've ever seen you quite this vulnerable before. Being with a woman can be highly emotional," Deb spoke quietly.

"It was a level of intimacy I was not familiar with. You know what I'm talking about, don't you?"

Deborah sighed. "Yes, I do but Julia...what if this woman..." She hesitated.

"Just tell me what you think, Deb," Julia said.

"As incredible as it was, this...encounter may not have meant to her what it meant to you. I'm sure it meant something to her, but it meant...everything to you." Julia nodded at Deb, answering the unspoken question before Deb continued. "Even if you had the chance to see her again, what if she can't be with you openly?" Deb asked quietly.

Julia shook her head. "I don't know."

Deb raised an eyebrow, in apparent disbelief. "Julia Sinclair, you are not the kind of woman who can be someone's dirty little secret," Deb stated firmly.

"No, I'm not, you're right about that," Julia said quietly. "I've just never felt like this."

"I can see that, hon."

"She would have called by now, right?" Julia watched as Deb met her gaze.

Deb nodded. "I think she would have, yes. I'm sorry, Julia. What can I do?"

"You're doing it, Deb."

Julia inhaled deeply and tried not to feel like a foolish girl who had misinterpreted a simple sexual encounter as some sort of sign of genuine emotion. Julia waved at the server to order another round.

Maddie cursed under her breath as she ran to catch the elevator, just stepping through the quickly closing doors. She rubbed her forehead and tried taking deep breaths to slow her quickly beating heart. As a rule, she was never late for work but this would be the second time this week that she would be cutting it close. She knew it was because she had been having trouble sleeping and that was due, in no small part to constant thoughts of Julia.

Maddie had thought about Julia almost constantly since she had left her in her hotel room. She thought about how much she had enjoyed Julia's company, how Julia had paid attention to everything she said and how Julia had made her laugh. Maddie thought about how it felt when Julia had touched her and how the sensations had been so powerful, how the orgasms had been so sharp and intense. How Julia had made her feel beautiful and sexy and so many other things when she had touched her.

Maddie thought about watching Julia sleep, how Julia's face had looked so calm and so beautiful, her arms resting above her head, and how the sheet had barely covered her full and beautiful breasts.

She stepped out of the elevator and walked quickly down the hallway, pulling open the heavy glass door that led to her department. She rushed to her desk, throwing her purse into her

69

left bottom drawer as she reached over to start up her desktop before her boss came out of his office. She noticed that it was already logged in, open to her e-mail.

She blinked in confusion before she saw the yellow sticky note beneath her keyboard. It read, *"You owe me. Cocktail tonight? Steven."* She smiled, thanking her friend silently as she quickly checked her e-mail.

After work, Maddie met Steven at the bar on the next block. It was a little too upscale for Maddie's taste but she knew Steven liked it. She spotted him standing at the quiet end of the bar, his dark hair mussed from pulling his tie off, his shirt unbuttoned, and she smiled. They had worked together for over 5 years, becoming close over the last two. He was the closest thing she had to a girlfriend besides her sister-in-law, Maria, and she was very grateful for him.

She sat in the bar chair he had saved for her and ordered a sidecar for him as usual, and a lemon drop martini for herself. She saw his eyebrows rise in surprise because she always drank white wine.

"Since when do you drink lemon drop martinis?"

Maddie thought of the lemon drop as Julia's drink and had ordered her very first one a few days after being with Julia. That night, she had gone to a bar alone for the first time in her life, trying to drown her sorrow over her decision to walk away from Julia. It seemed only right to order one now.

"Since they remind me of someone I'm missing."

"Okay. Who are you missing?" Steven was watching her closely. Steven's light blue eyes gazed at her through his rimless glasses.

"Her name is Julia." Maddie inhaled deeply and let it out slowly. "Steven, this stays between us, okay?"

He nodded. "Of course, as always. What's going on?"

Maddie paused as their drinks were placed in front of them and she slid some cash across the bar, waving off the bartender's offer of change. She swallowed deeply from her glass and nodded at Steven. "Okay. I met a woman...Julia... at the hotel bar Friday night. We started to talk, had a drink, she took me to dinner and I...I spent the night with her."

His eyes widened before he blinked and pulled over the nearest bar chair, falling into it heavily. "Sweet Maddie, you're serious."

Steven looked understandably shocked, as he knew this was completely out of character for her. Maddie bit her lip, trying hard to stop from tearing up. "What am I going to do?"

"Why do you have to do something?" He asked quietly. "It was a one-time thing, wasn't it?"

"No, I've never and she's never...with a woman. It was more than sex and she's all I can think about."

Maddie tried to wipe away the moisture on her cheek discreetly, thinking that she had cried more tears over Julia in the last few weeks than she had in years. Steven placed a soft hand on her arm.

"Okay, just tell me what happened," he said quietly.

Maddie relayed the events of the evening to him, skipping over the most personal details but managing to convey how Julia had treated her, how she had made her feel. She told Steven how Julia wanted to see her again and how she had walked away, afraid of starting a relationship with a woman and having to come out to her family, especially her mother.

"I know your mother can be difficult, but how bad would it be? She's very nice to me."

"Until you're out of earshot. Every time she has seen us together or I mention doing something with you, she reprimands me, reminding me that I'll never meet a real man if everyone thinks I'm dating you!"

"Why didn't you ever tell me that?"

"Because I didn't want to hurt your feelings."

He smiled. "Maddie, stop thinking about everyone else's feelings and start worrying about your own feelings."

She rubbed her forehead. "I know."

"You have to live your life, Maddie. Don't you want to be yourself? Be happy?"

"Of course I do but at what cost? What if I lose my family?"

"What if you lose yourself?"

Maddie shook her head. "I don't even know who I am anymore."

Steven smiled. "I know who you are. You're my beautiful, smart, kind lesbian friend."

Maddie looked around self-consciously to ensure that no one had overheard him and then realized what she had done. He shook his head. "Don't do that. Don't be ashamed of who you are."

"I'm sorry."

"Are you ashamed of me because I'm gay?"

Maddie was horrified. "What? No, of course not! Steven, you know I'm not."

"Then don't be ashamed of yourself. Tell me you're a lesbian."

"What? You know I am."

"But you've never said it. You've always said that you're attracted to women. Say 'I'm a lesbian.'"

Maddie looked at him, annoyed with him and embarrassed with herself at the same time. He was right, of course. She had never uttered those words out loud. She bit her lip. She thought about Julia, how she had touched Julia, had made her moan and arch and how Julia had done the same to her.

"I'm a lesbian." Her voice sounded quiet, but sure to her own ears.

Steven smiled widely. "Yes, you are. If you want to have a life, Maddie, you need to come out to your family, to your mother. It will not be easy. Trust me I know. My father is still not comfortable but we do have a relationship. If your mother loves you, she will get over it."

"What if you're wrong?"

"You cannot control other people's actions, Maddie, just your own, but you need to give her the chance to make her own decision." Maddie nodded as she finished her martini. "Give her a chance, Mads, that's all you can do."

Chapter 8

It was Friday night and all Maddie wanted to do was kick off her pumps and put her feet up while she sipped on a chilled glass of white wine. Instead, she sighed as she struggled to attach a hoop earring as she reluctantly finished dressing for the monthly dinner with her family. Her mother had called earlier and told her where she and Gabriel were expected to be and when. Maddie knew better than to try to back out once she heard the angry clipped tones of her mother's voice, which meant her mother was in one of her obstinate moods. Maddie dreaded having to smile and socialize, still shaken by the events of her morning and wanting nothing more than to be alone to think.

Maddie had not even been fully awake that morning when she had reached her hand out to the empty space in her bed, expecting Julia to be sleeping there beside her. Even half asleep, she had immediately realized that she was alone and woke completely, blinking in the dim light. She had inhaled deeply, trying to center herself when she realized that her nipples were stiff and hard and that her center was hot and damp with arousal. She had closed her eyes and tried not to cry as sensuous images of Julia played in her mind's eye.

She remembered Julia straddling her, naked and panting, her full breasts bouncing wildly as Maddie curled her fingers inside her, her neck taut as her head fell back in ecstasy. She thought about how Julia's gaze had locked on hers as they pleasured each other. She could still envision the stark pain on Julia's face when Maddie had told her good-bye.

This morning had not been the first morning that a half-asleep Maddie had reached for Julia in her bed, and like every other time it had happened, it left her feeling empty, alone and altogether unsettled.

Maddie tried to stop thinking about Julia as she and Gabe walked into the restaurant where they were meeting their family. She spotted them across the busy dining room, but stopped short when her sister-in-law, Maria, caught her gaze and widened her eyes in an obvious sign of warning.

"Who's that?" Gabe asked, referring to someone she didn't recognize sitting at their family's table. Maddie saw her mother's shrewd gaze jump from Maria across the crowded dining room to meet her own disbelieving look.

Maddie's parents had always helped both of their children, financial and otherwise, but that help had always come with conditions. The main condition being the relentless pressure and expectation to do what they wanted, specifically, what her mother wanted. Unfortunately, what her mother wanted was for Maddie to be married by now. They had repeatedly tried to set her up with what they considered eligible suitors and Maddie had repeatedly asked them not to do it.

The last time they had tried this, Maddie had threatened to stop speaking to them. Apparently, they had not taken the threat seriously, but why would they? She had rarely pushed back, but tonight, with memories of being with Julia bolstering her, she found that she was angry and fed up with being disrespected and having her feelings completely disregarded.

Gabe looked at her. "Mom, are they kidding with this again?" Gabe knew how his mother felt about these blind dates and he sounded as angry as she felt.

Maddie watched Gabe march to the table ahead of her and take the seat next to this evening's eligible candidate so she would not be forced to. She smiled gratefully at him as she slipped into the seat beside Maria, her hand instantly clasped in silent support. Maria had become family when she had married her brother, Lorenzo, years before, but she had become her friend almost as soon as they had met. Maddie loved Maria like a sister, mostly because she was the only person that dared to defy her mother, something that even her brother never dared to do.

She glared at him now. "Enzo, did you lose my phone number or your balls?" she hissed, only loudly enough for his ears.

Enzo had the good sense to look mortified at the uncomfortable situation they all found themselves in and Maddie found herself becoming increasingly angry that no one had dared to challenge her mother. Maddie knew that defying her mother was always a worse choice than capitulating to her but she was disappointed that no one had given her any advance warning.

Maddie's mother smiled at her and indicated the mystery man. "Layna, this is Tony. He's a friend of your father's."

Maddie knew that was a lie since she knew all of her father's friends. She wondered where her mother had found the latest contestant in this tedious game. Tony was a bit older than Maddie, his obviously dyed black hair combed straight back, and she could detect the unfamiliar scent of cheap cologne masking the smell of stale cigarette smoke. When he smiled, Maddie noticed what appeared to be tobacco stains on his teeth. Everyone who knew Maddie knew that she detested smoking. She thought her parents must have been getting desperate if this was the best candidate they had to offer.

"You must be Layna," Tony said.

Maddie sighed. "I must be."

He held out his hand to her. "Anthony Salvador. Call me Tony."

Maddie pointedly glared at her parents as she reached across her brother to shake Tony's damp, cold hand. "Mr. Salvador. That is my son, Gabriel."

Gabriel nodded at Tony and started to make polite small talk with him. Maddie turned to Maria. "Did you know?" She kept her voice low.

"Not until I got here. I was texting you when you walked in," Maria whispered. "What is your mother thinking, querida?"

"I don't think she is." Maddie smiled at the waiter as he approached. "A lemon drop martini for me please."

Tony smiled at Maddie, apparently completely unaffected by her less than enthusiastic welcome. "So, Layna, your mother tells me you work for a big company. What do you do?"

Maddie noticed how his eyes had strayed to the cleavage peeking out from her collared blouse before returning his gaze to her face. She tried not to shiver in revulsion. "I'm the Executive Assistant to the Vice President for an advertising and public relations firm."
"So, like a secretary?"

Maddie heard Gabriel snort as she shook her head. "No. It's a little more involved than that. A degree is required for my position."

Maddie heard Julia's voice in her head, telling her that she was an impressive woman, that she was a real catch and how much she enjoyed her company. She was suddenly overcome with a desperate longing to hear Julia's sexy raspy voice.

Tony's voice interrupted her thoughts. "I own my own business ya know...a cleaning company. They call me the 'King of Office Cleaning'."

"Tony does well for himself," her mother chimed in with a tight smile.

Tony nodded. "Yeah, I make good money."

Maddie heard Maria stifle a horrified gasp and felt Maria's hand tighten against her thigh beneath the table. Maddie managed not to roll her eyes at the boastful statement.

"How nice for you," she managed to say. The waiter placed a large martini glass in front of Maddie and she reached for it, sipping deeply.

"You like this place? I can take you out to dinner to a place way nicer than this, just the two of us," Tony said, smiling as his gaze once again strayed to her cleavage.

Maddie wondered if Tony realized he had just insulted her parents and she smiled when she heard Maria mutter a profanity in Portuguese under her breath.

With the taste of the lemon drop on her tongue and thoughts of Julia in her head, Maddie managed to find her backbone. "I'm sorry, Mr. Salvador, but I'm not available to have dinner with you...or for anything else."

"But your mother said–"

"I'm sorry, my mother is mistaken. I'm seeing someone." Maddie glared at her mother as she rudely cut him off.

"O quê? Você está namorando quem?" Her mother displayed her fury by hissing at Maddie through her teeth in Portuguese, demanding to know who Maddie was dating. No one dared to challenge her mother, and certainly not publicly like Maddie had just done.

Maddie inhaled deeply, thinking about what Julia had said to her about not selling herself short and she turned to her mother to say what she had never before dared to say to her. "Ma, I have asked you over and over again to stop doing this. Since you have absolutely no respect for my feelings, I'm going to excuse myself for the evening."

Maddie heard her mother gasp as she finished the rest of her drink in one long swallow and pushed her chair back. Gabriel instantly got to his feet and followed his mother as she walked briskly across the restaurant, heading directly out the door without looking back. Maddie had never before openly defied her mother and she wondered where the courage to do so now had come from.

Once seated in their car, Gabe turned to his mother. "Let's get out of here. Did you see Vavó's face? She is off-the-hook pissed at you."

"Yeah, well, I'm off-the-hook pissed at her." Maddie could not insert the key into the ignition and realized that her hands were shaking.

Gabe reached over and held her forearm gently. "Let me drive, Mom. Okay?"

Maddie simply nodded and they both exited the car, switching places quickly. "Be careful, Gabe," she reminded him as he pulled out into traffic. "Let's go to the pub. You can get a burger and I can get drunk." She noticed Gabe's eyes widen at that, since she rarely drank and certainly never got drunk.

As soon they were seated across from each other in a back booth of the pub near their home, Gabe looked at his mother. "You okay, Mom?" She simply nodded. "That Tony was a real creep, wasn't he?" Gabe asked.

Maddie nodded again, and waved a server over, ordering herself another lemon drop martini and Gabe a Coke. Maddie tried to stop the whirlwind of thoughts and emotions swirling inside her. Hiding her true self from the rest of the world had always been something that Maddie had simply done unconsciously, without thought or question. Since being with Julia, she had done nothing but question every little thing that she automatically did to keep up the charade. She realized that she had not been completely honest with anyone in her life, not with her own son and not even with herself. To her intense mortification, Maddie could not blink back her sudden tears and they spilled over her lashes and down her face.

Gabe reached for her hands across the table. "Mom, c'mon, you don't have to go out with him."

Maddie quickly wiped her face. "I know. It's not that." She gathered her courage and inhaled a deep breath, looking directly at her son. "Gabriel, would you freak out if I was gay?"

Gabe blinked and shook his head in confusion as he threw himself back against the leather seat of the booth. "Whoa. What? Gay? Uhmm, okay, no, I don't think I would freak out. Jesus, Mom, please explain yourself."

Maddie smiled as Gabriel used her own words on her. She often used that exact phrase with him when she wanted him to give her details.

Maddie inhaled deeply. "When you were visiting your father, I picked up a shift at the hotel and a woman came into the bar. She was very high-end, attractive, but not showy, just...classy. She was alone and she just wanted to sit and have a drink but men kept bothering her, trying to pick her up, so I offered to sit with her when I got off shift. She was smart and funny and we hit it off right away. She invited me to have dinner with her…in the hotel."

"At the Essex? You ate at the Essex?" Gabe asked, his eyes wide.

"Yeah, I felt underdressed so she let me wear her very expensive designer jacket and she took me to the Essex and it was amazing. The food…the wine…her company. I had the best time. We talked for hours and I realized that I liked her. A lot. More than a lot." Maddie looked up and met her son's gaze squarely. "More than I have ever liked any man."

Gabriel swallowed hard, watching his mother carefully. "Was she…hitting on you?" He asked quietly.

"No, Gabe, no, she wasn't. She was more than respectful. She actually treated me better than any man I've ever dated. We just…I don't know…had a connection. After a few glasses of wine, she said some things that let me know that she was feeling the same way I was feeling."

"So, what happened? How did you leave it? She's too high-end to date a mina?"

Maddie smiled at her son's use of the slang word for a Brazilian girl. Instead of being upset by her revelation, he was being protective of her. "No, she wanted to see me again, but I said I couldn't."

"Mom, why? You haven't dated anyone in a long time, but I know you get offers all the time, from men and from women. I'm not blind to that. If you finally met someone you like that much, even if it's a girl…I mean a woman, you should do it."

Maddie inhaled a deep breath. "I'm afraid."

Gabe's head jerked up in apparent surprise. "I didn't think you were afraid of anything."

Maddie nodded. "Everyone is afraid of something and I'm afraid of this, of what this would mean, of what your grandmother would do if she found out. I...Gabriel...I was involved with a woman before you were born...and I didn't have the courage...to live that life."

Gabriel watched his mother carefully. "Wow. I'm really surprised at that."

"That I was with a woman?" Maddie asked, her stomach dropping at the possibility that her son might disapprove of her true self.

"No, that you were afraid. What happened to my mother, who told me you can only be brave when you're afraid?"

Maddie smiled at her son. "I love you, Gabriel, but sometimes I hate it when you pay attention."

Gabriel returned the smile. "I love you, too and I always pay attention."

"You're really okay with this...if I'm...you know...?"

"Gay? Well, as okay as I can be. I'd rather see you with a nice woman than with someone like the 'King of Office Cleaning' that's for sure." Gabe shrugged. "It's just a little weird because you're my mother." Gabe leaned forward. "Seriously, if you like this woman...what's her name?"

"Julia," Maddie said and smiled.

"If you like Julia that much, I think you should go for it."

"I can't stop thinking about her."

"Have you talked to her since then?"

"No."

"She hasn't called you?" Her son asked with a frown.

"I didn't give her my number. She gave me hers but..."

"Jeez, Mom, you just left her hanging?" Gabriel asked, his voice high.

"I told her I couldn't see her again," Maddie admitted quietly.

"Was she okay with that?" Gabe asked.

Maddie paused. "No." Maddie had been so absorbed in her own personal struggle that she had not really spent a lot of time thinking about how she may have hurt Julia. "Shit...maybe she doesn't even want to see me again."

"You won't know..." Gabriel began the statement that his mother often repeated to him.

Maddie smiled. "...until you try."

Maddie stared down at Julia's number in her phone. She looked up at her son and he smiled at her in encouragement.

"What should I say?" Maddie asked him as she held her phone.

"Just say hi, Mom."

She inhaled deeply and slowly typed out a text.

Hi. It's Maddie

Maddie stared at the text, trying to think of something else to say, something meaningful or witty. She decided that the brief message was enough if Julia wanted to hear from her. If Julia did not want to hear from her, then there was nothing more to say. She pressed the send button.

Chapter 9

Julia sat on her deck in the dark, wrapped in a blanket against the spring night air, sounds from the nearby marina and an occasional distant voice carried over the water on the cold breeze. It was chilly and Julia knew she should go inside, but the house was too quiet, so she sipped on her Absolut Citron and pulled the blanket closer around her. She shook her head. She would usually relish some time alone, but all she could dwell on was what Deb had said about Maddie.

She heard her phone vibrate against the coffee table in front of her and she sighed as she put her drink down to pick up the phone. It indicated that it was a text, the number unfamiliar, but she opened it. She read the short message and blinked.

Hi. It's Maddie

Julia inhaled sharply, stunned at the words in front of her. She had hoped every day for weeks that she would hear from Maddie and when she finally decided to let her go, this happens. Julia had no idea what to do or what to text back, if anything. She cursed the amount of alcohol she had consumed with Deb but then she laughed at herself for feeling like a nervous teenager. She stared at the text and sensed the hesitancy in those three little words staring back at her, or maybe she was simply imagining things. She remembered telling Maddie to get in touch if she ever needed anything or if she just wanted to talk and maybe it was as simple as that.

"Nothing ventured, nothing gained," Julia muttered to herself. She saved the phone number, carefully typing in "Maddie" before she inhaled deeply and texted back.

Hello Maddie.

A response was almost immediate.

How are you?

Julia smiled. Now what? Julia stared at the message. Deb's words from earlier in the evening echoed in her head. *You are not the kind of woman who can be someone's dirty little secret.* Liquid courage made Julia throw caution to the wind and simply be honest.

Other than missing you, I'm fine.

Maddie looked down at her phone, excited and frightened. She smiled so widely her eyes nearly closed. She could hear Gabe laughing quietly as she stared at the text message. She texted back.

I miss you, too. Can I see you?

Maddie waited long excruciating moments and she thought that Julia might not respond before a return text appeared.

I'd like that

Maddie stared at the message. She had not thought this through. Would Julia be willing to travel into the city, or should she head to Fairhaven, where Julia lived? Maddie considered the constant calls from her mother that she had been ignoring since she had left the restaurant, how she had avoided going back to her own home to escape from dealing with the pressures of her family.

She wanted to see Julia where she could relax and be herself. She made a quick decision and went with it.

Are you free tomorrow? I can come to you

Julia breathed deeply, staring at the offer. As well as the overwhelming desire to see Maddie, she also liked the feeling of being pursued, but she did not want to seem anxious. Julia texted back.

You know where I am.

Deb's voice was a nagging reminder at the back of her mind. *It may have meant something to her, but it meant everything to you.* Julia took a deep bracing swallow of vodka, shuddering slightly as she wondered what it had meant, what she had meant to Maddie. Something or everything?

"I guess I'll find out." Her quiet words were carried off by the cool ocean breeze.

Once Julia faced the stark reality of the morning, she did not change the tentative plans she had already made for her Saturday, not quite convinced that Maddie would actually make an appearance. Julia was a great believer in keeping her expectations within reason so she wouldn't be constantly disappointed and this situation seemed tailor-made for that. She did have a moment of optimism, though, and dressed in a lightweight short-sleeved sweater and a pencil skirt, swallowing deeply when she pulled stockings up to attach them to the garters she decided at the last minute to wear beneath the skirt.

Since Eleanor was with her Dad until the following morning, Julia had planned to head into the office and get some work done. Julia's plan was to catch up on e-mails and return some calls. Being out and about on this sunny spring day was also doing wonders for her frame of mind. Julia parked her car near her office and forced herself to walk over to get coffee on the next block. The brisk walk, as well as interacting with people seemed to help her mood and once she was inside the office she opened all the blinds, cracking a window for fresh air in the conference room that she liked to work in as she sat down to check her e-mails on her laptop.

She could not help but glance down at her phone regularly, checking for any contact from Maddie, but she did manage to get a bit of work accomplished. She was just hanging up from confirming an appointment for a showing later in the week when she heard the sound of the tiny bell on the front door.

"Hello?" Julia called out.

"Mom?" It was Vivienne. Julia had not expected to see her in the office today.

"In the back," she said.

Vivienne strolled in and smiled and Julia marveled at the beautiful combination of her father's long leanness, dark hair and eyes with Julia's own features. "I didn't think I'd see you today," Julia said quietly.

Vivienne looked at Julia. "I came in to print the price sheets for today's open house and...Mom?"

Julia had covered her mouth with her hand. "The open house. I almost forgot."

"You almost forgot an open house?" Vivienne asked. "Since when?"

Julia scrambled mentally. "Since Deb and I went out for too many cocktails last night." She rubbed her forehead. "Shit...shit."

"It's under control, Mom, relax." Julia's cell phone vibrated and she jumped, shaking her head in embarrassment as she checked the message. When she looked up, Vivienne had her arms crossed. "Why are you so jumpy and why are you so dressed up if you forgot about the open house?"

Julia sighed, annoyed at Vivienne's perceptiveness. "I'm not...really dressed up."

"Yes, you are. You always look professional, but this is...more than that. What's going on? You've been so...prickly lately."

"Prickly? I'm not prickly. What does that even mean?"

"Touchy...cranky...and evasive. Also, your attitude has been very 'glass half-empty' instead of 'glass half-full' so spill it. What's going on?"

Julia rolled her eyes. "Nothing, really. I just...I did something a little crazy and very unlike me, Vivie, that's all, and I feel a little foolish and embarrassed about it."

"What did you do? Buy discount Chardonnay?" Vivienne smiled, knowing her mother's love of a fine glass of wine.

Julia laughed. "I wish it had been that kind of crazy, but no."

"Well, what kind of crazy was it?" Vivienne asked.

Julia sighed. "The kind of crazy that should not be discussed with one's daughter."

Vivienne's eyebrows rose in what Julia knew was a fairly accurate impersonation of her. "We discuss everything."

Julia smiled. "Yes, usually we do and I love you, Vivie, but we are not discussing this."

"Why? Oh my God, did you— "

Vivienne stopped talking as they heard the tiny bell over front door jingle. Vivienne turned to head out. "Probably a walk-in. I'll take care of it." She turned back to her mother. "But we are not finished with this conversation."

Julia heard quiet voices in the front before Vivienne came back and popped her head in the doorway. "Mom, there's someone here for you."

Julia put a professional smile on her face as she walked out and through the cubicles that separated the conference room from the reception area. As she cleared the last desk, she froze mid-step.

Maddie stood just inside the door, a tentative smile on her face, the sunlight pouring in from the large windows behind her. Julia realized she had forgotten how utterly beautiful Maddie was as she took in her dimpled smile and the warmth of her deep brown eyes, her dark, hair curling around her shoulders. Maddie was dressed in jeans, sandals and an embroidered cotton top, looking young and gorgeous. Julia simply stared at her for a long moment.

"You're here," Julia finally said.

"I am." Maddie's smile widened. "It's really good to see you."

Julia felt every emotion she had ever associated with Maddie, but she did not trust her feelings right now and she was not certain if she trusted Maddie either. Julia glanced around, wondering where Vivienne had gone and if she could overhear them.

Julia swallowed. "Sorry. You've caught me by surprise. How did you know where I was?"

"I'm sorry, I didn't." Maddie shook her head. "I still have your card so I took a chance you might be here but...I've obviously shown up at a bad time so I can meet you...somewhere else...later?" Maddie backed up a step toward the door, as if to leave.

Julia closed the short distance between them and reached for Maddie's arm, afraid if she let Maddie leave now, she might never see her again. "No, please don't go." Julia knew that she sounded desperate and probably looked frantic. She quickly released Maddie's arm and stepped back, embarrassed at her blatant insecurity. She lowered her gaze. "I'm almost afraid to let you out of my sight."

"Ouch," Maddie said quietly. "I guess I deserve that."

Julia was mortified that she had blurted out exactly what she was thinking. "No, no, you don't. I'm sorry, it's just that...I'm not sure what to think and I don't want to get ahead of myself."

"And get hurt again?" Maddie asked, tentatively reaching for one of Julia's hands. "I can see that I've hurt you, Julia, and I never intended to do that. I honestly wasn't sure if you'd thought of what happened between us as casual...or not...until this very moment."

Julia stared at Maddie. It had not occurred to her what Maddie may have assumed about her intentions or their encounter. It had not occurred to her that Maddie knew as little about her as she knew about Maddie. Julia wanted to give her the benefit of the doubt, but she would not let her off the hook quite that easily.

"I told you I wanted to see you again. I gave you my card," Julia said.

"I know you did, but that didn't necessarily mean it wasn't casual to you. I couldn't be sure of anything...including myself to be honest...but I'm here now."

"May I ask why exactly?"

Maddie nodded. "I haven't stopped thinking about you and I realized how much I missed you...just talking to you. I kept thinking of things I wanted to share with you. I kept waking up and..." Maddie paused, swallowing deeply. "...and reaching for you in my bed." She whispered the last few words. When Julia did not respond, Maddie took a step back and started to release her hand. "It's okay if you're not sure. I'm in town until tomorrow."

Julia squeezed her hand, keeping hold of it. "Please...wait." Julia's emotions were in free fall and she lowered her gaze, not wanting Maddie to see her panic at the thought of her walking out the door. Julia tried to control her emotions, but she could not and her eyes burned as she blinked away impending tears.

Maddie stepped closer, looking at her carefully. "Are you okay?"

"I didn't think I would ever see you again." Julia heard her own voice break.

Maddie cupped Julia's cheek as she wiped away some wetness beneath her eye with a gentle swipe of her thumb. When Julia raised her head, Maddie leaned in and pressed a soft and chaste kiss to Julia's mouth.

"Oh, querida, I'm so sorry," Maddie whispered.

The kiss was soft and fleeting, but it stunned Julia in how deeply it affected her. "It's...can we...let's go into the conference room in the back, okay?"

As Julia turned around, she noticed Vivienne was sitting in the cubicle closest to the conference room, typing at the desktop there. Julia heard the printer in the far corner of the office come to life and sighed. Vivienne looked busy, but there was very little chance that she had not overheard at least portions of their conversation or seen that kiss, however brief, and Julia had no idea what she would say to her daughter. As they approached, Vivienne simply smiled at them.

Julia turned to Maddie. "Maddie, this is my daughter, Vivienne Cantara. Vivie, this is Madalena Francisco." They shook hands and said hello politely and Julia indicated the conference room with her hand. "Go on ahead, Maddie, I'll be right in."

Julia watched Maddie walk through the doorway before she turned to Vivienne. "So how much of that did you hear?" Julia whispered as she felt herself blushing.

"Enough to know that she is the something crazy that you did," Vivienne whispered back as she glanced toward the conference room. "Are you okay, Mom?"

Julia smiled at her daughter. "I have no idea. Are you?"

Vivienne smiled back. "Just a little surprised. I didn't think you had it in you."

Julia placed her hands on her waist in a defiant pose. "Give me some credit, Vivienne."

Vivienne stifled a laugh with her hand. "Is this a mid-life crisis type of thing?" It was barely a whisper.

Julia bit her lip, looking her daughter in the eye. "No, this is...serious," she mouthed almost silently.

Vivienne looked surprised. "Wow. Okay. Do you want moral support or privacy?"

"Privacy now, moral support later?"

Vivienne smiled as she grabbed her purse. "I'm just going to grab my price sheets on the way out. I'm assuming I should cover the open house alone?"

"Do you mind terribly?"

"No, it's good experience for me," Vivienne said as she rounded the desk. She stopped and hugged her mother, placing a warm kiss to her cheek. "She's gorgeous, Mom. Good luck," she whispered as she walked away, stopping to pick up her copies on the way out.

Julia walked into the conference room and Maddie met her gaze from across the room.

"Hi." Julia smiled as she walked toward Maddie.

Maddie met her halfway and they tentatively embraced until Julia pulled her close, sighing deeply as Maddie's hands pressed firmly against her back. Sense memory washed over Julia as she inhaled Maddie's familiar scent and she pulled her impossibly closer. Julia melted into the embrace, her intense physical attraction for Maddie nearly overwhelming her.

Julia made a conscious decision to reign in her desire, to keep her wits about her and take things slowly. Julia wanted to talk to Maddie, to determine where they stood with each other and what they both wanted. Julia had to force herself to release Maddie and pull away.

Julia found Maddie running her gaze slowly over her face, and then down her body, a small frown on her face.

"You feel thinner. Are you thinner?" Maddie asked.

Julia blinked in surprise at the uncannily accurate scrutiny. "How did you—?"

"I remember everything about you," Maddie said quietly. "Some days, it's all I can think about."

Surprised at the response and the open look of longing on Maddie's face, Julia lowered her gaze and stepped away, rubbing her forehead to get her bearings. "I may have lost a little weight," Julia admitted.

Maddie moved to keep Julia's gaze on her own. "I think it was more than a little and you didn't need to lose any weight."

"Well, thank you, but I wasn't really trying to," Julia told her.

"Jule, are you ill?"

The shortened version of her name caught Julia off guard and she turned her back to Maddie and tried to slow her breathing. The last time Maddie had called her that had been in the throes of passion and Julia could not think about that right now. Julia shook her head. "No, no, I've just...it's been difficult."

Maddie closed the distance between them and touched Julia's shoulder. "What's been difficult? What happened?" Maddie asked her quietly as she moved in front of Julia.

Julia rubbed her forehead. "You happened, okay? You happened and then you disappeared and...it hit me pretty hard."

Julia could see that her revelation had stunned Maddie. Julia watched the color leave Maddie's face as she swallowed repeatedly. "Oh Julia, I never meant to hurt you."

"I know that. We made no promises." Julia shrugged. "I needed to lose some weight anyway."

"You most certainly did not," Maddie said firmly, sounding indignant.

"I was getting a little–"

"What? Curvy? Sexy?" Maddie asked loudly.

"Fat." Julia sighed. She had never been entirely content with her body, but in the brief time they had been together, Maddie had made her feel comfortable, sexy, and even beautiful.

Maddie shook her head. "That's ridiculous. Julia, you're gorgeous." Julia saw Maddie's gaze wander over her body. "So incredibly gorgeous."

Julia shivered, her desire for this woman making her head spin. "I'm glad you think so."

"Querida, I do."

Julia blinked at the term of endearment. "So...you're Portuguese?"

Maddie looked surprised by the unexpected question. "Yes. Half Portuguese actually, half Brazilian."

Julia ran her gaze over Maddie's face. "It's a beautiful combination."

Maddie blushed. "Thank you. Vivienne's last name is Portuguese, isn't it?"

"Yes, her father is Portuguese. Apparently, I may have a type." Julia rolled her eyes.

Maddie smiled. "So, Eleanor's Dad, is he...?"

Julia shook her head. "No, Jason is fair skinned, and the one exception to my apparent preference, if I think about it."

"So, Vivienne's father...that's how you're familiar with the language."

"Well, that and it's a part of the culture in this area. So, are you going to tell me exactly what you said to me in Portuguese the night we were together?"

Maddie blinked in surprise. "You remember that?"

"I remember everything about that night." Julia stared at her, instinctively knowing that Maddie did not want to reveal what she had uttered to Julia in the throes of passion. "And I know you weren't being completely honest with me about what you said."

Maddie shook her head. "No, I wasn't and I'm sorry. I just didn't expect to feel the things you made me feel."

Julia exhaled. "So it wasn't just me, then?"

"I'm here, aren't I?" Maddie whispered, her eyes wide, her expression open.

Unable to resist any longer, Julia pulled Maddie into a hard kiss, lips pressing and tongues seeking as she tried to control the incredible attraction simmering between them. Julia finally pulled away from the kiss, but held onto Maddie tightly, trying to slow her breathing. She wanted nothing more than to get lost in Maddie, but she would not let herself completely trust this, not yet.

"So I guess I didn't exaggerate in my mind how good it feels to kiss you," Julia whispered near Maddie's ear.

"Kissing you makes me forget my own name," Maddie whispered against her neck.

Julia pulled away and looked at Maddie. "What are we doing here...exactly?"

"Spending time...getting to know each other...figuring things out. Is that okay, for now?"

Julia felt herself smiling. "Yes, I think so."

Maddie's answering smile was brilliant. "So...can I take you to lunch?"

Julia tried not to stare at Maddie as they settled into their chairs on the oversized deck of the restaurant called Ishmael's. They both ordered a glass of Riesling before Julia became completely distracted by Maddie pulling her sunglasses up onto her head to hold her hair away from her face. Maddie's gaze moved over the fishing boats in the harbor, the ocean breeze lifting loose strands of her curly hair.

Maddie turned to her and smiled. "This is a great view."

Julia kept her gaze on Maddie. "Especially from where I'm sitting."

Julia watched Maddie's smile get bigger and she ducked her gaze for a moment before looking back up at Julia. "Thank you." Maddie inhaled deeply. "So...Vivienne is beautiful, although I wouldn't know she was yours at first glance."

Julia laughed. "If you spent a little time with her, you'd see the resemblance. Sometimes I want to scold her for her sarcasm or snarky remarks and then I realize she sounds just like me, so I can't.

I'm sure I will be further interrogated about you the first chance she gets."

"Will she be okay...with this?"

"She already is."

Maddie looked surprised. "Oh, okay. How is Eleanor?"

Julia smiled. "Getting way too smart for me, thank you for asking. How's Gabriel?"

Maddie nodded. "Good. I told him...about you, that I wanted to see you again."

Julia was pleasantly surprised by the revelation. "Oh?"

"I was having a bad day, missing you...and then my parents did something that really upset me. Gabe and I were talking and I started to cry. Poor Gabe. I told him everything after that."

"Is he okay about it?"

Maddie smiled. "Yeah, he encouraged me to get in touch with you."

"You needed encouragement?" Julia asked quietly.

"I did because, well, the way you make me feel scares me...and I thought I'd waited too long."

Julia nodded, thinking about what Maddie had said about her life and how her family would not approve of this. "Can I ask what your parents did to upset you so much?"

Maddie sighed. "Sure. They ambushed me at a family dinner with a blind date when I have repeatedly told them I am not interested in dating any man, and even if I was, it would never be this man." Maddie shuddered. "He had a bad dye job and a mustache straight out of bad 70's porn. He reeked of cheap cologne and cigarette smoke." Maddie shook her head. "I hate smoking. He tried to impress me by how much money he makes. I do just fine on my own, thank you very much...and have my parents met me?"

"Apparently not," Julia said with a small smile. "You watch bad 70's porn?"

Maddie smiled. "No." She looked at Julia. "It was pretty awful. He wasn't even interested in me as a person. He just kept staring at my breasts."

Julia leaned forward. "Oh, honey, I'm so sorry, your parents should not have done that, but I can't really blame him for staring. Your breasts are magnificent." Julia hoped that the comment was the right blend of flattery and humor and she was delighted as Maddie laughed, letting out a small snort.

"I wouldn't have minded if you'd been the one staring at them," Maddie said.

Julia smiled at the blatant desire on Maddie's face. "Good to know."

"God, Julia, I've missed you."

Julia relaxed just a little bit. "I've missed you, too."

Chapter 10

When Julia tried to pay for lunch, Maddie took the billfold from her. "Don't even try it. I asked you."

Julia smiled and allowed her to pay, then reached for her hand. "Would you like to see my house? We can talk there."

Maddie agreed and she followed Julia's car into the driveway of a Victorian style home overlooking the water, the sunlight glittering along the water's surface beyond the sloping lawn. There was a separate garage and carriage house on the property.

Maddie stepped out of her car and looked around. "This is your house?"

"Yes. Vivie lives in the carriage house." Julia turned toward the front porch. "Please come inside."

Maddie had known that Julia was successful and had expected her to have a nice house, but never imagined this property on the water that was worthy of being featured in a magazine. Maddie followed Julia silently onto the large front porch, through the front door and into a large foyer. Maddie looked into the living area on the left and a small dining room to the right as Julia locked the door behind them. The house was bright, the woodwork painted white, with gleaming hardwood floors, Native American style area rugs and simple but tasteful furnishings. Maddie could easily picture Julia living here. She turned and found Julia watching her.

"Your home is somewhat like you," Maddie said.

Julia raised her eyebrows. "Oh? Older? High maintenance?"

Maddie smiled and shook her head. "No. Classic and beautiful," she whispered.

"Thank you." Julia crossed her arms in front of her and Maddie suspected that Julia felt as nervous and uncertain as she did. Julia averted her gaze and threw her purse and keys on a table by the door and Maddie did the same.

"Would you like a tour?" Julia asked quietly.

Maddie wanted nothing more than to have Julia in her arms again, to kiss her, to touch her, but Maddie did not know if Julia wanted the same thing or if she should tell Julia that. She tried not to let her gaze linger on Julia's curves.

Maddie shrugged and smiled, "Sure. Of course."

Julia stared at her, licking her lips, an undercurrent of hot and thick sexual tension flowing between them. "What would you like to see first?" Julia whispered, one of her eyebrows cocked in what Maddie assumed was amusement or challenge.

Maddie shook her head and smiled, thinking that Julia was either teasing her or giving her the opportunity to ask for what she wanted. It also occurred to her that Julia was afraid to make herself vulnerable again. Maddie inhaled deeply and threw caution to the wind.

"I would really like to see your bedroom."

Julia exhaled a long, shuddering breath and reached out her hand to Maddie. Maddie took it and Julia led her slowly up the slightly winding wooden staircase to the second floor. They entered a bedroom at the back of the house and Julia pulled her inside. Maddie was momentarily distracted by the view of the water through the windows overlooking the harbor as Julia shut the door quietly behind them. Julia's headboard was wrought iron with a design of vines and leaves, the bedding white.

Maddie returned her gaze to Julia and inhaled sharply as her body reacted to Julia's intense gaze, her nipples contracting to hard peaks and a torrent of wetness gushing warmly between her legs. Maddie watched Julia walk slowly toward her and her desire for Julia was making her heart race. She reached for Julia, pulling her into a slow but deep kiss, their tongues dueling erotically as Julia cupped her face and head gently.

Julia slowed the kiss and pulled away, staring at Maddie for a moment. "I can't believe you're here. I can't tell you how often I've thought about you, how badly I wanted to see you again."

Maddie grasped the edges of Julia's sweater and pulled it up as Julia raised her arms, allowing her to remove it. Julia kicked off her pumps as she reached for Maddie's blouse. They continued to remove each other's clothing as they moved toward the bed until Maddie was pulling Julia's skirt down over her thighs, revealing the garters and stockings she wore.

Maddie smiled as she stared at the garters at Julia's thighs. She brought her gaze up to look at Julia. "Do you always wear these?"

Julia rolled her eyes. "No, almost never. I just couldn't find any pantyhose the morning of the conference."

"And this morning?"

Julia bit her lip. "This morning I wore them for you."

Maddie ran her hands over the garters. "I'm not sure I can adequately express my gratitude." She caressed the soft skin on Julia's thighs and ass.

Julia gasped as her hips bucked. "You just did. God, Maddie."

Julia's obvious arousal caused Maddie to roughly pull the garter belt and stockings down and off, taking Julia's panties with them. Maddie was desperate to touch Julia so she pushed her back onto the plush bed, following on her hands and knees. Maddie slid her own body gently against Julia's.

"I had almost forgotten how good you feel, how truly beautiful you are," Maddie whispered to her.

Maddie heard Julia moan as she brought her lips to Julia's neck before she moved to her shoulder and chest, quickly working her way down the silken landscape to take a nipple into her mouth, sucking deeply. Julia bucked up against Maddie's thigh, spreading warm arousal over it and Maddie reached down to cup Julia's center gently, sliding her fingers into the overflowing folds.

Every time Maddie had thought about being with Julia, and she had replayed every moment of that night repeatedly in her mind, she only regretted the things she had not done, the ways she had not touched Julia. She had kissed a myriad of soft spots along the landscape of Julia's body, but she wished she had had the courage to kiss Julia's most private area, wished she had brought her pleasure in the most intimate way. Maddie had promised herself that if the opportunity ever presented itself again she would rectify that. It was all that Maddie could think about now.

Julia bucked and moaned. "Maddie, baby, please..."

Maddie appreciated Julia's intense and obvious desire for her and she wanted to hear more of it. She pressed her forehead to Julia's. "Do you want me, Jule?"

"I ache for you...please."

Maddie kissed her way down Julia's body as she ran her hands along the inside of Julia's thighs, gently spreading her legs open. She placed a line of soft kisses along her inner thigh before she brought her mouth to Julia's triangle of soft curls, placing a soft kiss there.

"Oh God," Julia moaned softly as she bucked up into the contact.

Maddie boldly spread Julia open, gasping at the shiny pool of wetness spreading over her fingers and the clean aroma wafting under her nose. Maddie dipped her tongue in for a taste, then another before she ran the flat of her tongue slowly and deliberately through the soft and wet folds, savoring the subtle salty flavor. Julia bucked up into the contact, but Maddie held her down with firm hands at the juncture of her thighs as she began to explore every part of her intimate folds, learning the feel and the taste of her.

Maddie enjoyed feeling that Julia was under her command as she held her down, but did not stop to examine her feelings. She found Julia's clit and licked it, causing Julia to moan and jerk sharply. She started licking steadily and firmly up and down at the same cadence that Julia was setting with the rocking of her hips. Maddie paid close attention to Julia's responses, concentrating on the exact spot and the exact pressure and speed that caused the greatest reaction. After long moments, Julia clutched the back of Maddie's head and ground her hips faster. Maddie waited until she thought Julia was almost there, her wildly jerking hips, her loud moans telling Maddie what she wanted to know. Maddie took the stiff clit into her mouth and sucked gently and Julia exploded against Maddie's mouth, as she shouted her release loudly, the sound echoing in the large bedroom.

Maddie held Julia for a long time as she recovered, watching an occasional tear escaping as her breathing gradually steadied. Maddie ran her gaze over Julia's body, over her features, amazed at the responses she had managed to elicit from this beautiful and sensuous creature. She ran her tongue over her own lips, tasting Julia on herself and she shuddered, amazed at how much she had enjoyed the experience, and how much she wanted to do it again. When she saw Julia's eyes flutter open and look at her, she smiled.

Julia considered herself to be an experienced woman, but it hadn't been until Maddie was bending her knees open to settle herself between them, until Maddie was kissing her inner thigh, that she had known with any certainty what Maddie was about to do. For some reason, she had not imagined this young woman would touch her in this way, but it hadn't been the first time Maddie had surprised her.

She could not recall an orgasm ever being so incredibly, sharply intense and the force and strength of it had stunned her. It had been a very long time since Julia had experienced the powerful physical sensation of having someone's mouth on her and she had let herself surrender to the sensuously patient attention. It had been glorious, the warm and wet concentrated touch, the tactile roughness of Maddie's tongue, the overwhelming exquisiteness of it.

Julia opened her eyes and stared at Maddie for a long moment until Maddie moved in to kiss her. Julia detected her own scent on Maddie's face, tasted herself on Maddie's lips and gasped into the kiss, moving against her. When she pulled away from the kiss, she found Maddie watching her with a small smile. Julia felt her heart leap at what could only be called the adoring gaze that met her own.

Maddie caressed her face gently. "Hi."

"Hi." Julia heard her own husky response.

Julia said nothing else, every other response that occurred to her sounding inane and inadequate to express what she was feeling at the moment and she was frightened to reveal what that was. She wanted to tell Maddie how incredibly good she felt, how much all of this meant to her, but she did not. Instead, she reached for the back of Maddie's head, pulling her forward into a soft kiss.

Desire exploded between them and they surged together, moving into the kiss as they both sought to get closer. Julia pushed Maddie over onto her back, moving over her, taking control of the kiss, plunging her tongue deeply and erotically into her mouth. Maddie pulled her closer as she cradled Julia's thigh between her legs.

Julia pulled her mouth away to move it to Maddie's breasts, paying enough attention to her nipples to make Maddie squirm in pleasure. Maddie clutched the hand Julia had rested against her stomach and she slid it down into her own folds, Julia's fingers instantly engulfed in her warm wetness.

"Something you want?" Julia whispered in her sexy rasp.

Maddie pulled her close, whispering against her ear. "You...inside me."

Julia slid two fingers slowly and deeply into Maddie, pumping steadily, the way that she remembered that Maddie preferred. Julia watched Maddie react to her touch, her hips bucking, her breasts swaying, her hands looking for purchase before trying to pull Julia closer. Julia thought she had never seen anything more beautiful in her life.

"Oh...Jule," Maddie whispered.

Maddie's breathing gradually changed with the cadence of her hips, increasing steadily until Julia curled her fingers up inside her and pushed harder and Maddie moaned out her pleasure loudly.

Julia kept up her efforts as she watched Maddie orgasm, loudly and openly, and she thought that she could watch this lovely creature do this very thing for the rest of her life. She closed her eyes tightly in an attempt to block out that insane notion.

Maddie seemed to be lost in the aftermath for long moments as Julia pulled her closer against the chill settling on their overheated and slightly sweaty skin. Julia's instinct was to keep Maddie warm and safe, even as she tried to settle her own emotions. When Maddie finally opened her eyes, Julia touched her mouth with a gentle finger.

"You are so beautiful and so sensuous and I love, love, love being with you," Julia whispered.

Maddie kissed Julia's finger lightly. "It scares me a little, how much I want you…want to be with you."

"But you do? Want to be with me?" Julia asked, trying not to reveal every insecurity.

"God, yes, Jule."

Julia smiled. "Will you stay with me tonight?"

"Will I…wait…where's Norie?"

"Eleanor is with her father, but thank you for asking. Is that a yes?"

Maddie smiled. "I would love to, yes."

Julia kissed her deeply and Maddie responded by pulling her closer, cupping her ass as they surged against each other, the desire between them once again flaring to life as the dance started again.

In the morning Julia woke slowly, immediately aware of Maddie's scent and her warmth and she opened her eyes to find Maddie smiling down on her.

"Are you watching me sleep?" Julia's voice sounded rough to her own ears.

Maddie visibly shivered. "Yes."

"You okay?"

"Your voice does things to me," Maddie said.

"My voice?" Julia asked.

"Yes, your voice has the sexiest husky tone I have ever heard."

"You got it bad for me, don't you?" Julia wanted it to be a teasing remark, but it sounded serious to her own ears.

Maddie smiled at her, looking beautiful with her dimples showing, her hair tousled around her. "You have no idea."

Julia smiled. "Will you stay and have breakfast with me?"

"Yes, thank you. When can I see you again?" Maddie asked.

Julia smiled, thrilled that it was Maddie who was doing the pursuing. "I'll be in Boston on Friday. I have an appointment."

"What time will you be free?"

"I don't know. It depends on the wait between tests."

Maddie hesitated. "What kinds of tests and where...if you don't mind me asking?"

Julia sighed, seeing the concern on Maddie's face. "I don't mind at all. At Dana Farber starting at one o'clock. It's just my semi-annual cancer check."

"Okay. Text me when you're done or better yet, tell me where I can find you, just in case. That place is a maze. We can have dinner. Will you stay...with me...overnight?"

"Yes."

Maddie smiled as she reached for Julia. "Good."

Chapter 11

Maddie shivered as she shook thoughts of being with Julia from her head and came back to the present, finding her sister-in-law, Maria, watching her carefully.

Maddie had called and asked to see Maria alone, but now that Maria sat across from her, she found that she was beyond nervous. She was fidgeting with the cocktail napkin under her lemon drop martini as they sat in a quiet booth on Sunday afternoon. Maddie always looked forward to spending time with Maria, but she was apprehensive about her reaction to the news about Julia, about herself.

Maria reached across the table and covered Maddie's fidgeting hands with her own, giving them a light squeeze before sitting back. "What's up, chica? It's gotta be big if we had to come here to talk alone."

Maddie tried to smile. "Yeah, it is. I just don't know how to say...what I have to say to you."

Maria looked surprised by Maddie's reluctance and she leaned forward. "Hey, it's me. You can tell me anything....and I tell no one what you tell me...you know that. So what's going on? Is it your mother?"

"I'm still not speaking to her after that blind date fiasco the other night, but no."

"So, are you really seeing someone?" Maddie nodded and Maria continued. "I thought that was just a lie just to piss off your mother, but I'm glad it's true. I thought you were getting ready to join a convent. So what's the big secret? Oh my God, he's not married, is he?"

Maddie smiled at Maria's usual exuberance. "No, Maria, he's not married." Maddie inhaled deeply. "I'm not sure I can tell you."

"What do you mean? We tell each other everything."

"Not everything."

Maria nodded. "Yes, everything. You're the only person who knows how freaked I was about becoming a mother when I was pregnant with Michael. You're the only person who knew when your brother and I were talking about separating."

"You never said things were that bad."

"No, I didn't but you knew, didn't you?"

Maddie swallowed and nodded. She had known, and she had supported the both of them through that tough time. "Yeah, I knew."

"And you didn't push me to say more than I wanted to, but you were there and you knew because you know me, just like I know you."

Maddie swallowed deeply. "There are things you don't know."

"I know more than you think. Do you remember the night of Lena's wedding shower...when we went to your place after?"

"Yeah, sure. We got shit-faced drunk."

Maria smiled. "I was feeling pretty good. You were shit-faced. Do you remember what happened at the shower?"

116

Maddie swallowed, the memory and the accompanying emotions washing over her. "Yeah, Lena's cousin Diego kept hitting on me. He even sent his sister over to sit with me to try to get my phone number."

Maria shook her head. "He didn't send his sister. His sister was trying to get your number for herself and you knew it. That's when you started drinking."

Maddie swallowed, staring at Maria. "You knew?"

"Of course I knew. I've seen more than one woman trying to get your attention over the years. I know, Layna, so just tell me already."

Maddie swallowed, actually feeling slightly nauseated. "How can you know?"

Maria sighed and took one of Maddie's hands into her own. "I can know because there have also been a lot of nice good-looking guys trying to get your attention over the years and you always have an excuse why not. I'm also not your mother. I see you, Layna, and I love you and I don't care." Maria squeezed her hand. "Tell me."

Maria knew. Maddie released a long tight breath she had not even realized she was holding and blinked for long moments. Maria knew and she didn't care. "I met a woman. That's who I'm seeing."

Maria nodded and smiled. "Okay. Good. What's her name?"

Maddie inhaled deeply, her chest slowly loosening. "Her name is Julia."

"Where did you meet her?"

"She was having a drink when I was working at the hotel," Maddie said quietly.

"I'm assuming your mother doesn't know?"

"Are you crazy? Of course not."

"Oh my God, querida, she's going to flip a shitburger over this!" Maria said a little too loudly.

Maddie could not help herself as a laugh bubbled out of her. "Flip a shitburger? Where did you get that one from?"

Maria smiled. "I overheard Michael say it to Laney. I was going to scold him, but I couldn't stop laughing. Oh, querida, your mother might call a priest when she finds out."

Maddie nodded and lowered her head. "I know, I know, and that's why I tried to stay away from Julia, but I can't. I want to keep seeing her."

"Of course you do. So tell me...who is she? Is she...what's the word...butch? Oh my God, did she seduce you?" Maria rapid-fired questions at Maddie.

Maddie smiled at her. "Ria, slow down. One thing at a time. She's in real estate, has two daughters and she did not need to seduce me. I was flirting with her all night. I wanted her...and no, she's not even gay. She's never been with a woman before."

Maria looked surprised at that particular revelation. "But you have? What women have you been with?"

"It was before I met you, before I had Gabe...and not since then," Maddie explained.

"You've been attracted to women all this time and did nothing about it?" Maria rubbed her forehead. "Why, Layna?"

"You've met my mother, right? I couldn't take the chance she'd find out. I just ignored the way I felt about women. I tried to be straight and I got pregnant...and then I had Gabriel to worry about."

Maria reached for Maddie's hands and held them firmly. "Oh my God, I never knew that, but querida, you have to live your life, you have to do what makes you happy."

"I never had a good enough reason to...until now."

"Until Julia?"

Maddie inhaled deeply and nodded before she held her phone up to Maria. "This is the photo from Julia's agency's website."

Maria enlarged the photo, looking closely at it. "Wow, Maddie, she's pretty."

"She's gorgeous."

"She's a little older than you," Maria stated quietly.

"Yeah, I don't think that's the part that's going to upset everyone," Maddie said dryly.

Maria snorted out a laugh. "I guess not. So is this serious?"

Maddie felt her cheeks get warm. "It feels serious. I know it's asking a lot, but please keep this to yourself until I figure out what the hell I'm doing. I've only told you and Gabe."

"I won't say anything to Enzo for now. Gabe knows? He's okay with this?"

"Yes. He convinced me to get in touch with Julia."

"Because your son wants you to be happy. Listen to me, querida. Anyone who truly loves you will want you to be happy, okay?"

Maddie's eyes filled with tears. "Well, I guess we'll find out if my mother really loves me."

Anyone who truly loves you will want you to be happy. Maria's words reverberated in her head and Maddie decided to stop by to see her parents. She had been ignoring her mother's calls but she knew this couldn't go on forever. She hadn't seen them since she'd walked out of the restaurant two days earlier. Could it only have been two days ago?

Maddie was relieved when her father answered the door, hoping that his presence would help to keep her mother calm, as it often did. Her hopes were immediately dashed.

"Why haven't you answered your phone when I call you?" Her mother's angry voice came from within the house and she and her father looked at each other in silent communion.

"Be nice," her father whispered as he always did when he knew Maddie was upset.

She inhaled deeply. "I'm tired of being the only one who's nice," Maddie responded quietly.

"Oh boy," he said.

Maddie walked past her father until her mother came into view, wanting to keep him near for moral support, if nothing else. He rarely interfered, always assuming the role of mediator or referee, depending on one's point of view.

Maddie hoped the slight internal vibration of nerves in her core were not visible to her mother. "Well, I will be respectful enough to answer your calls when you start being respectful enough to care about what I want."

"I'm your mother!" Her mother's voice was loud.

"And I'm your daughter," Maddie answered in a calm voice. "Pushing strange men at me when I have asked you not to…"

"I didn't know you were dating anyone," her mother said.

"Not the point, Ma."

"Who is it? And why haven't you told me?"

"Because it's none of your business!" Maddie silently berated herself for losing her cool and raising her voice. She couldn't tell her mother who she was dating. Not yet anyway.

"I just want you to be happy."

Maddie rolled her eyes. "I am happy. I would be happier if you left me alone and let me live my life."

"Why can't you just tell me? I should know what's going on in your life."

"No, you shouldn't because you never approve of anything I do…and criticize everything…and I'm tired of it…so tired."

Maddie regretted her honesty for a brief moment as her mother looked stunned and hurt by her words. Maddie hated confrontation and she could feel her head throbbing.

"What do I criticize?"

Maddie shook her head. "Really? Where I work, where I live, the decisions I make about Gabe, my friends, you even criticized me for having fresh flowers in my house!"

Her mother shrugged. "It's a waste of money."

"In your opinion, not mine. That's why I don't tell you anything."

Her mother actually looked like she was thinking about what Maddie had said, something that had never happened before. "Okay, I won't say anything about flowers in your house."

Maddie shook her head. "Wow, great, I can have flowers now."

Her mother missed the sarcasm and seemed to be pleased with herself. Maddie sighed deeply and realized that her mother loved her, but she would never understand her, and she didn't even know how to try to fix that.

Sunday had turned out to be a warm day so Julia rolled up the cuffs of her sleeves when she got out of the car and walked toward the oversized and pretentious house belonging to her ex-husband to pick up their daughter. His family was one of the wealthiest in the area and when younger, Julia had aspired to live like they did, but she had never felt comfortable while living under this roof.

Eleanor's father, Jason Tate, still ruggedly handsome, came out of the mingling crowd of his social gathering when he saw Julia walk in the front door and they greeted each other warmly as they always did with a light hug. Their mutual love for their daughter helped to keep things cordial between them and Julia was grateful for that. They made polite small talk for a moment before Jason informed her that he had last seen their daughter in the solarium.

Julia was not really in the mood to make polite small talk with anyone inside, so she decided to go back outside and through the extensive gardens to reach the solarium at the back of the house. It was the one thing she missed about living here, the meandering paths overflowing with flowers that led to garden sculptures and small fountains throughout the property. Julia inhaled the warm spring scents and thought about her morning, waking up with Maddie, how they had talked and laughed, how good it had been to be with her and how badly she wanted to see her again.

Julia walked slowly, enjoying the weather and the spring blooms of forsythia, azalea, and the peonies that she so loved. She stopped near a small fountain to check the surrounding blooms when she heard footsteps behind her. She turned to see her ex-husband striding toward her.

Jason smiled as he caught up to her. "Can we talk? It was too busy in the house."

"Sure." She nodded as she strolled slowly through the area, breaking off a stem of a blooming peony and inhaling its scent. She found Jason smiling at her.

"What?" She asked.

"You always loved this garden," he said smiling.

She nodded. "Still do. It's lovely. Something on your mind, Jace? Is Norie okay?"

He nodded. "Eleanor is wonderful except that her vocabulary is frightening and she's much too self-assured. You're a great mother, Julia. I know I don't tell you that enough."

"Thank you, but it's easy with Norie. She likes school, she likes to read and tagging along at work with me has made her comfortable around different kinds of people. She's a joy, really."

"You were a good wife, too, Julia," Jason said.

Julia stopped, rather surprised by the compliment and wondering where her ex-husband was going with this. "Okay. Thank you."

Julia wondered if Jason had forgotten that he had allowed some stray remarks from a friend about her flirtatious behavior convince him that she was having an affair. He had been foolish enough to accuse her and then had been insecure enough to hire a private investigator to follow her, even after her shocked and vehement denials. There had been no affair and when Julia had discovered she was being followed, the subsequent fallout had been the beginning of the end of their marriage. Julia tried to stay in the present and was surprised when she noticed his gaze run slowly over her body.

"Have you lost some weight?" He asked.

Julia felt herself stiffen at the comment. "Maybe...a little." Jason had always preferred her to be on the thinner side, always commenting whenever she had put on a few pounds, as if she had needed him to point it out to her.

He nodded. "You look good...keep it up."

Julia could not help but hear Maddie's voice in her head, adamantly telling her that she did not need to lose any weight and how curvy and sexy she was. The thought of Maddie and not the compliment from Jason made her smile.

"Thanks."

"I've always hoped, Julia, that we would somehow get beyond my past mistakes...and try again."

Julia was surprised at the unexpected turn the conversation had taken. She had no idea that he still harbored romantic feelings for her or held onto any hope for a reconciliation. Her first reaction had been to laugh nervously, but she controlled that impulse and simply tried to deflect. "It's water under the bridge, as they say."

"Julia, would you ever consider...giving me another chance?"

Julia stared at his familiar and handsome face, stunned at the question. He was a good father and had been a fairly good husband until the end of their marriage. She still felt a certain affection for him, but she knew that she no longer loved him and realized that she had never had the kind of connection with him that she already had with Maddie, had never wanted him with the same passion that she wanted Maddie. That recognition staggered her and she inhaled deeply to find her bearings before speaking.

Julia shook her head. "I think we both know that ship has sailed Jason, but I'm flattered."

Jason leaned in for a close hug and Julia allowed it, knowing she had, at the very least, hurt his feelings. His rough cheek reminded Julia of how soft Maddie's skin felt, and the sharp scent of his cologne reminded her of how clean and fresh Maddie always smelled. She pulled away from him and the uncomfortable situation and quickly hurried into the house through the solarium door, leaving him alone in the garden.

Julia heard the joyful and familiar notes of her daughter's giggle and spotted her talking to a group of adults in Jason's social circle. Eleanor spotted her and politely excused herself before hurtling toward Julia.

Julia bent to hug her close, grateful that her daughter still allowed these public displays of affection. "Hey, kiddo."

"Hi, Mom. Did you see Dad? He wanted to talk to you."

"I did, and we talked. Are you ready to go?"

It was not until they were in the car that Eleanor asked the tough question. "Are you and Dad getting back together?"

Julia tried to maintain her calm façade. "No, of course not. I would tell you something like that. Why would you ask me that?"

"I heard Auntie Linda tell Daddy that he should beg you for forgiveness instead of wasting time with his latest bimbo. What exactly is a bimbo?"

Julia pressed her lips together hard to prevent herself from laughing. "Well, it's really not a nice word, Norie, so maybe you shouldn't repeat it. Obviously your Auntie Linda is not happy about someone your Dad is spending time with."

"Yeah, I know. Her name is Sally. Auntie Linda said Dad would never find another Julia and then she called Sally a gold digger. I know what that means."

Julia pressed her lips together again and reminded herself to call her former sister-in-law to thank her and to warn her about Eleanor's eavesdropping abilities. On second thought, maybe she would leave out the part about the eavesdropping.

"Who is Sally exactly?" Julia asked.

"Dad's new girlfriend. She smells like hairspray and is really skinny. Auntie Linda keeps telling Dad to feed her before she passes out."

Julia smiled. "Maybe you should stop listening to other people's conversations."

"I'm not! They leave the door open or talk right in front of me! Dad keeps calling Sally his 'friend'. I'm 13, but I'm not deaf...or stupid."

Julia pulled into the driveway of her home and put the car in park, killing the engine. "No, you most certainly are not." Julia thought of her situation with Maddie and realized she needed to tell Eleanor about it. "So, Norie, if I met someone I really liked and wanted to start dating, you would want me to tell you, right?"

Eleanor's gaze was intense. "Yes, I would want you to tell me right away. Have you been dating?" Her voice was quiet.

"No, not technically."

"What does that mean, Mom?"

"It means that I had no intention to date anyone, but I met someone I liked. I thought we would just be friends so when we had dinner together, it wasn't a date, but now I think I want to be...more than friends."

"Why did you just want to be friends at first and why do you want to be more than friends now?"

Julia hesitated, trying to think of the proper approach to take with this. "At first, it was because I didn't consider...this person...suitable for me to date."

Eleanor looked confused as she contemplated the possibilities. "Why not?"

"Well, because this person is a girl."

Eleanor's eyes widened. "A girl? Mom, you like a girl?"

"I think I do, yes, but since I've never actually liked a girl before, I obviously thought we'd just be friends."

"But now you *like her* like her?"

"Yes, now I *like her* like her," Julia said.

"Like Ms. Finley likes Ms. Lucci?"

Julia smiled. Ms. Finley was Eleanor's physical education teacher and Ms. Lucci was her art teacher. It was rumored that they were dating. "Yes, like that."

Eleanor frowned. "Does she look more like Ms. Finley or Ms. Lucci?"

Ms. Finley dressed in track pants and sneakers and her short blond hair added to her boyish look. Ms. Lucci had shoulder length brown hair and wore dresses. "A bit more like Ms. Lucci. Are you okay with...if I started dating...a girl?"

Eleanor nodded. "If she's nice to you then you can. What's her name?"

"Her name is Madalena, but I call her Maddie."

"Can I meet her?"

"If and when we decide we're getting serious about each other."

"Why not now?" Eleanor frowned.

Julia sighed. "Well, because if it doesn't work out, it will be hard not to see her anymore, for me and for you, too."

Eleanor thought for a moment. "Okay, but you need to keep me posted until then. I want to know everything."

Julia smiled at her youngest. "Of course you do."

Maddie was gazing out the window watching the colors of the sunset when she realized her son had stopped watching the baseball game on television and was simply watching her. She smiled at him. "What?"

"Did you have a nice time with Julia?"

Maddie felt herself blushing. "Yes."

Gabriel snorted at his mother's embarrassment. "Yeah, I can tell."

Maddie closed her eyes and rubbed her forehead. "I'm sorry if this makes you uncomfortable."

Gabriel gently nudged his Mom. "Not as uncomfortable as it's making you."

Maddie opened her eyes and found her son smiling at her. "So...you're okay with this?"

He shrugged. "Sure. I want you to be happy, Mom. She makes you happy, doesn't she?"

"Yeah, I think Julia is pretty wonderful."

"Good, because you're going to owe Tia Maria big time. According to Michael and Laney, she's been avoiding almost constant phone calls from Vovó asking about your 'new boyfriend'." He made quotation marks with his fingers.

Maddie sighed. "I went to see your grandparents earlier today. Your grandmother just doesn't see how intrusive she is, how judgmental. I tried to talk to her but she simply does not understand me. I guess that's only fair, since I really don't understand her."

"You can't just tell them that you're seeing a girl?"

"I will have to tell them eventually. I think your grandfather will be okay but not your grandmother. She'll never accept it, never be okay with me being with Julia."

"How do you know?"

"You know my cousin Jamie? Well, when he came out, Uncle Manny disowned him and your grandmother said she couldn't really blame him."

"That's why they don't speak?"

"Yeah, it's ridiculous but Jamie is excluded from some family invitations now."

Gabe rubbed his hands on his knees and swallowed deeply. "Would you ever...what if I...what would I have to do for you to disown me?"

The question stunned Maddie for a moment before she recovered. "Nothing." She pulled her son in for a firm hug. "There is nothing you could ever do that would make me disown you, Gabriel, don't even worry about it." Gabriel hugged her back for a long moment and when she felt his deep inhalations, she suspected he was trying not to cry. "You are my son and I love you unconditionally. That does not mean I don't expect you to study hard, clean your room and to not play video games all the time. Understand?"

She heard Gabriel's relieved laugh as he pulled away, wiping his eyes. She waited until his gaze met her own and she smiled at him. "Speaking of?"

He rolled his eyes at his mother. "I already did my homework and folded my laundry and put it away."

Maddie smiled. "Thank you."

That evening, Julia sat on her back deck and watched the calm water of the inner harbor glisten with the last rays of the late day sun as it dipped near the horizon. Her phone chirped and she smiled at the display, thrilled to see Maddie's name on her phone. "Hello, beautiful."

"Hello yourself." Maddie's voice was quiet.

"What are you wearing?"

Maddie's surprised laugh made her shiver. "Flannel lounge pants and a t-shirt that says 'Well behaved women rarely make history.'"

Julia laughed. "That sounds like you."

"Does it?"

"Yes, politely defiant," Julia said.

"That's actually...uncannily accurate. What are you doing?" Maddie asked.

"Watching the water from the back deck and sipping a fabulous glass of Riesling." Julia said quietly.

"God, that sounds like heaven."

"The wine or the view?"

"Being there with you."

Julia smiled. "I wish you were here and I'm so glad you called me. I've wanted to talk to you just to share things that have happened today."

"I've wanted to talk to you, too. So tell me now...what's going on."

Julia smiled as she started to share the conversation she'd had with Norie and a previous conversation she'd had with her friend, Deb.

"Do you have any idea why Deb thinks you've won a toaster oven?" Julia asked.

Maddie laughed, the sound warming Julia. "Watch the Ellen episode...the one where she comes out."

"Okay, I will. So...tell me what you've told Gabriel."

Julia stretched out, sipping her wine as she listened to Maddie share her life with her, things about her son, about a movie she had seen. Julia was still amazed at how easily they talked and she wondered if the sexual chemistry was coloring these interactions or if these interactions were contributing to the overwhelming attraction between them.

Maddie paused. "I could talk to you all night, Jule, but I have to go."

"Yes, it's getting late," Julia whispered.

"Besides waking up beside you, this was the best part of my day," Maddie said.

"Oh sweetie, me too. I can't wait to see you on Friday."

Chapter 12

Julia tried to distract herself by gazing out the window of the waiting room that overlooked a parking garage as she sat quietly and waited to be called in to begin her battery of tests at the Dana Farber Cancer Institute. Her thoughts once again wandered to Maddie, as they had all day, and as if by magic, she appeared, strolling casually into the large and busy waiting area.

Julia jumped up. "Maddie." When Maddie reached her, she pulled her in for a hug, holding her for a long moment. Julia inhaled the already familiar fresh scent of lemons and vanilla that seemed to surround Maddie and whispered against her ear. "What are you doing here?"

"I came to offer moral support. I was worried about you...here alone, so I just took the rest of the day off, in case you needed me."

Julia pulled away and Maddie quickly placed a chaste kiss on each of her cheeks in a decidedly European fashion.

"You took the rest of the day off? For me?" Julia asked.

Maddie smiled widely. "Yes."

Maddie looked as beautiful as ever in her work outfit of wide-legged trousers and a fitted button-down collared blouse, low-heeled pumps on her feet and an overcoat draped on her arm.

"You look adorably professional," Julia said.

"You look adorably sexy," Maddie whispered.

Julia looked down at her own jeans, sneakers and thin hooded pullover, her leather jacket thrown on her chair. Julia pulled Maddie into the chair beside her. "You're joking, right?"

"Not at all. You are the sexiest thing I have ever seen." Julia simply stared at her at her and Maddie smiled. "Are you waiting for the doctor?"

Julia clutched her hand. "No. I have to go in for vitals and blood work first, and then a mammogram, then an MRI and then I see the doctor. It will take hours."

Maddie smiled at her. "Make it worth my while then. Flash me that gorgeous ass through your hospital gown."

Julia laughed lightly. "I'll flash you anything you want."

"And then after you're done we can get something to eat and have a nice glass of wine?" Maddie suggested.

"That sounds perfect. I can't believe you're here. Thank you...so much."

"It's my pleasure, Julia. Now I get to spend the day with you."

Julia was pleasantly surprised at how Maddie's mere presence made what had always been a tedious and stressful ordeal suddenly seem like fun. Maddie held her hand while they drew vial after vial of blood from her arm and then helped her change into a hospital gown and laughed as Julia flashed her as promised. She gave Julia a kiss for luck before she went in for her mammogram and then another before she went in for her MRI. When she heard her name called while they sat in the waiting area for the doctor, Maddie was distracting her with a funny story about her job.

Maddie smiled at her. "I'll be right here."

Julia clutched at Maddie's hand. "Will you come in with me?"

Maddie did not hesitate. "Of course, querida."

Maddie did not let go of her hand as they walked into the office and rubbed it with a gentle thumb after they sat side by side. Maddie squeezed her hand when her doctor walked in and smiled at Julia. "Hello, Julia, it's good to see you."

"Doctor Cuddy."

The doctor smiled at Maddie and held out her hand. "Helen Cuddy. I'm Julia's doctor."

Maddie shook her hand. "Madalena Francisco. I'm Julia's...plus one." Julia smiled widely at the description.

Dr. Cuddy nodded. "It's nice to meet you, Madalena, and good for you, Julia." She made her way to her desk, sitting down and looking directly at Julia. "Everything looks good, Julia. You can relax."

Julia closed her eyes for a moment and exhaled, the relief washing over her. "Thank you."

"Are you still checking your breasts regularly? Watching your diet? Exercising?"

Julia nodded. "Yes, yes and yes, ma'am."

"Good, then I won't keep you. If you have any issues or questions, please feel free to call me, but otherwise, I'll see you in six months."

Julia pulled Maddie behind her out the door. "God, what a relief. Let's get out of here."

Julia smiled as Maddie brought the hand she still held to her mouth and placed a kiss to the knuckle. "Would you like to go for an early dinner somewhere?"

Julia pulled Maddie closer. "Can you just take me home with you?" Julia loved how Maddie's gaze slowly drifted from her eyes to linger on her mouth before returning to her eyes. It made her feel warm and attractive, and desired.

"Yes," Maddie whispered.

Maddie led Julia up the concrete front steps of her building. She could not help but glance around nervously, well aware of her mother's propensity to show up unannounced and not wanting to have to explain Julia's presence, or why she was home from work much earlier than usual. She quickly unlocked the front door and ushered Julia into the foyer with an old-fashioned tiled floor. She pointed to Julia's backpack. "Is that all you brought with you?"

Julia nodded. "Yeah. My laptop and a change of clothes. I figured anything else I needed I could either borrow from you or get at the hotel."

Maddie stopped short in surprise. "Hotel? What hotel?"

Julia shrugged. "You didn't specifically invite me to stay here...and I didn't want to presume anything...with Gabe and all."

"My mistake then. I wasn't specific because I thought you understood that you would stay here with me. You are not staying at a hotel. Gabriel is spending the night with my brother and Maria and their kids."

"I'm sorry."

"No, don't be. Gabe offered and he stays over there all the time and Enzo's kids are here a lot, too."

"You have nieces or nephews?"

"One of each. Laney is 16 and Michael is 15."

"Is Laney short for–?"

Maddie smiled. "Madalena, yes, named for me."

Maddie quickly unlocked one of the mailboxes in a small row in the wall and removed a small pile of mail.

"Are you and your brother religious?" Julia asked quietly.

Maddie smiled at the question. "Why would you ask me that?"

"Because Gabriel and Michael are both archangels."

"Well, we were raised Catholic and my parents are still devout, but no. Enzo and I, we just liked the names. How did you know that, anyway?"

"I was raised Catholic as well, but no longer practice." Julia said.

"What do you practice now?" Maddie asked, moving closer to Julia.

Julia smiled. "I try to practice kindness and I believe in fairness and second chances and everyone's right to be happy."

"You would make a fine Buddhist."

"Would I? Are you a Buddhist?" Julia asked.

"A part-time one, but no one but Gabe knows that since my mother would flip if she didn't think I was going to Mass every Sunday. Buddhism and meditation make me feel...calm." Maddie pointed up the staircase. "I'm on the second floor." Maddie led Julia up the polished wooden staircase and had a brief moment of apprehension as she thought about the glaring difference in Julia's large, beautiful house and her own modest apartment.

"This is a great old building," Julia said.

"Yes, it is." Maddie walked to the door at the rear and unlocked it. "Gabe and I have been here a while."

Maddie could feel Julia's gaze on her as she led her through the door, then shut and locked it before she shed her coat and hung it on a row of hooks on the wall by the door. Julia was looking around and Maddie tried to see her living room through Julia's eyes. It was neat and clean, and brightly decorated. The leather sofa and the matching easy chair that surrounded a mission style coffee table were both slightly worn, but were helped by brightly colored pillows. Maddie's ever-present stack of books was on the floor by the armchair and Gabe had left his video game controller on the coffee table. Maddie's small kitchen was located to the right separated from the living area by a breakfast bar and stools.

Julia smiled as she looked around, her eyes moving over everything. "Your home is very much like you," she said, parroting what Maddie had said when she'd first seen Julia's home the last time they had been together.

Maddie smiled. "Okay, I'll bite."

"Warm and sensuous with splashes of rebellious color."

"Thank you." Maddie sighed, thinking that Julia always said something that made her feel accepted and understood. "Let me take your jacket," Maddie offered, careful not to look directly at

Julia, lest she see the almost overwhelming desire that had suddenly come over her now that they were alone.

Julia dropped her backpack where she stood and shed her jacket, handing it to Maddie. Maddie took the jacket from Julia and hung it beside her own before she inhaled deeply and leaned back against the door, meeting her gaze and watching Julia watch her.

"You okay?" Julia's voice was a throaty whisper, the natural huskiness of her voice actually making Maddie's nipples harden.

Maddie shook her head before she reached her hand out and clutched the front of Julia's thin pullover hoodie, pulling her forward until their lips met in a searing kiss. Julia kissed Maddie back deeply, pushing her against the door. Maddie snaked her hands beneath her shirt and Julia gasped when Maddie's cool hands met the warm skin at her sides. Maddie felt her shiver as her hands moved to Julia's back and snaked inside of her jeans.

Maddie reluctantly pulled her mouth away and waited for Julia to look at her. She smiled at Julia. "Miss me?"

"More than I thought possible." Julia's raspy whisper made Maddie wet.

"Yeah, it's a little intense, this thing with us," Maddie said.

Maddie stared at Julia, wanting nothing more than to drag her to her bed and slowly remove every article of clothing from her body. She hesitated, feeling a little nervous and inhaled deeply, forcing herself to relax. She just wanted to touch Julia so very much, wanted to taste her, wanted to be inside her. She shuddered at the realization.

Julia frowned. "Are you alright?"

Maddie bit her lip. "I don't know. I can't even think, you've got me so turned around."

"What can I do?"

"Let me make love to you."

Maddie heard Julia inhale a sharp breath, staring at her. "Let you? You're kidding, right?"

Maddie smiled in relief and pushed away from the door, moving past Julia. She turned to look at her. "Coming?"

Julia shook her head. "Too easy."

Maddie laughed lightly as she led Julia through the large open living area of her apartment, past the kitchen on the right and a small study alcove in the corner to the left. Julia followed her into the hallway, past Gabe's bedroom on the left and the bathroom on the right into Maddie's master bedroom at the back. Julia walked through the doorway as Maddie was standing beside her queen-sized bed kicking off her heels and unbuttoning her blouse.

Julia put a hand out. "Maddie, wait...please."

Maddie froze, staring as Julia approached her and covered her stilled hands on the buttons of her blouse with her own. Julia smiled at her. "Is it alright if I do this?"

Maddie nodded. "God, yes."

Maddie dropped her hands to her side and Julia stepped back, pulling her sweatshirt over her head and dropping it to the floor before returning to Maddie's buttons. Maddie lifted a hand to Julia's face, gently caressing as she straightened the wisps of hair that had come loose from Julia's ponytail. Julia wore a simple white t-shirt under the sweatshirt. Maddie noticed the small black print on the front.

"'Be the change.' Is that Gandhi?"

Julia nodded. "Yes, one of my favorite quotes, actually."

"I like everything I learn about you," Maddie said.

Julia leaned into Maddie and placed small kisses against Maddie's neck and chest and the tops of her breasts as she removed her blouse. "I will remind you of that the next time I get bitchy in your presence."

Maddie laughed gently as she tugged at Julia's t-shirt and pulled it over her head. Julia unzipped Maddie's slacks, pushing them over her hips as Maddie snaked her hands along the warm skin at Julia's waist and slid them into the back of the loosened jeans and beneath her panties, grabbing Julia's ass roughly. Julia gasped and Maddie pulled the jeans and the panties past her hips as Julia toed her sneakers off and Maddie stepped back to pull off her own pantyhose. Julia reached for Maddie's bra as Maddie reached for Julia's, hooks quickly unfastened before they were being thrown aside and then they kissed, open-mouthed and hungrily.

Julia slowly pulled away from the kiss and stepped back just enough to look at Maddie, her gaze slow and appreciative. Maddie watched Julia's gaze prowl slowly down her body, lingering on her breasts before drifting down to her center, unabashedly staring as they both breathed deeply. Maddie pushed Julia back onto the bed and watched as her luscious body settled against the comforter, thinking how right Julia looked in her bed.

Maddie stopped and simply stared at Julia for a long moment. Julia pushed herself up onto her elbows. "What?"

Maddie shook her head. "Just memorizing this vision of you in my bed...and trying not to get ahead of myself."

"I'm already way ahead of myself with you," Julia whispered.

"Are you?" Maddie moved toward Julia.

"Yes, I think so. I knew my feelings for you were getting serious when my ex-husband was asking for another chance with me and all I could think was that I never wanted him the way I already want you...that I never felt like this with him."

Maddie froze for an instant at the stunning revelation. "You...what...how do you feel...with me?"

"Let me just say it's intense, sweetie, what I feel. Are you okay with that?"

Maddie nodded, the admission overwhelming her for a moment. "Yes. And your...he wants you back?"

"Apparently, yes, but that will never happen," Julia assured her quietly.

Maddie inhaled deeply, deciding to be honest, as well. "I think that just made me feel a little jealous."

Julia smiled. "You have absolutely nothing to worry about."

Maddie moved onto the bed over Julia and kissed her softly, running her tongue over her lips before dipping into her mouth. She kissed her chin and her neck before moving her mouth to Julia's breasts. She sucked Julia's nipples into her mouth, moving back and forth between the two until Julia was covered in a light sheen of sweat, her breathing labored, her nipples hard, her center swollen and wet with need. Maddie's lips blazed a trail up the inside of her thigh and Julia clutched at the edge of the mattress over her head, her heels sliding against the sheets. Maddie had been teasing her for long minutes, and Julia squirmed and moaned.

"God, please— "

Maddie stopped and waited for Julia to look at her. "Please what?"

Julia stared at Maddie, as desperate for her touch as she had ever been for anything in her entire life and overwhelmed by this aching sexual need. God, what this young woman could do to her. She breathed deeply, trying to form a coherent request.

"I need you to fuck me." Julia barely recognized her own desperate voice.

Julia let out a long and loud moan as Maddie plunged inside her with her fingers, filling her deliciously and stealing her breath. It was overwhelming and glorious and Julia became a panting, heaving and slightly desperate mess as Maddie continued to push inside her in a deep and steady pace. Maddie seemed to know how much force and speed and hit every spot as she fucked her perfectly and Julia lost herself in the breath-stealing sensations for endless moments.

At some point, Maddie began a soft rhythm against her clit, rubbing in perfect sync to her thrusts, the added stimulation starting to push her over the edge. Julia surrendered herself to Maddie until her world exploded into sensation and color as an orgasm sent her jerking and shuddering while Maddie still held her tenderly. It took Julia quite a while to come back to herself as she lay in Maddie's arms, surprised when she realized those were her own tears drying on her face. The orgasm was so intense that she could still feel her inner walls clenching against Maddie's fingers.

Maddie was kissing her chest and shoulder while gently wiping her cheeks. She placed a firm hand against Julia's face. "Okay?"

Julia simply nodded, her eyes closed, still trying to even out her breath. Maddie continued to place kisses against her warm skin, at her chest and down her torso to her abdomen because Julia could still feel herself moving sensually against Maddie's touch, her vaginal walls clenching against the still warmly encased fingers. She wasn't sure she had ever had an orgasm as powerful.

Julia loved the way that Maddie pulled her close, seeming to envelop her for long moments until Julia had fully recovered, until her vaginal walls stopped their spasms against Maddie's fingers and Maddie gently and slowly pulled them out of her.

"I've missed you...I've missed this, but I've missed talking to you, telling you about my day," Julia whispered her admission.

Maddie's full and sudden smile conveyed how pleased she was by that admission and it filled Julia with warm emotion and the overwhelming desire to give Maddie pleasure in the most intimate way possible. The last time they had been together, Maddie had taken Julia with her mouth and Julia had spent a great deal of time since then thinking about what it would be like to have her mouth on Maddie. Julia had never gone down on a woman and she was hesitant to disappoint Maddie in any way, but her need to take her overruled any lingering insecurities.

Julia gently pushed Maddie over with intent as she moved down Maddie's body, caressing with her hands, kissing and sucking with her mouth. She squeezed Maddie's breasts as she lowered her mouth to one, sucking the nipple deeply as Maddie moaned and arched. Julia was more aggressive than she had ever been with Maddie, her touch a little more forceful, her mouth sucking hard, her teeth scraping against the nipple. Maddie moaned and bucked and Julia reached between her legs, dipping into the warm and slick pool gathered there. Julia wanted desperately to taste Maddie so she ran two fingers up Maddie's slit and then stilled, waiting until Maddie opened her eyes and met her gaze.

While Maddie watched, Julia brought her wet fingers up and inhaled Maddie's scent from them before she placed the tips of them into her mouth, closing her eyes as she sucked them, shuddering at the first taste of her. Julia groaned around the fingers, the taste of Maddie sweet, tangy, and incredible. She found Maddie's gaze locked on hers when she opened her eyes and slowly pulled her fingers from her mouth.

"Can I have you?" Julia's voice was a rough and raspy whisper.

"You can have anything you want," Maddie said.

Julia slid down between Maddie's legs, lowered her head and ran her tongue through the wet warm folds. Maddie's moan reverberated through the air as Julia explored, the first touches of her tongue tentative as she licked up and around her clit and back down. Julia was amazed at the appealing taste of Maddie and the utter and exquisite softness of her folds against her tongue. She felt Maddie's hand pressing at the back of her head and she smiled. She had apparently found the pressure and the tempo that Maddie needed and she focused on bringing her pleasure.

Julia moved her hands to the juncture of Maddie's inner thighs to hold down her jolting hips as she feasted. She more than enjoyed her ability to make Maddie moan and squirm and beg and she fed on the hard and fleshy clit and the warm wetness that poured from her. Maddie arched sharply and Julia found herself moaning against Maddie's folds as she realized how much she was enjoying this, especially Maddie's response. Much too soon, Maddie's moans changed their pitch and her hips changed their cadence and Julia followed suit, increasing her efforts.

Julia felt the increase in the intensity of her movements and she heard Maddie muffle a small shout into her own fist as her hips bucked wildly, as wave after wave of sensation shook her. Julia held onto Maddie as she orgasmed, beautifully and openly, shuddering against Julia's loving mouth.

"God, Julia," Maddie whispered as she finally opened her eyes long moments later.

"I think I enjoyed that almost as much as you did," Julia said, smiling.

Maddie returned the smile. "Not possible." Maddie inhaled deeply. "Are you sure you've never done this before? Any of this?" Maddie asked.

Julia blinked in surprise. "I'm fairly certain I would have remembered. Why?"

"Everything you do...the way you touch me...the way you...just now...with your mouth..."

"It was okay?"

Maddie widened her eyes. "Okay? It was earth-shattering."

Julia smiled. "Maddie, I've never wanted to touch anyone the way I want to touch you."

Julia kissed her, moving over her and sliding their warm bodies together. Maddie pulled her closer and deepened the contact, the unmistakable scent of Maddie's arousal in the kiss. Julia moaned into the kiss, their tongues sliding firmly and wetly before it intensified, their mouths opening wider in an attempt to become as close as possible. The kiss slowed gradually and they pulled away, watching each other closely for long moments. Julia shuddered at the glorious intimacy of it.

Julia smiled. "I wish I had the words to express to you what I'm feeling right now, just looking at you. You are so beautiful and you make me feel so damn good."

Maddie hesitated. "Do you really want me more...than...?"

"More than I wanted my ex-husband? Yes. I wouldn't have said it if it wasn't true." Julia inhaled deeply as she caressed Maddie's face. "This intensity was never there when I was with him. I loved him and it was good, but it wasn't this." Maddie swallowed deeply. "Too much too soon?" Julia knew her insecurities were showing.

Maddie shook her head. "No. I appreciate your honesty."

"So be honest with me. This scares you, doesn't it?"

"Of course. It's a lot to take in. And you?"

Julia smiled and nodded. "Yeah, sure, but I couldn't stop it even if I wanted to and I don't want to."

"I feel the same way." Maddie suddenly widened her eyes. "Oh my goodness, I am a terrible hostess. I haven't even offered you a glass of water."

Julia smiled. "You offered something much better."

"I'm glad you think so, but querida, you must be starving? Let me make you something to eat." Maddie slid from the bed and strolled into the closet, emerging a moment later in track pants and a long sleeved t-shirt.

Julia watched her with a small smile, simply enjoying the sight of Maddie moving. "Do you have something I can throw on?"

Maddie pulled an oversized white men's shirt from the bedpost and handed it to Julia before she pulled a pair of yoga pants from a drawer, tossing those to her. Julia turned the shirt over in her hands as she slid to the edge of the bed. "Can I ask whose shirt this is?"

Maddie laughed lightly. "It's mine, thank you very much. That shirt is my favorite thing to wear when I'm home alone. Would you like me to find you something else?"

Julia slipped the shirt on, the scent of Maddie on it unmistakable. "Absolutely not. Thank you."

Julia sat at the small island in Maddie's kitchen while Maddie quickly prepared a plate of fruit and cheese and poured her a glass of white wine. Julia smiled. "Thank you. This is lovely."

"Now, what would you like for dinner? I can do Shrimp Mozambique or Thai Coconut Curry Chicken..."

Julia smiled and pointed at the plate. "Isn't this dinner?"

Maddie shook her head. "No, that's just to stimulate your appetite."

"You've managed to stimulate everything else," Julia whispered.

"Funny."

"Not trying to be. Can I see the take-out menu?"

Maddie stiffened and then smiled. "There is no take-out menu. Those were the things I could whip up for you quickly. I just didn't know what you were in the mood for. I could make you an omelet if you wanted something lighter."

I took another moment for Julia finally understood that Maddie was offering to cook a meal. Just for her. She inhaled a breath. "You're going to cook for me?"

"Yes."

"And I just insulted you by asking for a menu, didn't I?"

Maddie smiled as she walked over to Julia, leaning on the island beside her and reaching out to caress her face. "No, you didn't insult me, you just surprised me. I have the ingredients for the Thai dish or the shrimp dish if you're interested."

"I am, I just can't remember the last time someone made dinner for me...if ever."

"Well, I'm going to make dinner for you."

"I would really love that."

"Do you like Thai?"

"I love it, thank you. Can I help?"

"Maybe next time. Relax, finish your wine." Maddie kissed Julia lightly on the lips. "Make yourself at home. You can put your things in my room, if you'd like."

Julia smiled. "I would like, thanks."

Chapter 13

Maddie plated two servings of dinner and refilled Julia's wine glass. Julia moved behind Maddie and wrapped her arms around her, kissing the side of her face. Maddie leaned back into Julia, thinking how good it felt to be simply held by this woman.

Julia whispered. "Dinner smells amazing. Thank you so much."

"It's a simple meal and it's my pleasure."

They sat close together and Julia moaned at the first bite. "This is incredible."

"Not too spicy?" Maddie asked.

"No, just spicy enough, like you."

Maddie smiled. "Was that a line, Jule?"

"No, not at all. You seem to be everything I ever wanted in a...partner," Julia said, her gaze steady.

Maddie inhaled sharply. "Wow, you really know how to charm a girl, don't you?"

Maddie's cell vibrated on the coffee table in the living room for the second time since they had come out of the bedroom and she glanced over at it.

Julia looked at her. "I won't be offended if you answer your phone."

Maddie smiled. "Thanks, excuse me."

Maddie had not answered because she knew it was her mother. She walked away to speak to her, keeping her responses short until her mother mentioned stopping by.

"It's not a good time right now. No, I have company."

Maddie ended the call and sighed.

"Everything okay?" Julia asked.

Maddie shrugged. "Just my mother...being nosy...and intrusive. She thinks she has a right to know what's going on in my life."

"She doesn't know...about me?" Julia asked quietly, sighing.

"She knows I'm seeing someone, but I didn't tell her it was a woman." Maddie could not meet her gaze. "Baby steps."

The loud knocking at the door startled them both.

"Layna...Layna!" The loud voice on the other side of the door caused Julia to sit up straight while Maddie groaned and lowered her head.

"Who is that?" Julia whispered.

Maddie was horrified because she knew that her mother had a key that she would not hesitate to use. "Shit. I'm so sorry, Julia. It's my mother and she has a key."

"She wouldn't let herself in?" Julia asked.

Maddie nodded, feeling sick. "Oh yes, she would."

"Bit of a control freak is she?" Julia asked as she poured herself some more wine. She smiled at Maddie as she buttoned the next two buttons on the shirt she had borrowed from her. "I guess I'm going to meet your mother."

Maddie slowly walked to the door, complete and utter dread at what might happen next. Even with their recent discussion, she knew her mother would not be afraid to push her weight around. Maddie inhaled deeply as she opened the door as her mother walked in, speaking loudly in her usual combination of English and Portuguese. Her mother and the ranting both immediately stopped as she noticed Julia sitting at the kitchen island.

Julia smiled brilliantly. "Hello, I'm Julia Sinclair. You must be Madalena's Mom."

Maddie watched, mesmerized, as Julia turned into a charmingly exaggerated version of herself as her mother was caught completely off-balance by it. Maddie watched her mother's confusion as she tried to determine Julia's sincerity and who she might be. Her mother stared for a brief moment and then smiled politely.

"I'm sorry. I didn't know Layna had company," her mother said, her pleasant tone and lilting accent belying the glare of suspicion that Maddie could plainly see on her face.

"I just told you I had company," Maddie said as she stepped forward, feeling as though she was caught in some weird experimental theater as her lover and her mother stared each other down, each of them smiling falsely.

"I thought you were just saying that," her mother said and Julia's eyebrows rose at the excuse.

Maddie realized that her mother had not bothered to introduce herself. "Julia, this is my mother, Celeste Francisco."

"It's nice to meet you, Celeste." Julia looked at Maddie. "You didn't mention your mother would be stopping by, Maddie. I wouldn't have changed into something so casual."

Maddie's eyebrows shot up slightly in surprise at Julia's falsely polite, but pointed tone of voice. She tried not to smile. "I wasn't expecting her, Julia, I'm so sorry."

Maddie's apology seemed to make her mother angry, her glare jumping from Maddie to Julia. "I'm her mother and I can stop by whenever I want."

Maddie caught the gasp that threatened to escape her throat. Maddie could plainly see the challenge on her mother's face and she felt stuck between a rock and a hard place, knowing that she could not take sides here and wanting this to end as quickly as possible.

"But you shouldn't, Ma. Julia's a client at my agency and we're behind schedule with a project, so we decided to have a working dinner. I'm working." The convenient lie came too easily and Maddie internally cringed at her own cowardice.

Maddie saw Julia's surprise which she hid by taking a generous swig from her wine glass. Her mother's shrewd gaze indicated that she did not believe the lie, but Maddie shrugged, indicating to her mother clearly that she would say no more.

Her mother pressed her lips together in an expression all too familiar to Maddie. She was angry, but would not dare challenge her and jeopardize Maddie's job. "Well, I can stop by another time." Her suspicious glare jumped from Julia to her daughter, but Julia kept smiling at her and she had no choice but to retreat. "I'll call you tomorrow," she said to Maddie.

Maddie smiled at her. "Tell Dad I said hi."

She held the door open for her mother and ignored her pointed glare as she shut it quickly behind her before she turned to look at Julia. She was embarrassed that she had lied about who Julia was and what she meant to her.

"Your mother is charming," Julia said and Maddie could not mistake the sarcasm.

"I'm sorry." Maddie sighed. "I told you she was...difficult."

"I can see that. She's also a bit of a control freak. I understand that she's your mother, but you shouldn't allow her to treat you the way that she does."

"Well, that's very easy for you to say, but you don't know what my parents have done for me, and I can't just blurt out something like this to her. I've already told Gabe and Maria, but I need to work up to telling my mother."

Maddie breathed deeply as she thought about how her mother would react to her being with Julia. Maddie knew that her mother would never simply allow her to have this relationship. Maddie knew that if her mother discovered this, she would make Maddie's life an absolute hell. Maddie knew that her mother would threaten and rage, would involve her brother Enzo and sister-in-law, Maria, and possibly even Gabriel. She had done it before for things that seemed petty and insignificant in comparison.

Maddie swallowed down her fear and shook her head as she realized that Julia was right. Her mother was a control freak, but she was still her mother.

Julia sighed. "And in the meantime? Are we supposed to continue to pretend that I'm a client? For how long?"

"I don't know, Julia. I'm sorry but I need to do this my way. I know my mother can be difficult, I know that better than anyone." Maddie inhaled deeply. "But I also know what she's done for me. When she found out I was pregnant she flipped out, I won't deny that, but she was also by my side for every doctor's appointment and for the 15 hours I was in labor and scared out of my mind." Maddie started to slowly pace as she continued. "For the first 7 years of Gabe's life, she was there for both of us every day, taking care of him or picking him up from school, so that I could finish high school and then keep going to get my Associate's degree. And she was working a full-time job the entire time. When I finally moved out on my own, she gave me some of her furniture and dishes and she sewed curtains for my windows. She's difficult and she expects a lot but she gives a lot, too. I don't expect you to understand how hard this is for me."

Maddie did not want to lose her family but did not want to sacrifice what she had with Julia to keep them either. She felt sick and hollow and could not meet Julia's intense and knowing gaze because she knew her denial had hurt Julia and she also knew that right now, she could see no way out of this corner she found herself in.

Julia could see the struggle of emotion on Maddie's face and she could only imagine what she was going through. Julia could also easily imagine a series of clandestine weekend meetings and rushed trysts squeezed in between Maddie's real life while Julia remained a secret to Maddie's family and friends. Julia saw herself becoming the one thing she had promised herself she would never become.

"I do understand," Julia whispered. "I can't imagine how hard this is and I allowed you to deny our relationship to your mother, but I will not be your dirty little secret." Julia licked her suddenly dry lips. "And I need to know where this is going. Or is this what it's going to be?"

"What do you mean?" Maddie asked.

"Is this what we're going to be, Maddie? We'll sneak around to meet up for sex?"

Maddie looked shocked as she shook her head. "No. No. I'm sorry. I never want to make you feel the way I apparently keep making you feel. I want to be with you, Julia, I do...and...I want this...with you. Please don't doubt that."

"Honestly, Maddie, how can I not doubt it? I don't know what to think. This is crazy. How can you live like this? Your mother is not stupid. It's clear, to anyone who wants to see, what's going on here."

"She won't take the chance that you actually are a client and I'm not sure that she really wants to know what's going on here."

"Well, that's very sad. Will she come back?"

Maddie shook her head. "I don't think so."

"You don't think so? How can you live like this?" Julia tried to control the level of anger in her voice. "Can't you just change your locks?"

"I could but then she'd ask Gabe for his key and that's not fair to him and she would make my life hell in the meantime."

"She's already making your life hell. Can't you see that?"

Maddie nodded, rubbing her forehead. "I know. You're right, but it's easier to just go along to get along."

"That is ridiculous and your mother is completely unreasonable." Julia sighed. After Maddie's denial of her to her

159

mother, Julia knew she had no choice but to put all of this on hold. The realization made her feel as though she was going to vomit. "Listen, I'm not going to sneak around and pretend to be your colleague or any other ridiculous thing. I will introduce you to anyone and everyone in my life as my girlfriend, my lover, my...anything you want, but I will not lie and I will not sneak around. It goes against every fiber of my being. Honestly, I can't even imagine it. I will not come between you and your family, but I will not let you into my life, into my daughters' lives until you're sure you can do this."

"I can do this," Maddie assured her.

"Then tell your family what I am to you," Julia said, rubbing her forehead, her head starting to throb.

"I will, I just need time," Maddie insisted.

Julia nodded. "I know. I can see that very clearly. You can have all the time you need." Julia turned toward Maddie's bedroom. "I'm going to get dressed and go."

"Go? Where? It's getting late."

"I can get a hotel."

"Julia, please."

"I can't stay here knowing that your mother will just let herself in whenever the mood strikes."

"Please, Julia, don't go."

"I can't stay here," Julia repeated firmly.

"When will I see you again?" Maddie asked, closing the distance between them.

160

"That's entirely up to you, Maddie."

"What does that mean?"

"You know what it means." Julia sighed and felt her shoulders sag. "We can't go forward the way things are. I'm afraid of getting in any deeper. This is already hard enough...walking away from you."

"Then don't. If you felt about me the way I feel– "

"Don't you fucking dare, Maddie, because I'm falling for you."

Maddie gasped. "What did you say?"

Julia surprised herself with the unintended declaration, but she was even more surprised at the stunned look on Maddie's face. "You have to know how I feel about you. Are you telling me you don't have feelings for me?" Maddie simply lowered her gaze and the lack of response made Julia feel as though she had been sucker punched, all of the breath leaving her body. She stepped away from Maddie. "My mistake then."

"Julia, please, don't, you can't just say something like that."

"Yes, I can because it's how I feel." Julia swallowed deeply, feeling sick.

Julia went into the bedroom and dressed quickly, grabbing her backpack as she walked to the door as Maddie watched from the sofa silently. Julia stopped and looked at Maddie and silently urged her to say something, to say anything that would make her change her mind or give Julia some idea how she felt about her.

"Julia, please don't leave," Maddie whispered.

161

Julia closed her eyes against the wave of pain that washed over her. "Bye, Maddie. Call me if things change." Julia kept going, out the door, shutting it silently behind her because Maddie telling her not to leave was not what she needed to hear.

Eleanor returned from her father's on Sunday morning and as was the norm, Vivienne walked over from her place so they could all have breakfast together. Julia decided to eat outside, hoping the beautiful day would lift her spirits. When they sat down to eat, Vivienne looked at her closely.

"You okay, Mom? How's Maddie?"

Julia tried not to reveal anything but she had to bite her lip to stave off sudden tears and she simply shook her head. "I'm not sure I'm going to see Maddie again."

"What happened?" Vivienne asked.

"It's complicated, but I'm fine."

Eleanor sighed. "That wasn't very convincing, Mom."

Julia tried to smile, feeling both annoyed and grateful that her daughters knew her so well. "Okay. I'm...sad."

Vivienne reached for her hand. "Tell us."

Julia sighed. "Maddie's mother unexpectedly stopped by while I was there and Maddie lied to her about who I am. I can't be with someone who is ashamed of being with me."

Eleanor looked at her. "Why did she lie, Mom?"

Julia paused, as always, when trying to explain the complications of life to her youngest child. "Maddie's family is Catholic and her mother is...difficult. Maddie is afraid to defy her and be honest about who she is...about being gay because they apparently don't approve of that."

"She's still not told her family?" Vivienne asked.

"No and until she does, I'm not going to sneak around or pretend to be something I'm not and I told Maddie that."

"Did she break up with you?" Eleanor sounded indignant.

Julia smiled. "No. I simply told her we couldn't continue like this, especially with the way I feel about her."

"You really like her?" Eleanor asked quietly.

To her dismay, Julia had to blink back tears. "Yeah, I really do...and I'm not sure she feels the same way." Julia hastily wiped her eyes and tried to make light of it. "What was I even thinking? I suck at relationships." She looked at Eleanor. "Don't repeat that word, Norie. I should have said 'I am unsuccessful' at relationships."

Vivienne smiled. "Norie does not say 'suck' as her vocabulary is more refined than yours and mine."

"It is," Eleanor agreed.

"And you don't suck at relationships, you just suck at men," Vivienne said. "Luckily for you, Maddie is a girl."

Julia cocked her head and stared at her oldest daughter for a long moment. "What are you talking about?"

163

"Now that Maddie knows how you feel, she's going to realize what she needs to do. Give her some time and wait for her to call you."

"Why do you say that?" Julia asked.

"If the situation was reversed, isn't that what you would do?"

Julia nodded, thinking. "Yes, as a matter of fact, that is what I would do. I think you might actually be right."

"I think you might actually be a lesbian," Vivienne said.

"Are you a lesbian?" Eleanor asked her mother.

Julia looked at her younger daughter and smiled. "I don't know, Norie, and I don't think it's that black or white. It doesn't have to be something that you label. What I am is...crazy about Maddie." Julia gave Vivienne and Eleanor both a pointed look. "But I am not buying Birkenstocks, regardless."

Despite how she was feeling, her daughters' delighted laughter echoed in the air around her for long moments and she found joy in it, as she always did. She decided to try to stay in the moment with her daughters and not dwell on what may or may not happen with Maddie.

Despite her best efforts, Julia could not help but check her phone more often than she wanted to, simply waiting for some contact from Maddie. Julia could not remember ever being this twisted up over a man. She laughed to herself. Maybe that explained the two failed marriages. Maybe Vivie was right and she simply sucked at men, or maybe she was a lesbian after all, or maybe she had simply not met the right person, male or female, until now. Maybe Maddie's mother had finally worn Maddie down and she decided that being with Julia was simply too much trouble.

She was sitting on the deck with Vivienne later that afternoon when her phone vibrated with a text from Maddie. "It's her."

Vivienne nudged her mother. "What does it say?"

"She wants to talk." Julia inhaled deeply, shuddering. "It probably means she never wants to see me again."

Vivienne leaned closer to her mother and looked her in the eye. "Mom, if jumping to conclusions was an Olympic sport, you'd have a gold medal."

Julia barked out a laugh, grateful for her daughter's quirky sense of humor. "Thank you, Vivie, I needed that. Excuse me."

Julia walked into the house, just settling into an armchair when the phone rang in her hand. "Hello."

"How are you doing, querida?" Maddie asked.

Julia felt herself relaxing at the affection in Maddie's voice and she decided to listen to Vivie's advice. She inhaled deeply. "I'm upset and I miss you."

There was a brief pause before Maddie responded. "God, Julia, I miss you, too."

"Are you telling me you want to be with me?"

Maddie hesitated a moment. "I think you know that I do. You caught me off guard by what you said and I didn't...and we didn't have time to talk it out and I want to...need to talk about things with you...can I see you?"

"Have you told your parents about me?"

"Christ, Julia, no, not yet!" Maddie sounded angry.

Julia sat forward in the chair. "Do you have any idea how that makes me feel? Like you're ashamed of me...of what we are together."

"That's not it at all."

"It's how it makes me feel."

Julia heard Maddie stifle a sob. "I'm sorry. I never want you to feel this way."

"But that is what you're doing."

"Jule, please...just give me some time. I need to do this in my own way."

"I know you do, and I'll give you all the time that you want. You know where I am. But until then, I simply can't do this."

"Julia, please..."

"It hurts too much." Julia knew she would not be able to resist Maddie, that she would allow Maddie to convince her to give her another chance, to open herself up to more of this awful feeling of being in a painful limbo. "I'm sorry, but I have to go, Maddie."

Julia ended the call and stared down at the phone, feeling crushing disappointment. She leaned over, wrapping her arms around her middle. She watched as her tears splashed on the hardwood floor between her feet. She knew she had been falling for Maddie, but she never thought it would hurt this much to let her go.

Chapter 14

Maddie sat in her car, staring up at her parent's home, the home she had grown up in, the home her family celebrated almost every holiday and birthday in. She was here to tell her parents that she was gay but found she could not leave the safety of her car just yet. She had always known that this day was inevitable, but she had always thought of it as being far into the future, when she had her degree, when her son was grown. The future was suddenly upon her and still, she hesitated.

This decision had less to do with making things right with Julia than simply realizing that it was time, and that she could never go back to pretending to be something she was not. Spending more time with Steven recently had opened her eyes in many ways. He had insisted on taking her out to lift her spirits and they had gone to what he called a club "with a mixed crowd." She hadn't realized until after they'd arrived that he'd meant a mix of gay and straight clientele, but mostly gay.

Maddie was embarrassed at how naïve she had been. Seeing women together, kissing and dancing, and simply just being affectionate, without any hint of self-consciousness had been a revelation for her. Instead of being shocked or uncomfortable, Maddie had simply felt at ease, the same way she had always felt when with Julia. That same sense of freedom and comfort was intoxicating, and she realized that she wanted more of that and less of the awful fear usually lurking deep in the pit of herself.

She took her time getting out of the car, inhaling deep breaths as she walked the same path to the door she had taken thousands of times over the course of her life. Everything seemed to speed up when she walked into their home, grateful for that because she was afraid her courage would fade.

She wiped her sweaty hands on her jeans as she greeted her parents. "Could I talk to the two of you?"

They looked at each other before they sat on their sofa. She remained standing in front of them. "Is Gabe in trouble?" Her mother asked.

"No, Mom, Gabe is not in trouble, but if he was I probably wouldn't tell you." Her mother started to respond but Maddie put a hand up, realizing it was shaking slightly. "For once, please let me talk."

Her mother looked annoyed. "Talk."

Maddie sighed. "I've tried to tell you this a dozen times, since I realized it in high school, but I never could. I don't tell you a lot of things Ma, because you're never happy about anything and you won't be happy about this." She inhaled deeply and averted her gaze, unwilling to see the looks of disappointment or worse that she might see on their faces. "I'm gay."

There was a momentary silence, and when she looked, her father returned her gaze the way he always had, with a calm and steady affection.

Her mother looked furious. "What are you saying? Is this a joke?" she asked in a loud voice.

"This is not a joke. I'm gay. I always have been. I'm sorry you're upset but I am. It hasn't really mattered until now, but I met someone, a woman that I want to be with."

"No!" Her mother shouted as she rose. "You are not like that. I forbid it! Take it back."

169

Maddie didn't know whether to laugh or cry. "I can't take it back. It's who and what I am." She shook her head and smiled in equal parts disbelief and disgust. "Taking it back will not change it."

"You think this is funny?" Her mother's voice was low but angry.

"No, I don't, I think it's sad that you don't care about me, about my happiness."

"I care about what people will say. Who knows about this?"

"That's what you're worried about?" Maddie's voice rose.

"It's that...that fancy puta that was in your apartment," her mother accused.

"Don't call her that. It's Julia, yes, but she's gone because I lied to you about what she is to me."

"Good!" Her mother practically spit the word at her.

"Good? Really, Ma? Look at me. I haven't slept, I can't eat." Maddie bit her lip to stop the impending tears burning her eyes.

Her father rose and placed a hand on her mother's arm, but she shook it off.

"Don't be stupid," her mother said. "All of this over a woman? You would risk your family for a puta?"

"Risk my family? Are you threatening me?"

"No," her father said.

"Yes," her mother said loudly. "I forbid this. It's your puta or your family."

Maddie's father reached out and once again put a hand on his wife's arm. "Celeste."

Her mother shook off his hand and took a step toward Maddie. "You don't need her. You'll get over it."

Maddie inhaled and looked her mother in the eye. "You will have to get over it, if you make me choose."

Her mother took another step toward her. "You would choose her?"

"Why do I have to choose? Could you choose between me and Enzo? Between your husband or your children?"

Her mother took another few steps, stopping in front of her. "Stop talking stupid. That puta is not your family. We are."

Something snapped inside of Maddie. "Stop calling her that! I love her," she yelled.

Maddie saw the slap coming, but could not quite believe it was happening, so did nothing to stop it. Her mother's hand caught her full on the side of the face, the burning sting exploding into pain. Her father was suddenly in front of her, keeping her mother back and reaching for her shoulder to check on her.

She tried to focus as her mother screamed over her father's quiet words, asking if she was all right and his pleading protests to his wife to calm down.

"I knew you were not working with that puta," her mother screamed and Maddie knew at that moment that Julia had been right. Her mother was not stupid or in denial, but simply more concerned about what she wanted than about Maddie's happiness.

171

"Get out of my house!" Her mother's shout brought Maddie back into focus.

"Celeste! Layna, don't go," her father said.

Maddie did not hesitate to head for the door. When her mother screamed at her retreating back, forbidding any contact between Maddie and the rest of her family, Maddie knew that her mother was purposefully trying to hurt her. Maddie was so shaken that she had no recollection of how she had gotten herself home that night, feeling as if her world had imploded.

Her mother had apparently called Enzo and Maria and forbidden them to speak to Maddie. Thankfully, Maria had immediately and openly defied her mother-in-law and gone directly to Maddie's home that night and for many nights after that, sitting with her as she cried more tears than she knew a body could produce. Maddie's tears covered a long and vast list of hurts, but the biggest one was the realization that her mother loved being in control of her more than she actually loved her.

That Friday, her brother called her at work to invite her and Gabe to his home for dinner. Since it had always been Maria who extended these invitations, Maddie knew that the gesture was her brother's way of showing his support.

Maddie and Gabe had always spent a lot of time with her brother and his family and Maddie was afraid that her revelation would change the way things had always been. She found herself holding her breath when her brother answered the door. He briefly greeted Gabe on his way in with a smile and a gentle tap on the arm. When Maddie stepped inside, he pulled her close into his arms. Maddie could not remember the last time her brother had hugged her like this.

"I'm sorry about Ma," he whispered. "I don't care who you're with, as long as they treat you right."

Maddie kissed his cheek. "Thank you, Enzo. I love you," she whispered as she wiped her eyes. She went into the kitchen to have a glass of wine with Maria, as she always did. Her niece Laney followed her into the kitchen.

"Tia, can I see a picture of your girlfriend? Mom said she's really pretty."

The utter normalcy of her niece asking about her girlfriend caused Maddie to bite her lip to keep from crying as she found a picture of Julia in her phone and showed it to Laney. "I hope she's still my girlfriend. She's upset with me right now."

Laney leaned against her and Maddie hugged her close. "Just tell her you're sorry for hurting her feelings."

Maddie smiled. "Thanks, I'll do that."

Gabriel had been momentarily distracted by Michael's new video game, but he came into the kitchen to greet his aunt, kissing her cheek politely.

"Hey, Tia, how are you?"

Maria smiled. "Good, sweetie, you?"

He shrugged. "Okay, thanks."

Maria watched Gabriel walk out and then looked at Maddie. "What's going on with him?"

Maddie sighed. "I asked Gabriel to stay out of the fight between his grandmother and me and he has, speaking to her whenever she's called, but something happened yesterday. She must've said something pretty awful to him because he now refuses to speak to her."

173

"What did she say?"

"He won't tell me. He said he would not repeat her 'crazy bullshit.' I told him that I did not want him in the middle of this battle and he said he wasn't in the middle of it, but totally on my side and always would be."

"You're a better person than me, querida," Maria said softly, "because your mother's calls will not be answered by any of us until she stops this."

"I feel awful that all of you are stuck in the middle."

"Why do you feel awful? You are not the one who has put us all in this position. You are not the one trying to control our lives and telling us what to think and how to feel." Maria moved closer, placing a soft hand on Maddie's arm. "Have you talked to Julia?"

Maddie bit her lip, trying to stave off the impending tears. "No, I can't, not yet. Everything is such a mess. She doesn't deserve to be in the middle of this, either. Maybe in a week or two when I get my shit together."

"Don't wait until it's too late. You deserve to be happy."

Maddie swallowed, wondering if it was already too late.

Julia had expected to miss Maddie, had expected to feel bad about how they had left things, but she hadn't expected this painful longing. She expected to hear from Maddie on each day, convinced that she would get a call or a text. When the end of each day proved her wrong, her nights became long and lonely, second-guessing herself for giving Maddie an ultimatum.

Julia also spent too much time doubting Maddie's feelings for her and trying to decide if this thing between them had been much more serious for her than it had been for Maddie. She was afraid that she had assumed too much about Maddie's feelings for her, had read too much into Maddie's behavior, her loving concern, the incredible way that they had made love. Like Deb had suggested, maybe it meant something to Maddie, but it had meant everything to Julia.

Julia was aware that she was not handling this as well as she should, but she had no point of reference for what had happened with Maddie, because she had no point of reference for the feelings she had for Maddie. She knew that the glass or two of wine she was having on those evenings when she could not quiet her frenzied mind were not helping her to sleep, but that did not stop her from indulging. She was mortified when she noticed the worried glances between Vivienne and Eleanor so she tried to limit her drinking in front of them.

By the second week, Julia was convinced that she had permanently pushed Maddie away with her insistence that she tell her family. That conviction brought out incredible anger at herself and at Maddie, as well, and she did not quite know how to find her way out of all that negative emotion. The secret nightly glass or two of wine were gradually upgraded to vodka martinis since she was not sleeping well.

That second Saturday night found her sitting alone on her deck since Norie was spending the weekend with her father. She quickly lost track of the number of martinis she slowly sipped as she mentally reviewed every moment with Maddie, every touch, and every word. Of course, she hadn't planned on getting quite that drunk, but by the time Vivienne stopped by to check on her, it was after midnight. She was still out on the deck, as intoxicated as she could ever remember being.

"Mom, what are you doing out here?" Julia wondered why Vivienne was talking so loudly and why she seemed to be upset.

"What's the matter?" Julia asked, vaguely aware that her voice was slurring. "You okay, baby?"

"Are you okay?" Vivienne was in front of her, her hands on her hips. "Jesus, Mom, you're drunk," Vivienne said.

"So? I can be drunk in my own damn house," Julia said defiantly, angry that her words sounded thick to her own ears.

Vivienne smiled at her mother's display. "Oh my God, should I make you some coffee?"

"No coffee, I'm going to bed," Julia said as she lurched to her feet, not realizing that she was seriously swaying until Vivienne clutched her around the waist and helped her back down into the chaise. When her head finally stopped spinning, Vivienne was sitting beside her, placing a large mug of coffee in her hands.

"Drink this," Vivienne said sternly.

"Don't talk to me that way," Julia asked.

Vivienne shook her head. "Then don't make me."

Julia smiled when Deb suddenly appeared, strolling onto the deck from the darkness of the back lawn with a small smile on her face. "Deb, hi. Hey, you wanna a martini?"

"No, she doesn't want a martini," Vivienne said.

"She likes tequila, get her some tequila," Julia said to Vivienne.

Deb laughed lightly and looked at Vivienne. "Okay, you're right. I've never seen her this wasted." Deb sat on the other side of Julia and rubbed her back. "No tequila for me, hon, but thanks. How are you doing?"

Julia thought about how she was doing and realized she was crying as Deb and Vivienne each clutched an arm and pulled her up to her feet. They walked her into the house and Julia had no recollection of much of anything after that.

When Julia woke the next morning, she felt sick, her head throbbing painfully. She gratefully drank the water and managed to keep down the painkillers she found beside her bed. She could not remember how she had gotten into bed or why she was wearing a satin nightgown that she'd forgotten she even still owned. She realized that someone had helped her dress for bed, and she was mortified as bits and pieces of the night before started to return. She waited for her head and her stomach to settle somewhat before she took a shower and dressed in jeans and a t-shirt.

When she shuffled into her kitchen, she was surprised to find Vivienne and Deb at her kitchen island, drinking coffee and watching her closely. "Oh, God, I'm so sorry." She cringed at the roughness of her own voice. "Did you two spend the night here?"

She noticed the long glance between them before Deb smiled at her. "Yeah, we did. We were worried about you."

Julia slumped onto the bar stool near Deb and moaned as she rested her head in her hands as Deb placed a mug of coffee in front of her. "It won't happen again."

"Mom, it can't happen again. You were here alone. You couldn't even walk. You could've fallen and hurt yourself."

Vivienne was on the verge of tears and Julia felt awful that she had upset her daughter so much. "I know. I promise I won't drink alone anymore."

"I think you should stop drinking altogether for at least a week." Vivienne stared down her mother. "Don't think I haven't noticed the number of bottles in the recycle bin."

Julia nodded. "Okay, that's probably a good idea." Julia looked at her daughter. "I'm so sorry, baby. Did you put me to bed?"

"With Deb's help," Vivienne said.

Julia groaned as she put her head down on her arms. "I'm so embarrassed."

Deb nudged her. "C'mon, drink your coffee." Julia picked up her head and brought the mug to her lips, sipping slowly. "Don't be embarrassed, Julia," Deb said with a smile. "It's not like I didn't already know you were built like a brick shithouse."

Deb winked, Vivienne laughed and Julia shook her head, moaning loudly. "I can't believe you just said that."

"You're welcome," Deb said before her smile faded. "Seriously, hon, why didn't you just call me?"

Julia sighed. "Because I'm so tired of this and so tired of me like this. I figured you must be, too."

Deb smiled. "Not even close. Besides, how many nights did you sit with me when I was sick and scared?"

Julia nodded, reaching for her hand. "Okay, I'll call next time I get the urge to do this to myself."

Deb squeezed her hand. "Listen to me, hon. If you and Maddie are meant to be, it will work out, and if it's not meant to be, there's probably a good reason for that."

Julia nodded, trying hard to hang onto Deb's words.

Julia stared at the computer screen in her office and sighed. She leaned forward on her elbows and rubbed her face. She could not concentrate once again and was losing patience with herself. This inability to focus was frustrating, but it was a far sight better than the drunken and heartbroken stupor she had been in over the last few weeks. Julia shook her head and pushed her chair back, walking over to the windows in the conference room. She watched the boats in the harbor and let her mind wander.

Julia still hadn't heard from Maddie and that hurt more than she had expected it to. She missed Maddie with an intensity that sometimes took her breath away, but the hurt settled inside her, like an unshakeable illness, like a vast emptiness. She hadn't felt this void of hope when she was fighting breast cancer.

As it was now, she was in no less pain or turmoil, but had simply started to become resigned to the situation. Julia was still holding onto a tiny sliver of hope that Maddie was simply taking the time that Julia had insisted that she take. That hope was greatly overshadowed by the growing acceptance that she would most likely never see Maddie again. Julia knew that she could simply end all of this painful uncertainty by simply calling or texting Maddie, but she was afraid to do that. If Maddie actually declined her call or told her that it was over, she would have no hope to hold onto and she couldn't take that risk.

One of Julia's hard and fast rules was to keep her expectations within reason so she wouldn't be constantly disappointed, but she now wondered what she believed anymore. Julia had admitted to Deb that she was finding it difficult to know what to consider a reasonable expectation because simple disappointment did not even begin to scratch the surface of what she was feeling.

Regardless of her state of mind, Julia had made sure to spend time with her daughters and worked diligently at her business to keep herself occupied. She managed to make a good deal of money, but felt no joy or pride in it. She was finding it hard to find enjoyment in anything, so when Deb had suggested that she and Vivienne quit work early on Friday to take advantage of the glorious weather, she had readily agreed. They were all meeting for lunch and Julia wanted nothing more than a cocktail, pleasant conversation and an afternoon free from responsibility. Deb and her daughters had been her saving grace these past few weeks and she was grateful for them.

Julia sighed and decided to call it a day, closing down her office computer. She knew she would be early to meet Vivienne and Deb, but it was a beautiful day and she could simply take the time to try to enjoy it. It would give her some time to clear her mind and try to think of positive things. Julia was determined to keep a brave front even though she could now readily admit that Maddie had broken her heart, and for the second time. Julia inhaled deeply when she thought of the impossible demand she had made of Maddie and wondered if she might have broken Maddie's heart as well.

Maddie glanced down at what she thought of as her dressy watch as she walked away from her parked car. She felt slightly overdressed in her pencil skirt and pumps from her earlier appointment and she took her time since she had a few minutes to spare. She was trying to enjoy the sunshine and the cool breeze coming off the ocean in the town that Julia called home. Maddie found herself smiling because she realized how much she liked this quaint town and because she was having a relatively good day, especially when compared to the last few weeks' worth of days.

Maddie inhaled deeply. In some ways, the last few weeks had been some of the worst of her life, but she was grateful to have been through them. She had decided to go to counseling, knowing she had many things to deal with, but wanting most of all to keep moving ahead. She thought of the quote that she had repeated like a mantra to herself over the last few weeks. *Not all storms come to disrupt your life; some come to clear your path.* She knew this to be true because the experience of the last few weeks had left her feeling like a completely different person with a much clearer path. She hoped she was finally becoming the person that she was meant to be even though that had come with a cost.

Maddie's father had unexpectedly appeared at Maddie's workplace on the second week of the siege and taken her to lunch. Maddie had cried when she had seen him in the lobby of her building and he had immediately apologized to her. He told her to give her mother time to get over the fact that not everything could be the way she wanted it to be. That actually made Maddie angry and she thought about how Julia had once described her as politely defiant. That gave her the courage to tell her father clearly that they would no longer have a daughter if her mother could not get over it. Her father had looked surprised, but had nodded in agreement and told Maddie he loved her. In that moment, Maddie knew she had to stay strong to have the life she had always wanted.

As day after day passed, Maddie could clearly see how she had allowed her mother to dictate her life and hold her back from so many of the things she wanted. She also knew, without a doubt, that the thing that she wanted most of all was Julia Sinclair, but she did not know if she would ever get another chance to show her that.

She missed Julia more than she knew she could miss anyone. She longed to simply hear Julia's voice, to see her smile, and to hold her. Maddie did not realize that Julia had become so important to her until she no longer had her. Maddie's sorrow had become a constant companion.

Knowing that Julia was almost certainly nearby was weighing heavily on Maddie's mind as she walked along the busy waterfront. It was so very tempting to simply go to Julia's home or office right now, but she was almost afraid to do that. She and Julia had had no contact in nearly a month. Maddie was taking the time that Julia told her to take. She did not realize that it would be this long, but she decided that a little more time would make no difference at this point. She needed to get all her ducks in a row before she offered herself to Julia. She hoped that Julia could forgive her and give her another chance. She hoped she could forgive Julia for letting her go so easily.

Maddie arrived at Ishmael's and walked up the steps to the raised outdoor seating deck. Maddie had picked this restaurant because she knew that Gabriel would enjoy the view of the harbor and the fishing boats on the working waterfront. She spotted her son waiting for her at the outdoor host station and she smiled widely at him. She didn't know what she would have done without him these last few weeks.

Gabriel hugged her unexpectedly. "What's this for?" She asked as she returned the hug.

She felt him shrug against her. "It's good to see you smiling. Good day?"

She smiled at him. "Yes, finally, a good day. Are you hungry?"

"C'mon, Ma, always."

Maddie was smiling at her son as they followed the host to their table. She was just about to sit down when a flash of movement in her peripheral vision caused her to glance quickly over to her left. She froze in place when she saw Julia rising to her feet at a nearby table to stare openly at her.

Maddie gasped. "Julia."

Gabriel stopped and turned to look at the woman that had captured his mother's attention. "That's Julia?"

"Yes."

Maddie thought Julia looked like a vision, even dressed casually in khakis and an untucked button-down shirt with the sleeves rolled up. She looked so beautiful with the ocean breeze blowing strands of her hair away from her face. She was as still as a statue for a long moment and Maddie suspected that Julia was waiting for her to do or say something, but Maddie was paralyzed, unsure of Julia's feelings at seeing her, until she met her gaze.

Julia looked as if she was about to cry, her lower lip trembling and Maddie could not help but take a step forward, smiling at her in encouragement. She saw Julia inhale deeply before she returned the smile. Maddie moved toward Julia, with Julia doing the same until they walked into each other's arms, holding each other tightly for a long moment.

"Jule, querida, it's so good to see you," Maddie whispered, not wanting to let her go and embarrassed at the tears that had quickly spilled over her lashes. Maddie hung on, reveling in the familiar scent of her, the wonderful softness, the feeling of acceptance and safety that she always felt with Julia.

"Maddie, God, Maddie," Julia whispered back, her voice breaking.

Maddie finally pulled away to look at Julia, noticing her tears. She wiped Julia's face as Julia wiped hers, and they laughed, still keeping physical contact, Julia clinging to her arm and Maddie's hand at her waist. Maddie was somewhat surprised, but very relieved at Julia's warm welcome. Julia looked tired, but seemed more than happy to see her.

Maddie glanced over to the table Julia had been sitting at and noticed an attractive woman watching them intently. Her skin was the color of light coffee and her black, shiny hair was pulled back from her face with a colorful headband. Maddie lowered her gaze in embarrassment as if the woman could see the sharp and unexpected pang of jealousy she suddenly felt when she realized that Julia was having lunch with another woman. A very attractive woman.

"I'll let you get back to your...date. I'm here with Gabe," Maddie said softly.

Julia looked past Maddie and smiled. "Yes, I can see that. He's so handsome."

"Thank you," Maddie whispered.

Maddie saw Julia's daughter, Vivienne, approaching the woman Julia had been sitting with and she watched as Vivienne looked over and recognized her. Vivienne's eyes widened at the sight of Maddie and her mother clinging loosely to each other.

"Christ on a raft, that's Maddie," Vivienne said, loudly enough for her voice to carry over to them on the breeze.

Maddie could not help but smile at the surprised outburst. "Christ on a raft, there's Vivienne," she said, quietly enough for only Julia to hear.

Chapter 15

Maddie's comment and mischievous smile caused a warm wave of affection to wash over Julia and she realized just how much she had missed this part of being with Maddie, her quick wit and the way she made her laugh.

Julia shook her head. "Don't worry, I heard her. I think everyone heard her."

Maddie nodded. "Well, I don't want to keep you."

Julia stared at her, not wanting to let Maddie go. "Please...keep me."

"I'd like that." Maddie reached for Julia's hand, squeezing it, and Julia's heart soared. "Would you like to meet Gabe?" Maddie asked her.

Julia smiled. "Yes, I really would."

Gabriel smiled at her warmly as he shook her hand, making eye contact. "It's so good to finally meet you," he said to Julia. He seemed sincere and Julia wondered what Maddie had told him to cause him to seem so pleased to meet her.

"Same here, Gabriel. Would you like to meet my daughter Vivienne?" She asked.

Gabe readily agreed although Julia could see that Maddie was hesitant, so she reached for her hand and tugged gently, and Maddie smiled and followed her. Julia could feel the tension as she made introductions and was relieved when Vivienne politely told Maddie that is was nice to see her again. Julia introduced Deb as a friend and she saw Maddie swallow deeply at Deb's reserved greeting. Julia knew that Deb was being protective and she understood her reservations. Julia met Deb's gaze and smiled at the support from her friend.

Julia was pleasantly surprised when Vivienne asked Maddie and Gabe to join them for lunch. She knew that Vivienne was doing it for her so when Maddie tried to decline, Julia insisted. She quickly motioned to the host and two smaller tables were quickly moved together to accommodate their group.

When they were all seated, Vivienne looked at Gabe and smiled. "So, are you here to see your Dad for the weekend?"

Gabe smiled at his mother before turning back to Vivienne. "Yeah, but my Mom had a thing in New Bedford this morning so we came early and my Dad managed to get me a last-minute invite to tour the Vocational High School there this afternoon."

"I went to high school there," Deb said with a smile and Gabe started to chat with her and Viv about the school and the area.

Julia openly stared at Maddie, still in disbelief that she was sitting beside her. Maddie seemed to be having trouble taking her eyes from Julia as well.

"I wasn't sure I would ever see you again," Julia said to her quietly.

"I'm sorry," Maddie responded in a whisper. "You told me to take the time I needed, but things did not go as well as I'd hoped."

"Were you ever going to call me?" Julia asked quietly, internally cringing at the pleading tone of her voice.

Maddie licked her lips. "Of course." Maddie glanced toward the others, to ensure they were not listening, before continuing. "I was just waiting..." She paused and lowered her voice. "...until I could tell you everything that you deserved to hear from me...until I was worthy of being with you."

Hearing Maddie say that made Julia feel as though her insides had been emptied out, hollow and sick. What had she done by giving Maddie an ultimatum and insisting that she tell her family? She reached for Maddie's hand. "You have always been more than worthy. I'm so sorry I made you feel otherwise."

"You didn't, Julia." Maddie blinked repeatedly and Julia knew she was trying to hold off impending tears.

Julia squeezed her hand. "Can we talk about this alone? Do you have time...today...or tomorrow? Please, Maddie."

Maddie wiped her eyes, trying to catch the quickly escaping tears and all conversation at the table stopped. Maddie tried to smile. "Excuse me for a moment, please."

Gabriel automatically rose as his mother did, pulling out her chair like a gentleman and watched as she walked away, following her with his gaze for a long moment before he turned and looked at Julia.

Gabriel sat back down and Julia slipped into Maddie's empty chair. "Gabriel."

He smiled softly. "Julia."

She inhaled deeply. "Is she okay? Your mother?"

Gabriel looked thoughtful for a moment. "Well, no, she hasn't been okay...not at all...but today is the first day I've seen her smile, really smile, and look happy in weeks."

Julia stared, wondering if that meant what she wanted it to mean when Gabriel smiled and raised his eyebrows in the direction his mother had gone. Julia was instantly up and moving in that direction when she spotted Maddie standing alone on the side deck of the restaurant. Julia ignored the "restricted access" sign, pushing through the closed gate to approach Maddie slowly. Maddie inhaled deeply, wiping away her tears and Julia moved to stand beside her.

Maddie was still and silent for a few moments before she looked at her. "I'm so sorry I hurt you, querida, that it took so long. I never thought, when I told my parents...I knew it would be bad...but I never expected..."

Julia looked at her. "What happened?"

"I can't...not here."

"Where then? When? Unless..." Julia stepped back. "...you still can't do this? Just tell me now before you break my heart all over again."

Maddie looked stunned, her eyes wide. "Is that what I did?"

Julia looked away. "Pretty much."

"I never intended to do that and I don't intend to ever do it again."

"You know, I thought...before I saw you today...I thought 'wouldn't it be nice if Maddie and I could salvage a friendship out of this', because you know, I've really missed you, but now that you're here in front of me, it's clear to me that I can't be just your friend."

"I don't want to be just your friend either," Maddie whispered. "So, is Deb just a friend?"

Julia's anger rose, quick and hot, but she tried to control herself. "A very good friend. The friend whose shoulder I cried on after the first time we were together. And it was Deb and Vivienne that had to help me to bed when they found me blind drunk on the deck one night after I didn't hear from you after the *last* time we were together."

Maddie looked mortified, swallowing deeply. "I'm sorry."

"You should be. Do you think that I could make love to you, that I could have you inside me, that I could tell you I'm falling for you and then what? Fall into someone else's bed in a few weeks?" Julia kept her voice low, but it was obvious how angry she was.

Maddie's eyes filled with tears, but she held Julia's gaze. "Not really, no, but I couldn't blame you if you did. Deb is gay, right, and lives her life openly? She's very attractive. Why wouldn't you be with her? In comparison I must seem like a..." Maddie's voice faltered over a small sob. "...like a...train wreck."

Maddie's tears spilled over and Julia's anger faded instantly. She pulled Maddie into an embrace and inhaled deeply, giving them both a moment.

"You're not a train wreck. What you are is the woman that I cannot get out of my head or my heart," Julia said quietly.

Maddie wiped her eyes and looked at Julia. "Really?"

Julia could not help but smile. Even with her eyes red and swollen, Maddie was beautiful. "Yes, really."

Maddie inhaled deeply, wiping away more tears. Julia helped herself to a few paper napkins at the nearby wait station, returning to hand them to Maddie. Maddie smiled at her and dabbed at her face and eyes.

"Let's take a deep breath, okay?" Julia said. "I need a big fucking cocktail and then we can have some lunch."

Maddie smiled. "A cocktail sounds good."

Thankfully, Vivienne, Deb and Gabe were talking easily, dissipating any remaining tension and they managed to have a pleasant lunch, the conversation staying light and casual. Julia was relieved to see that Deb started to warm up to Maddie, finally speaking to her directly. When Julia smiled at Deb, she smiled back and winked at her, letting her know that all was well. When they finished eating Gabriel checked his phone and smiled at his mother.

"Dad is picking me up in 10 minutes. He wants me to have dinner with them after the tour and stay over."

Maddie smiled. "I assumed as much. I have a reservation at the Sea Breeze, so go, have fun."

Gabriel rose and smiled at Vivienne and Deb. "Thanks for the conversation and the insight, ladies. It was good to meet you." He looked at Julia. "It was especially good to meet you, Julia."

Julia was charmed and she rose, reaching across the table to shake his hand. "Same here, Gabriel."

Gabriel hugged his mother, whispered something to her and then made his way to the parking lot. Deb looked at Maddie. "Maddie, you should be very proud of Gabriel. He's really smart and personable. I can't remember the last time I met a teenager with such manners."

Maddie smiled. "Thank you."

Vivienne nodded in agreement. "He's really great, Maddie." Vivienne looked at her mother. "So, Deb and I are staying to have another drink if you're interested in joining us. We'll even let you have another."

"Vivienne..." Julia warned her daughter with her angry tone and a glare. Julia felt her anger rise until Maddie looked at her, eyebrows raised in a question. Julia pressed her lips together and sighed, her anger dissipating. "Vivienne is reminding me...again...that I...overindulged recently...but we won't be staying. Maddie and I need to talk about some things."

Maddie nodded in understanding at Julia before she turned to smile at Vivienne. "Since I assume I am somewhat responsible for that...overindulgence, what if I make it my responsibility to keep an eye on her?"

"She's all yours," Vivienne said with enthusiasm and Deb laughed.

Julia rose and Maddie followed suit, looking over at Vivienne. "It was nice to see you again." She looked at Deb. "It was nice meeting you, Deb."

Julia looked at Maddie. "Is it alright that we go to my house?"

Julia hoped that Vivienne and Deb took that as the hint she intended it to be. She wanted time alone with Maddie. She wanted to know everything, including Maddie's intentions toward her.

Maddie nodded. "Of course."

As soon as the door to Julia's home closed behind them, Julia tossed her purse on the large sidebar table in the foyer area. Maddie was afraid she might be angry as she leaned back against the table and looked at Maddie.

"Maddie, I'm so sorry that I gave you an ultimatum to tell your parents. I had no right to do that."

"Julia, don't." Maddie shook her head. "You simply told me what you needed. I knew I was hurting you." Maddie sighed. "I was hurting myself as well. I'm sorry I made you feel like I was ashamed of you, Julia. Please know that I never was and I never will be."

"If I had known...I wouldn't have done that. Maddie, please know that I would have agreed to anything...being discreet, sneaking around...anything if I knew I wouldn't get to see you at all."

"Julia, no. That was never my intention. Never. I was trying to make things right because you didn't deserve that...but my life...imploded." Maddie rubbed her forehead with her fingers.

"Tell me what happened with your parents," Julia said quietly.

Maddie inhaled deeply, giving herself a moment. She had recounted what had happened with her mother several times, including in a counseling session, and had been unable to say the words without crying, but she did not want to cry now. Maddie took a few steps away and then turned back to Julia.

"My mother...came completely unhinged. When I said I was gay, she asked if I was joking. She screamed at me to take it back, then threatened me...told me that I had to choose between you or them." Maddie swallowed deeply, her eyes stinging with impending tears. "When I told her I couldn't, she slapped me."

"What?" Julia stood up straight. "Oh sweetie...oh God. I'm so sorry."

"Julia, it's not your fault and it's not my fault, either."

"Where the hell was your father?" Julia asked angrily.

193

Maddie shook her head. "Trying to hold her back before she could come at me again, while she ranted and raved and kicked me out of their house. She has forbidden the rest of my family from talking to me. Thankfully, they've ignored her, but she has cut me off...completely."

Julia gasped. "Maddie, I'm so sorry."

"You have nothing to be sorry for. It's her decision."

"I'm sorry, nonetheless." Julia said as she rubbed the back of her neck and started to pace.

"I know you are." Maddie reached for Julia, pulling on her arm. "Hey, it's okay. You were right, you know."

Julia shook her head. "God, Maddie, I don't want to be right, I just want you to be okay." Julia turned to her and caressed her face. "Where did she hit you? Here?"

Maddie nodded and then closed her eyes as she felt Julia place a soft kiss to her left cheek and then another and then another until she was covering every inch of it, down to her jaw and then to her neck. Maddie shivered against the loving attention. Julia cupped Maddie's face and pulled her into an open-mouthed kiss and everything else seemed to fade away. Julia kissed her deeply, almost savagely, emotions taking over and Maddie was lost in the erotic kiss for long moments. The kiss finally slowed and Maddie pulled away, giving them both a chance to catch their breath as their eyes opened and their gazes met.

Julia looked as if she wanted to cry and Maddie cupped the side of her face. "Jule, querida, talk to me," Maddie whispered.

"I thought you were gone for good. I can't do this again if...if you're going to disappear."

Maddie felt a combination of guilt, anger and slight pressure by what could be construed as another demand and then she inhaled deeply and let it all go as Julia's gaze held onto her own steadily. Maddie reminded herself that Julia had been here the entire time, thinking that Maddie had abandoned her and she had still forgiven her immediately. That eased some of the defensive anger that Maddie was feeling.

"I didn't intend to disappear, you know. I thought I would only need a few days or a week to settle things but...I fell apart. I really was a train wreck. I had to pull myself together and...figure things out...before I called you. I had no idea you..."

"What? Was worried? Missed you desperately? Thought you simply walked away...again?" Julia stopped, obviously angry and upset.

Maddie tried to control her own anger and failed. "No, Julia, I didn't know because I didn't walk away. You did."

Julia rubbed her forehead. "I'm sorry, so sorry. I shouldn't have pushed you."

"It seemed so easy for you to walk away..."

"It wasn't easy, trust me. It damn near killed me...I was drinking too much. Every night. Promise me...no, don't, I'm sorry. No more ultimatums." Julia lowered her gaze.

Maddie suddenly realized that she was willing to promise Julia anything to make this work. "It's not an ultimatum if you just tell me what you need from me, querida, and I will do what I can to give it to you."

Julia's gaze shot up. "I just need to know you won't disappear, that you want to do this. I need to make plans with you."

Maddie nodded. "I'm here. I want to do this."

Julia moved closer, reaching up to caress her cheek. "And I will never push you away again."

Maddie felt herself relax. "Okay...so...I would love to see you again tomorrow, Julia and Sunday, too, if you're free. I would love to do something with you next weekend. I would love to take you out, on a real date, like the first night at the Essex, and keep taking you out until you can't imagine what it was like before me."

Julia's smile was tentative, but beautiful. "I already can't imagine."

Maddie leaned in slowly and kissed Julia gently, savoring the taste and the feel of her, their tongues swirling together. Maddie's hands ran through Julia's hair and Julia's hands held Maddie's waist, pulling her tightly against her. Their mouths separated slowly and reluctantly, Julia placing small kisses along the side of Maddie's face and up to her forehead.

"I've missed you so much, Maddie," Julia said.

"God, I've missed you," Maddie whispered back.

Maddie closed her eyes as Julia leaned back against the table, pulling Maddie along with her. Maddie settled herself against Julia and tried to keep her hips from bucking into her, her desire as out of control as the myriad of emotions coursing through her. Maddie failed when Julia's hands pushed up her pencil skirt, allowing Maddie to easily straddle Julia's thigh. Maddie brought her lips to Julia's throat and sucked on the spot that always made Julia a little crazy. Julia's hips bucked forward and Maddie tried to push her thigh firmly against Julia's center.

Maddie moaned as her throbbing center slid against Julia's thigh, as Julia's hands reached under her skirt to clutch at her ass roughly. Then Julia was plunging her tongue into her mouth and Maddie fell into the incredible sensations, her hips instinctively moving against Julia's firm thigh, against the delicious friction. One of Julia's hands reached for Maddie's breast, her fingers squeezing the nipple through her clothing. Maddie pulled away from the kiss and gasped, her hips still moving.

Maddie could not believe how quickly things had escalated, how very much she wanted Julia. Her hips pressed wantonly into Julia, her now damp center rubbing rhythmically against Julia's raised leg. "How do you always do this to me? God...I want you so badly...I need..."

"Shhh...I know what you need...let me...just like this okay?" Julia slipped her hand down into the back of Maddie's panties and gripped her bare ass cheek firmly, holding her in place. "I'll take care of you, honey....right here...right now."

Julia pulled Maddie against her, pressing her head down onto her shoulder, caressing her hair as Maddie slid herself harder against her leg. Julia whispered sexy sweet nothings into Maddie's ear as she squeezed her bare ass rhythmically and Maddie jerked wildly, wanting more friction. Maddie felt Julia snake her finger along the damp crevice between Maddie's ass cheeks and she felt her own hips jerk back against the forbidden and tantalizing sensation. Maddie had never even imagined anyone touching her there, but she wanted Julia to touch her there.

"It's okay...let me take care of you...I know you need to," Julia whispered as Maddie groaned into her shoulder and pressed her hips harder against her thigh.

Julia began to flex her thigh muscle against Maddie's center as she squeezed Maddie's ass in the same cadence. "God, you're so sexy...I can feel...on my leg...how hot you are," Julia whispered against her ear and Maddie could do nothing but simply whimper as one of her hands tried to find purchase on Julia's shoulders and the other gripped the back of the table that Julia was leaning against.

Maddie felt Julia slip her finger deeper into the damp crevice between her ass cheeks. "You feel so good against me...take what you need," Julia whispered. Maddie's hips began to move in shorter and quicker jerks as desire exploded, as her need escalated.

Julia licked Maddie's ear. "I'm going to take you upstairs...have you naked under me...I want to taste you...to be inside you...to claim you."

Maddie's hips jerked wildly, her breathing becoming ragged and sharp against Julia's neck. Maddie felt Julia slip her finger further between her ass cheeks until it was actually brushing against Maddie's puckered rear opening and Maddie gasped at the incredible sensation, rearing up wildly, shocked at how much her body wanted this.

"Can I have your ass?" Julia whispered loudly, her rough and raspy voice causing the cadence of Maddie's hips to increase.

"God...Jule...yessss..."

Maddie reached out and braced her hand against the wall behind Julia as the sensations and her desire spiraled out of control. She could hear the table Julia was leaning against thud rhythmically against the wall behind it with each wild jerk of her hips, but she did not care. Julia's teasing and probing finger against her ass was making her crazy.

"You are so beautiful...God, Maddie..."

Maddie felt Julia push the pad of her finger gently, but insistently, against her rear opening and she silently begged Julia to breach that last frontier, the taboo nature of the act as exciting as the sensations it was creating. As if Julia could read her mind, Julia's finger pushed inside the tight opening of her ass as her hips reared up wildly. Maddie ground her clit against Julia's leg as Julia's finger moved tantalizingly in her ass and she could not quite believe the intensity of sensation, her shout barely muffled against Julia's shoulder as she exploded in an orgasm that shook her violently.

Maddie slumped against Julia, her legs wobbly, her internal muscles still clenching from the intense orgasm as Julia held her up with a tight arm, kissing the side of her head. It was long moments before Maddie came back to herself and she could not quite believe what had just happened.

"What the hell was that?" Maddie finally whispered, her voice sounding hoarse to her own ears.

Maddie felt more than heard Julia laugh softly, shaking them gently. "That was the sexiest thing ever," Julia whispered. "You seemed to like that...a lot."

Maddie nestled further into Julia's shoulder, her face flaming in embarrassment at what she had allowed Julia to do to her. The forbidden nature of it, however, had not prevented her from coming like a freight train and feeling incredibly sexy.

"I didn't know...I've never..."

"It's okay, I've never...either. You make me feel things and God, Maddie, the things I want to do to you."

"Like what?" Maddie whispered against her shoulder.

Julia pulled her closer. "I never understood penis envy until I had you in my bed, wet and open and the sexiest thing I have ever seen."

"I can buy you one of those," Maddie whispered, surprised at herself.

Julia's laugh was low and raspy and Maddie felt it against her and inside her. "I'll keep that in mind. Come to bed with me." Julia's sexy, whiskey-soaked voice made Maddie shiver and she nodded again, willing to follow this woman anywhere.

Chapter 16

Julia watched Maddie walk into her bedroom in her bare feet, her pumps hanging from her fingers, as Julia waited to shut her bedroom door behind them. She heard the pumps hit the hardwood floor and when she turned, Maddie was already starting to unbutton her blouse and their gazes met. Julia toed off her own shoes as she moved quickly toward Maddie. She reached out to unbutton the last button on Maddie's blouse and they slowly undressed each other. They reached for each other's bras, impatiently unhooking and pulling at straps, yanking at panties until they were both naked and softly panting.

Julia shivered as Maddie's gaze prowled slowly down her body, lingering on her breasts before drifting down to her center, unabashedly staring as Julia tried to catch her breath. Julia could not ever remember anyone turning her on by simply looking at her, but Maddie's gaze was intense and Julia felt it as a caress. Maddie stepped toward her, bringing them together, skin to skin and Julia moaned. Julia hung onto Maddie as their mouths connected and they kissed deeply.

Julia let her hands roam over Maddie, pulling her close as she tried to kiss her deeper. She moved her hands down to squeeze Maddie's ass firmly as her own hips jerked toward Maddie, any self-restraint a distant memory.

"God...I want you," Julia moaned against her mouth.

Hearing that seemed to incite Maddie into action and she pushed Julia back onto the mattress, following her and waiting for her to scoot back to the middle of the bed before she ran her hands up her legs and across her middle, capturing both breasts in her hands. Julia arched up as Maddie's mouth found her nipple, latching on as her hand dipped into Julia's center. Julia heard Maddie gasp at the first touch and Julia knew that she was beyond wet.

Julia did not realize how much she had missed this part of being with Maddie, the excitement of being desired, the way that Maddie seemed to know what she needed and how to give it to her. How Maddie's touch was firm but gentle at the same time. Julia's hips seemed to be moving of their own accord, wanting more.

Julia felt Maddie work her way down her body, placing small kisses and gentle caresses up to her neck and back down to her nipples, pulling them into her mouth firmly, sucking as her hands continued to roam along the landscape of her body. Julia moaned and stretched at the delicious attention and she reached a hand to squeeze and pull at the hair at the back of Maddie's head.

Maddie pulled her mouth away from her nipple. "You want my mouth somewhere else?"

"God, yes, please," Julia whispered, not above begging at this point.

She felt Maddie quickly move down between her legs and gently spread her folds open. Julia could feel how incredibly wet she was as the cool air hit her clit, feeling like a touch.

"Hurry," Julia rasped out. She knew her whisper was a desperate plea, but she did not care. She wanted Maddie's mouth on her now and she was not disappointed as Maddie lowered her open mouth to cover her clit.

Julia nearly screamed as Maddie's mouth seemed to devour her, her tongue lashing, her lips sucking. Julia put her hand on the back of Maddie's head, giving her something to hang onto and holding

Maddie's mouth where she needed it. Julia could not believe how sharply intense every stroke of Maddie's tongue felt as she tried to control the wild bucking of her hips, tried not to bathe Maddie's entire face in her juices. The sensation was focused and intense and Julia tried to hang on, tried to make it last, but it was no use as her body had a mind of its own and her body wanted to come. Julia heard the shout explode from her throat as an orgasm tore through her in explosive waves.

When Julia came back to some awareness, Maddie was kissing her way back up Julia's body. Julia pulled her close, shuddering, a few stray tears escaping and Maddie kissed those away.

"I love doing that," Maddie whispered to her.

Julia let out a sound that was half-sob and half-snort. "Good because I love it when you do that."

They lay in each other's arms quietly for long moments before Maddie kissed her cheek sweetly. Julia ran her gaze slowly over Maddie's features. "So, tell me what else is going on. Why is Gabe touring the high school and what were you doing in New Bedford?"

Maddie seemed to hesitate and averted her gaze for a moment, but then she returned it to Julia. "Gabe's Dad, Sam, had asked Gabe a while ago to think about moving down here to live with him. Gabe really wants to so I'm trying to make that happen, sooner rather than later. My mother has been trying to prevent this for years, threatening all kinds of things, but that's no longer a consideration."

"Love shouldn't be conditional. You said that to me the night we met when referring to your family."

Maddie smiled. "You remember that?" Julia nodded and Maddie continued. "My mother has always tried to dictate how Gabe was raised, expressing her opinions and pushing her advice freely and constantly. Gabe and I have always talked about everything...we make a lot of decisions together. She thinks that's ridiculous...and once she finds out what my plans are...I shudder to think what she might try, but it doesn't matter, it's not going to work."

Julia frowned. "Gabe seems mature enough to make that decision. He seems to have a good head on his shoulders. Maddie, you should be more than proud of yourself and of Gabriel. You've done an amazing job with him. He's polite and...thoughtful and smart."

Maddie smiled. "Thank you. Gabe likes my 'girlfriend' by the way. He texted me as soon as he left the restaurant."

Julia laughed. "I haven't been anyone's girlfriend in many years."

"But you want to be mine?" Maddie asked.

"I want to be more than your girlfriend." Julia said clearly, meeting Maddie's gaze.

Maddie nodded. "I want that too, Julia. I just need to take care of some things, get Gabe situated."

Julia simply nodded, suddenly overcome with a fear that Maddie would leave and it would be weeks before she saw her again. Julia was painfully aware that Maddie had failed to answer her about what she was doing in New Bedford and Julia was afraid to jeopardize this delicate balance of trust and emotion and ask again. "Is there anything I can help you with?"

Maddie smiled. "Not right now, but probably at some point. Thank you for offering, Julia."

"And you won't disappear on me while you're taking care of these things?"

"I will not disappear. You have a phone, too, you know."

Julia sighed. "I know, but the more time that passed, the more I was convinced that you had decided I was too much trouble."

"You are no trouble, Julia, you never have been. So, maybe we should agree, right here and now, that no contact is unacceptable."

Julia nodded. "I need to have a lot of contact from now on, okay?"

"That actually sounds really nice."

"Maddie, I want to be with you."

Julia thought that Maddie's smile was magnificent, her dimples popping. "I want to be with you, too."

Julia pulled Maddie forward and covered her mouth with a soft, wet and glorious kiss. Julia closed her eyes for a moment and inhaled deeply. Just this morning she had wondered if she would ever see Maddie again and here she was, in her bed and making plans with Julia.

"Tell me again," Julia whispered.

"I want to be with you, Jule, querida, and everyone knows it," Maddie added.

"Who's everyone?"

"My son, my brother, my sister-in-law, my entire family. My friend, Steve, from work. Everyone."

Julia smiled as she kissed her lightly. "That makes me very happy, but I'm sorry if that's causing a rift in your family."

"Don't be. You're the best thing that's ever happened to me, Julia Sinclair." Julia was slightly stunned at the declaration, simply staring at Maddie, overcome with emotion. Maddie touched her face. "Did I say something wrong?"

"No. I've just never been anyone's best thing before," Julia whispered.

Maddie placed a small but firm kiss to Julia's lips. "Well then, you've been with idiots because that's just ridiculous. You're my best thing...by far."

They made love again, slowly and softly and Julia was overwhelmed at the emotion, the absolute joy of being with Maddie in this way. Julia actually found herself smiling as she brought Maddie to an orgasm, her tongue delving deeply into Maddie's soft warm folds, Maddie's thighs squeezing against her head as her hips bucked to completion. After Maddie lovingly brought her to another orgasm with her gently probing fingers while holding her in her arms, she could not stop the tears that flowed, but Maddie simply kissed them away.

Julia inhaled deeply, letting the emotions roll over her in a giant wave. Julia made an instant decision, taking the biggest leap of faith of her life. "Maddie, would you like to meet Eleanor?"

Maddie paced nervously in the foyer of Julia's home, the sound of her pumps across the hardwood floor keeping pace with the pounding of her nervous heart. They had quickly showered and dressed and Julia had walked down to the corner to greet her daughter at the bus stop. Julia wanted to talk to her about what had happened before meeting Maddie. Maddie shook out her hands and straightened her blouse as the front door flew open.

Eleanor stopped short and looked at Maddie. Then she smiled widely. "Are you Madalena?"

Eleanor was tall for her age, long and lean like her sister, but her hair was dirty blond, her eyes blue, and she looked like Julia. Maddie smiled back. "Yes, I am, but you can call me Maddie. It's good to meet you, Eleanor."

"You can call me Norie like my Mom does." Maddie saw the surprised look on Julia's face at her daughter's comment as she came in behind her and shut the door.

Maddie smiled. "Okay, Norie it is then."

"Is Gabe here? Can I meet him? How long are you visiting?"

Julia smiled at her daughter. "Hey, little miss hurricane, can you take it down a notch?"

Maddie laughed. "Gabe is with his Dad and we'll be here until Sunday so maybe you'll get to meet him." Then she looked at Julia, not wanting to overstep since she and Julia had been too busy making love to discuss the details of the remainder of the weekend. "If you already have plans..."

Julia smiled. "Not really and we haven't talked about it, but if you and Gabe are free tomorrow night maybe we could all go out and have dinner together, if that's alright with you?"

Maddie felt herself blush, warmed by the way Julia looked at her. "I'll check with Gabe, but I'd like that."

Eleanor clapped her hands together. "Can we go to Amelia's for dinner? We love Amelia's."

Julia looked her daughter. "You love Amelia's and maybe. Do you have homework, Nor?"

208

"Not while Maddie is here."

"Oh yes, while Maddie is here, but you can sit out on the deck with us while you do it."

Eleanor sighed dramatically. "Alright."

Maddie tried to stifle a smile at Eleanor's display. Eleanor looked at her, her blue eyes bright and Maddie realized how much of Julia she could see in her daughter. "It won't take me long to finish my homework."

Maddie smiled. "Don't rush on my account. I'm not going anywhere just yet."

Julia smiled as she ushered her daughter toward the stairs. "Put your stuff away and wash your hands and face please." When Eleanor was at the top of the stairs Julia walked back to Maddie. "That girl is more than a handful."

Maddie kissed Julia quickly and lightly. "I think she gets that from her mother."

Julia laughed and pushed Maddie back into the living room and against the wall, kissing her deeply, her tongue delving into her mouth before she pulled away. Maddie ran her gaze slowly over Julia's features and smiled at her. She knew it had taken a lot of trust on Julia's part to let her meet Eleanor.

"What?" Julia whispered.

"Thank you for letting me meet Eleanor. I know what it means. Thank you for trusting me."

"You're welcome."

"Do you mind if I run out to my car to get some things out of my bag? I would really like to change, get out of these pumps," Maddie said.

Julia's gaze was fixed on Maddie's. "Just bring your bag in with you. Cancel your reservation at the Sea Breeze. Stay here with me...with us."

Maddie took a moment and thought about spending the weekend with Julia, in her home, allowed into her life. She shivered as she thought about sleeping in Julia's bed, closely entwined with her. She reached for Julia's face, caressing it softly.

"I'd love that."

Maddie woke early, as she usually did, the unfamiliar but welcome scent and sounds of the ocean gently wafting in through the open windows in Julia's bedroom. Maddie watched Julia sleep beside her, inhaling deeply at the emotion stirred in her by simply looking at this woman. Out of respect for the fact that Eleanor was in the house, they had simply kissed each other good night and slept fully clothed, but Maddie had still slept deeply and contentedly, and she still wanted Julia with every fiber of her being.

The previous day had almost seemed like a dream to her. She had spent the remainder of the afternoon on the deck with Julia and Eleanor, drinking wine and nibbling on various snacks that Julia had put together for them. The day had been clear and warm, the view of the harbor beautiful, and the view of Julia even more so. Eleanor had joined in their conversation as she did her homework at a nearby table. Maddie had noticed her sneaking occasional looks at her.

"What kind of homework are you working on, Norie?" Maddie asked her.

"Language Arts." Eleanor answered as she turned to her. "We're reading *To Kill a Mockingbird* by Harper Lee. Have you read it?"

"Yes, but it was quite a while ago. Gabe had to read it for class, too."

"I read it last summer," Eleanor sighed, "and I'm glad I got to enjoy it before I have to read it again for class and analyze everything. I don't want to have to think about how a particular line of dialogue moves the story forward."

Maddie found Eleanor to be observant and intelligent, and a little scary, if she was honest. "I understand your frustration, but maybe you will feel differently after you learn things about the way the author wrote the novel or what she was trying to say about society, what the intent of the book is."

"What do you mean?" Eleanor asked politely.

Maddie smiled. "Have you talked about the theme of the novel yet?"

"Ms. Vaz, my teacher, said it had to do with the loss of innocence, but we would talk about it more on Monday. Do you know what she meant?"

Maddie shrugged. "Let's think about it. Was Scout innocent at the beginning of the story? What happened to her by the end of it...to Gem...to the town? Did they learn things about themselves or about society that they really didn't want to know?"

Eleanor had looked deep in thought for a moment before she smiled. "They lost their innocence when they realized how prejudiced people can be."

Maddie smiled back. "And how accepting people can be, too. And how life is complicated."

"What is the thing that you remember about the book?" Eleanor asked.

"I remember that I had to keep reminding myself that it was Scout as an adult who was telling the story because it is written for a child to understand. I had to keep in mind that the reader can understand certain things that Scout, as a child, cannot understand. That made me look at things...differently or more carefully, I guess."

"Thanks, Maddie."

"You're very welcome."

When Eleanor had gone into the house, Maddie looked at Julia. "She read it last year? *To Kill a Mockingbird* was part of a...what... 6th-grade summer reading list?"

Julia smiled. "Oh, no, she actually read it on her own, but she's already in some advanced high school level classes due to accelerated learning."

Maddie laughed lightly. "Oh, God bless you."

Julia joined in the laughter. "You have no idea. I haven't been able to help her with math homework for years now."

"She's amazing, Julia."

"Thank you. She likes you."

"Does she?" Maddie asked, thinking that Julia was simply trying to put her at ease.

Julia nodded, her gaze intense. "Yes, I can tell she likes you a lot."

212

Julia did not look particularly happy about that for a moment, but then she smiled. Maddie suspected that Julia was thinking about the consequences of their relationship for her daughter. It was not simply the two of them involved in this any longer. Eleanor, and to a lesser degree, Vivienne and Gabriel, would be affected by the decisions they made.

Maddie had reached for Julia's hand and held her gaze. "I'm glad. I'll try not to do anything to change that." Julia had smiled.

In Julia's bedroom, Maddie let the memory wash over her as she watched Julia sleep for another moment. She knew she would not be able to get back to sleep so she kissed Julia's cheek gently and quietly slipped out of bed. She closed the door to the attached bathroom and started to brush her teeth as she turned the shower on. She was leaning over the sink wiping her mouth when she felt arms snake around her, one hand slipping into the front of her sleep shorts and the other running up under her tank top to cup her breasts. Maddie smiled into the mirror and Julia's sleepy gaze met her own. Her eyes were half-open, her hair was tousled and Maddie thought she looked amazingly beautiful.

When Julia awoke and found herself alone, she glanced at her bedside clock and smiled. Eleanor would still be asleep for hours and Julia could hear the shower starting in the bathroom. She found Maddie bent over the sink and the sight of her filled Julia with an overwhelming combination of emotion and desire. She wrapped her arms around Maddie and sought out the warm skin beneath her shorts and tank, one hand seeking her breasts, finding and caressing a nipple, and the other playing with her soft pubic hair.

Maddie met Julia's gaze in the mirror and Julia lost her breath at the look of adoration on Maddie's face. Julia heard Maddie gasp as she gently squeezed her nipple.

"What are you doing, Jule?" Maddie asked quietly.

"Touching you...I can't help myself," Julia whispered.

Maddie turned around and Julia was forced to take a step back. She half-expected Maddie to push her away and remind her that Eleanor was down the hall, but she did not. Julia watched as she kicked her shorts off and slid back onto the towel that rested on the counter. She looked at Julia before she pulled her tank top off and wrapped her legs around Julia, pulling her forward. Julia froze, still surprised at how much Maddie seemed to want her.

"I thought you couldn't help yourself," Maddie whispered, teasing her.

Maddie cupped Julia's head and pulled her into an open-mouthed kiss, her spearmint flavored tongue tangling with her own. Julia moaned into the kiss and she pulled Maddie to the edge of the counter, her fingers squeezing and tugging at her nipples. Julia slid her hand down the soft skin of Maddie's abdomen and slid her fingers into her damp curls. Julia was pleasantly surprised to find Maddie already wet for her.

Julia quickly coated her fingers so she could slip two of them inside Maddie. Julia loved that Maddie moaned into her mouth, their tongues still tangling together. Julia tried to be gentle in her thrusts, but Maddie's heels pushed into the back of Julia's thighs and she grunted into the kiss, indicating she wanted more. Julia pulled her mouth away and pushed her hips into her own hand, forcing her fingers harder into Maddie, enjoying the panting sound Maddie made in response.

Julia sucked at Maddie's neck. "My beautiful Madalena."

The words seemed to inflame Maddie and she started to orgasm, in sharp jerks of her hips, in small whimpers of delight, beautifully and wildly, until she fell forward, shuddering in Julia's arms. Julia held her closely for long moments until her breathing and shuddering slowed. Julia removed her fingers carefully and pulled Maddie close while she caressed her warm naked skin, slightly overwhelmed by the way that making love to Maddie made her feel, powerful and joyous.

Maddie kissed her lightly and pushed her back, sliding gracefully from the counter. She wordlessly pulled off Julia's tank and tugged off her sleep pants before leading her by the hand into the still running shower.

The warm spray of the shower hit Julia as Maddie embraced her lightly, gently pushing her against the far wall, her lips attaching themselves to first one nipple, then the other. Julia moaned and caressed her wet, slick hair, holding her there. Maddie dropped to her knees and spread Julia's folds open, licking up to her clit with the flat of her tongue. Julia heard herself moan as she spread her legs, one foot finding the rubber mat, the other perched on the edge of the tub, and a hand gripping the shower railing for support.

Maddie teased and aroused her gently with her tongue gently before diving in with her mouth and her hand, sliding fingers up into Julia as she firmly tongued her clit. Julia's free hand attached itself to the back of Maddie's head and her hips began a frenzied dance, the dual sensations overwhelming every nerve ending.

Julia was in ecstasy, as Maddie seemed to be everywhere. Maddie had always been able to bring her to orgasm with just her fingers or with just her mouth, but it felt like both were happening independently of each other and at the same time. Julia tipped her head back to suck in oxygen and clutched at the railing in her hand as she pulled Maddie's head harder against her as her inner walls started to spasm, as Maddie's tongue did its magic. Julia started to shake as the orgasm started and then continued, washing over her in a frenzied wave until another one began and it seemed to go on forever. Julia hung on until her knees gave out and she started to slide down the shower wall, Maddie holding her firmly and guiding her down into her arms.

Julia felt spent and vulnerable in a way that was not familiar to her. It was a very long time before Julia was able to find her voice. "Water's getting cool," she managed to whisper.

"Are you okay?" Maddie's voice was near her ear and Julia realized that her eyes were still closed and she had no desire to open them and expose her most private vulnerabilities. Having Maddie here in her home, loving her this way seemed too perfect and she tried not to get ahead of herself.

She felt Maddie gently push her wet hair out of her face. "Let me help you up and I'll turn the water up. Okay?"

She nodded and Maddie pulled her up and they showered quickly, but gently, with kisses and caresses in between lathering and rinsing. Julia was relieved when Maddie stepped out of the shower first, without a word, possibly sensing that Julia needed some time alone. When Julia finally stepped out of the bathroom, wrapped in a towel, Maddie was in the bedroom dressing. Julia tried to smile, but could only swallow painfully. Maddie pulled her close and held her for a long moment.

Julia pulled away and placed a small kiss to Maddie's lips. "There's coffee in the kitchen. Please poke around and help yourself to whatever you can find."

"Can I get you anything?" Maddie asked.

"If you could throw an English muffin in the toaster, I'd appreciate it," Julia managed.
"Butter and jam, right?"

Julia smiled, pleasantly surprised that Maddie had remembered her preferences. "Yes, thank you. I'll be down in a few minutes."

"Take your time, querida."

Julia was relieved and grateful that Maddie seemed to know she needed some space and some time alone and she took that time to think through what was happening between them and exactly how that made her feel. Julia felt as though she was free falling and it was exhilarating, as well as frightening. She breathed deeply as she dressed, trying to ease her overwhelming emotions.

When Julia finally walked into her kitchen, she saw Maddie sipping from a mug of coffee, gazing out at the water through the window. Julia's muffin, with butter and jam, was waiting on a plate and there was a mug for her by the coffeemaker. Julia was not accustomed to being waited on and the considerate gesture eased some of the fear that gripped her. Julia inhaled a deep and shuddering breath as she closed the distance between them. She snaked her arms snaked around Maddie from behind.

Maddie put her mug down, allowing the embrace before she turned and met Julia's gaze. "Did I do something?"

Julia's heart clenched at the painfully bleak look on Maddie's face. "Oh, sweetie, no, of course not. I just had a little meltdown."

"Oh querida...why?"

"Being with you is so...overwhelming. You make me feel wonderful and this feels so right, having you here, and I realized there is no going back."

Maddie moved slightly away from her. "Do you want to go back, Jule? Having second thoughts?"

Julia's gaze snapped up to Maddie's eyes, surprised at Maddie's question until she realized that Maddie was afraid of her answer. She brought her hand up to caress the side of Maddie's face. "No, sweetie, not at all. I want to be with you and now I've had a taste of what that might be like, I'm...worried."

"Tell me why."

Julia blinked, holding off tears. "Honestly? It was hard the first two times we didn't see each other but now...I can't imagine what it would be like if you changed your mind."

Maddie looked stunned, but Julia could not take back what she had said and she wanted to be honest. "Changed my mind?" Maddie said quietly.

"Maddie, I didn't say that to hurt you. The more I'm with you, the more I want you and...I'm afraid."

Maddie nodded, her eyes blinking back tears. "I don't want to hurt you either. All I can tell you is that I will not disappear, even if you ask me to. I can't know exactly how you feel and you can't know what I'm going through. I'm not you, Julia, and I handle things the way I handle things. I have things I need to take care of, and in the meantime, all I can do is ask you to trust me."

"I'm trying."

"I know you are. I couldn't walk away from you, Jule, even if I wanted to and I don't want to. I have wanted this with you from the beginning, but I was afraid. I'm not afraid anymore."
"What do you mean, from the beginning?"

Maddie swallowed visibly. "That first night when I whispered to you in Portuguese..."

"When you seemed shocked that I recognized the language and you didn't tell me everything you said?"

Maddie smiled. "Yeah, because I was afraid you would think I was crazy."

"So...tell me now."

"Eu acho que te amo."

"What does that mean?" Julia asked quietly.

Maddie inhaled deeply. "It means, 'I think I love you'."

"You thought you loved me? The first night?" Julia's eyes were wide.

Maddie smiled and rubbed her forehead. "Yeah. I also thought I might be losing my mind, but apparently, I wasn't. I was just...starting to fall in love with you."

Julia pressed a hand to her chest as it seemed to fill with warmth. "You're in love with me?"

"Yeah, I am, Jule. I'm in love with you."

Julia watched Maddie's face, the love shining clearly in her open gaze. Julia knew that she had never wanted anything more than she wanted this woman, that she had never loved anyone quite like this before. She pulled Maddie into her arms and held her gaze.

"I'm in love with you."

Maddie's smile was blinding and Julia laughed lightly, the joy of the moment overwhelming her senses before Maddie kissed her softly. Maddie held her for a long moment before releasing her.

Maddie smiled as she slid the plate holding the muffin she had made Julia earlier toward her. "Now, eat the damn muffin."

Julia laughed lightly. "Too easy."

Maddie shoved her playfully. "Shut up." After a few moments of watching Julia chew her muffin, Maddie inhaled. "So...I have a work thing this Friday night."

Julia cocked her head. "A work thing?"

"Yeah, a cocktail party at the Long Wharf Marriott. It's an annual event for clients and I can bring someone."

Julia put down the rest of her muffin and felt her eyebrows rise as she tried to control her excitement and expectations. "Oh? Who did you bring last year?"

Maddie smiled. "I went alone...and hung out with my friend Steven."

Julia turned to face Maddie. "I've never been to the Long Wharf."

Maddie wiped a crumb from Julia's lip. "The views are beautiful."

"If I'm with you, the view is always beautiful."

"Wow." Maddie met Julia's gaze with her own. "So, would you like to be my date?"

Julia smiled widely. "Are we making plans?"

"We are."

"I would be thrilled to be your date."

Chapter 17

Amelia's turned out to be a casual and busy seafood restaurant with a view of the water and Julia had apparently made reservations as the five of them were immediately seated at a round table with a window view. Eleanor was busy telling Gabe about her favorite menu items while Julia looked on in amusement and Maddie took the opportunity to lean over toward Vivienne.

"Is there something you want to say to me, Vivienne?" Julia's oldest daughter had been exceedingly polite to her, but Maddie could feel her eyes following her constantly. At best, Maddie thought she was curious about her and her relationship with her mother and at worst, Maddie thought she did not trust her. Maddie would not blame her for either.

Vivienne glanced quickly at her mother, ensuring she was still distracted by Gabriel and Eleanor, and then looked Maddie in the eye. "Make sure this is what you want, please. Don't hurt her. She's had enough of that in her life."

Maddie reached for Vivienne's hand and squeezed it quickly. "I promise I will do my best to never hurt her again."

Vivienne smiled and then looked up to find her mother's gaze on her, an eyebrow slightly raised. Maddie was impressed at how easily Vivienne ignored her mother's obviously curious and slightly displeased look. "So, what looks good tonight, Mom?"

Julia's eyebrow managed to arch a little higher and Maddie could see that Julia knew that Vivienne was blatantly hiding something from her. Julia smirked as she ran her gaze slowly over Maddie's features. "I haven't decided yet."

"Oh, I think you know exactly what you want, Mom," Vivienne lobbed back.

Maddie tried not to smile as Julia shot Vivienne another sharp glance. "Oh?"

Vivienne smiled. "You always get the scallops here, don't you?" She winked at her mother to temper her snarky and self-satisfied response.

Eleanor nodded knowingly. "Yep, she always gets the scallops."

Maddie laughed, thinking about the first time she had met Vivienne and telling Julia that she would not know she was Julia's daughter at first glance. Julia had laughed and assured Maddie she would see the resemblance if she spent any time with her and now Maddie knew exactly what Julia had meant. Vivienne was as confident and as sarcastic as her mother.

"And now I see Vivienne's resemblance to you," Maddie whispered to Julia, making her smile. Maddie looked at her son. "What are you thinking about, Gabe?"

Gabriel smiled. "Eleanor recommends the fish and chips, but if Julia likes the scallops...what do you like here, Vivienne?"

Julia laughed lightly. "Gabriel, you are just as diplomatic and as charming as your mother."

Vivienne put her menu down. "Lobster roll and sweet potato fries," she announced.

Gabriel and Vivienne discussed the pros and cons of regular fries versus sweet potato fries until Eleanor claimed that onion rings trumped both. Julia leaned toward Maddie, placing a hand on her thigh. "What's your pleasure, beautiful Maddie?" She whispered.

Maddie smiled. "As lovely as this is…my pleasure would be you…me…alone…for days," she whispered back. "But I'll settle on the calamari appetizer and the seared salmon."

Julia nodded. "The last two I can easily do and I will definitely work on the first one."

Maddie glanced at Gabriel and the girls laughing about something and looked at Julia. "This is very nice, all of us here together. Thank you, Julia."

"I should be thanking you."

"Whatever for?"

"Being here. Coming back into my life. Loving me."

Maddie stared, her gaze locked on Julia's own. She placed her hand over Julia's and turned it over, lacing their fingers together. The server arrived and Maddie pulled her gaze away, finding her son looking at her with a small knowing smile on his face. She smiled back, Julia's fingers still laced with her own beneath the table.

Julia had invited Gabriel to stay at her house for the remainder of the weekend and he had readily agreed. Eleanor wanted to show Maddie her room so Julia offered to show Gabriel to his room when they got to the house after dinner. Julia smiled as Gabriel craned his neck to take everything in as they climbed the stairs together.

"Wow, this is a big house." Gabriel said.

"Yes, probably too big for just Eleanor and me, but when it came on the market I couldn't resist. I've always wanted to live on the water."

"The woodwork in here is incredible, the crown molding and these spindles." He touched the bannister.

Julia smiled. "I think so, too. Your mother mentioned you like wood carving and sculpture."

Gabriel nodded. "I do. My Uncle Enzo is a carpenter. I work for him during the summer. That's why I wanted to tour the vocational school, to check out the carpentry department."

"How did that go? Did you like the school?"

"Yeah, I did. The instructor knows my Dad so he let me use the lathe. That was pretty cool."

"Is that what you want to do?" Julia asked.

Gabe shrugged. "Possibly. I like to do finish carpentry work as well as woodcarving and sculpture. UMass in Dartmouth has a good Arts Program and they have a certificate program in sculpture."

"Their Arts Program is top-notch and a degree is something you can always fall back on."

Gabe smiled. "You sound like my Mom."

Julia laughed softly. "Thank you, I think." Julia opened the door to the bedroom at the end of the hall and the farthest away from her own. "This is your room while you're here. Make yourself at home."

Gabriel looked around the large but simply decorated bedroom with the queen sized bed and large windows as he set his bag on the bed. He looked at the small flat screen on the dresser. "Wow, I wasn't expecting a room this nice just for me. This is great, Julia. Thanks for having me."

"It's my pleasure. You know where the kitchen is so help yourself to anything. Don't be shy, Gabe, okay?"

Gabriel smiled widely, the resemblance to his mother causing Julia's breath to catch. Julia smiled back. "You look just like your mother when you smile."

"Thank you."

"I hope you won't be bored while you're here."

"Not at all."

"Are you always this agreeable?"

"I'm sure my mother would say no, but it's just nice seeing her this happy."

Julia paused at the sudden emotion she felt at his words. "Thank you for telling me that, Gabriel."

"You're welcome. Good night, Julia."

Julia wandered over to her daughter's bedroom, the bedside lamp washing over the scene inside. Eleanor and Maddie were huddled together on the bed as they talked quietly. Julia watched as Maddie simply watched her daughter talking, a small indulgent smile on her face. Maddie gently moved a wisp of hair from Eleanor's forehead before she noticed Julia in the doorway watching them.

Julia smiled. "Am I interrupting?"

Maddie shook her head. "No, Norie was just telling me about her art class."

"Maddie knows about art, Mom. She knows what chiaroscuro is."

Julia smiled. "Maddie knows about a lot of things, Eleanor. She's well-rounded."

Eleanor nodded. "That's what I want to be, too. Can we go to a museum soon, Mom, with Maddie?"

Julia walked over to the bed and leaned over to kiss her Norie's forehead. "We'll plan something soon. Now don't stay up too late on Snapgram, Instachat or whatever tonight. Okay?"

Norie giggled. "Okay, Mom, good night. Good night, Maddie."

Maddie placed a light kiss to the side of her head. "Good night, Norie."

Julia reached for Maddie's hand and pulled her up, leading her into the hallway, leaving the door slightly ajar. Julia pulled Maddie into her arms. "If I wasn't already in love with you, seeing the way you are with Norie would've sealed the deal."

Maddie smiled. "She's so much like you, how can I not love her?"

"I was just thinking the same thing about your son. He's thoughtful...and sweet...and looks just like you when he smiles a certain way. You should ask him about the school tour if you haven't already." Julia kissed her lips lightly. "Take your time. I'll be waiting in our room."

Maddie became very still and Julia realized what she had just said. Julia decided to simply wait for Maddie to address it or not. "Did you just say 'our room'?" Maddie finally asked.

Julia smiled softly. "Noticed that, did you?"

"It's mine already?" Maddie smiled back.

"Since you are the first and only person I've ever had in that bed...to ever share that room with me...you get dibs if you want 'em."

Maddie smiled as she walked down the hallway before she turned and slowly walked backward. "I call dibs on the bed, the room, and on you, Julia Sinclair."

Julia could not believe how ridiculously happy it made her simply hearing Maddie say that.

On Sunday morning, as was the norm, Vivienne walked over from her place so they could all have breakfast together on the deck, but this morning included Maddie and Gabe as well. Julia was afraid that her girls might resent the intrusion, but she had worried needlessly as Viv and Norie seemed more than happy with the imposition of Maddie and Gabe on their private time together. Julia tried to stay in the moment and not dwell on the fact that Maddie would be leaving soon. She tried not to show any of the fear or insecurity that she was feeling and she thought she had been doing well until Maddie followed her into the house.

"I don't use my phone in the car," Maddie said to Julia when they reached the kitchen.

"Excuse me?" Julia asked.

"It's a rule with me, no phone while driving, so I won't be able to call you until I get home."

Julia smiled. "Okay?"

"I don't want you to think I won't miss you as soon as I drive away, that I won't call you as soon as I can."

Julia and ran her finger lightly between her eyebrows. "Are my frown lines showing?" Maddie shook her head in confusion and Julia sighed. "Are my insecurities that obvious?"

"When you looked at me this morning, I saw happiness. When you looked at me a few minutes ago all I could see was worry and doubt."

Julia nodded. "I think it's going to take a while before I can...relax."

Maddie folded her arms in front of her. "Okay."

Julia saw the gesture as defensive or possibly protective so she reached for Maddie's arms, pulling them loose and moving them around her own waist as she stepped into Maddie's space. "I'm sorry for being...so..."

"It's okay, I understand, but we have plans for Friday, don't we?"

"Yes, we do and even if we didn't...if you disappear...I'll simply come looking for you."

Maddie pulled her close and rested her forehead against Julia's. "Promise?"

Julia heard many things in that request from Maddie, including fear, vulnerability and affection. They were both feeling the same things and somehow, ridiculously, that gave Julia the hope that she needed at the moment.

Julia smiled as her cell vibrated against her stomach. She had placed it there to ensure that she would not miss a call from Maddie. She picked it up and put it to her ear.

"Hello, beautiful."

"Hi, honey," Maddie said. "How was your day?"

Julia heard the smile in Maddie's voice and it made her happy. Maddie had called her as soon as she and Gabe had arrived home on Sunday and each evening since then. It had eased some of Julia's fears.

"Thankfully busy."

"Thankfully?" Maddie asked.

"Yeah, if I'm busy I'm not thinking about how long until I get to see you," Julia said quietly.

"Only two days and I miss you, too."

"That's nice to hear," Julia whispered, a few more doubts quieted. "So, this thing on Friday night? What should I be wearing?"

"It's up to you."

"What are you wearing?"

"Well, I've got a hot date, so I'm wearing a cocktail dress."

Julia laughed quietly. "Really? What color is it?"

"Black."

"Sweet Jesus, I can't wait to see that."

"I can't wait to see you. Are you staying until Sunday?" Maddie asked.

"Are you asking me to stay until Sunday?"

"Yes."

"I'm staying until Sunday."

Chapter 18

Maddie sipped from her martini glass as she glanced toward the doorway of the event venue for the hundredth time, barely noticing the beautiful views of Boston Harbor from the large windows or the soft jazz music coming from the DJ's speakers.

"Relax, she'll be here," Steven said, smiling at her.

"I know. I'm just dying to see her."

"Well, I'm sure she's dying to see you, too...and wait until she does see you."

Maddie frowned. "What? Why?"

Steven took a step back and looked at Maddie from her head to her feet. She was dressed in a vintage lace cocktail dress with a flared tulle skirt and simple pumps. "Maddie, girl, you look so hot tonight that even I would think about switching teams."

While she laughed, she saw Steven look past her, his eyes widening. "Wow, who the hell is that? A new client?"

Maddie turned and saw Julia standing just inside the door, dressed in a fitted dress, the fabric a colorful burst of blue and white flowers against a black background. The fit of the dress complemented her full figure and the color complemented her shining cobalt eyes. She had pulled her hair back, her lips covered in glossy red lipstick, gold chandelier earrings swinging gently from her ears.

Maddie smiled, her heart swelling. "That, my dear Steven, is Julia."

"Shut the fuck up," he whispered.

Maddie laughed lightly. "I told you she was attractive."

"That's not attractive. That's...magnificent."

Julia spotted her and smiled widely, walking toward her, their gazes locked. Maddie couldn't wait for Julia to reach her so she left Steven and her martini at the bar to meet Julia halfway and Maddie sighed deeply when Julia pulled her into a close embrace. They held each other silently for an extended moment.

Julia pulled away and smiled at her. "Hello, gorgeous." She cupped her face tenderly and then stepped back to run her gaze over every inch of Maddie. "You are certainly a sight for sore eyes."

Maddie inhaled deeply, overwhelmed at finally having Julia here with her. She looked down at Julia's dress. "You are a vision. This dress was made for you."

"For us, actually. I picked something so we would be coordinated."

Maddie laughed. "You're sweet and I'm not sure you've ever looked more beautiful...and that is saying a lot since I nearly swallowed my tongue the first time I saw you."

Julia's smile widened. "Really? You never told me that. So you liked the business suit?"

"Oh yes, until I saw the other suit." Julia frowned in confusion and Maddie smiled. "Your birthday suit," she whispered.

Julia laughed lightly and pulled Maddie close. "I can't believe you just said that."

"Me neither. I'm giddy because I'm so happy to see you, Julia."

"I think I like you giddy."

"So, come meet Steven and I'll get you a drink."

Julia realized that she was licking her lips as she watched Maddie greet some clients and direct them to a group of suits congregated in the far corner of the room. It had gotten busy since she had arrived and it was getting more difficult to track Maddie when she had to wander away to take care of something. She looked so beautiful and confident and Julia noticed several people look at Maddie with more than a passing interest.

"Don't worry. She has no idea how hot she is."

Julia turned to look at Maddie's friend, Steven, standing near her at the bar. "Oh I think she's aware there's interest...she just doesn't–"

"Really know how hot she is?"

Julia laughed easily. "Maybe you're right."

"Trust me, she doesn't. And even if she did, she only has eyes for you. I've never seen her like this."

Julia looked at the soft-spoken young man. He was younger than Maddie, with dark hair, blue eyes and rimless glasses. He looked more than handsome dressed in a navy suit with his white shirt unbuttoned at the collar.

She smiled at him. "Like what?"

"She's crazy about you. As far as I know, she's had no interest in anyone the entire time I've known her...and I'd never seen her so upset as when you two were...on a break."

Julia nodded. "Yeah, that was pretty rough for me, too. So, how long have you two worked together?"

"About six years or so. We hit it off right away, but she's always been very private, never talked about her personal life. It's taken me years to get past her natural...reserve shall we say, to get her to talk to me...and finally admit that we have something in common."

"Good looks and charm?"

He smiled at her. "You are as kind as you are beautiful." He raised her hand and placed a small kiss to her knuckles.

She laughed softly. "Oh, people are going to start talking now." Julia felt a soft arm around her waist.

"What will they say?" Maddie asked with a smile, moving closer and putting Julia between herself and Steven.

"They'll probably say that I'm stepping out on you," Steven said with a smile. He looked at Julia. "Some people actually think that Mads and I are dating."

"They might think that I'm the one stepping out on you," Maddie said, as she tightened her hold on Julia's waist.

Julia looked at Steven and then at Maddie. "Maybe they'll think that we're having a threesome," Julia said as she finished her martini.

Steven laughed. "Oh, Mads, I like her."

Maddie smiled. "Me, too."

"Mads? He calls you Mads?" Julia asked.

Maddie shrugged. "Yep."

"You've got an awful lot of aliases there, Tracy."

Maddie laughed. "Oh my God, you remember that?"

Julia nodded. "I remember every minute I have been graced with your presence, Madalena Francisco."

Maddie gasped. "Wow."

"Talk about charm," Steven said.

The music from the DJ changed and became a bit louder and Steven smiled as he looked at Maddie. "The dancing has started. Are we going to leave?"

"Leave? Where are we going?" Julia asked.

Maddie sighed. "This is when Steven and I usually leave."

"Why's that?"

"When Steven and I dance together, the rumor mill ramps up and if we don't dance together..."

"Then the trolls come out and line up for Mads." Steven completed the explanation. "But...then again, she's never brought a date before." He smiled at Maddie.

"Do you like to dance?" Julia asked Maddie.

Maddie smiled. "I do like to dance. Do you?"

"Yeah."

It was apparent to Julia that living closeted for so many years had caused Maddie to subdue her natural personality and she had noticed that she was not entirely comfortable with public displays of affection. Maddie had always seemed much more relaxed when they were in Julia's world, but tonight they were squarely in Maddie's own backyard and Julia wasn't sure what to expect. Maddie did not look pressured or uncomfortable though. She simply smiled as she cocked her head slightly, appearing to be listening to the music.

As soon as the music slowed down, Maddie turned to her. "Would you like to dance with me, Julia?"

"I would love to dance with you," Julia said quietly.

Maddie held her hand out and Steven squealed like a little girl. They both laughed before Julia took her hand and let Maddie lead her onto the dance floor.

There were only a few couples on the dance floor, mostly the management team at her agency dancing with their spouses. Maddie saw a few surprised glances in their direction, but shrugged them off as she led Julia to the middle of the floor. They came together, the fingers of one hand still attached and rested their foreheads together for a brief moment. Maddie felt her face heating.

239

"You okay?" Julia asked.

"I just realized that we've never danced before," Maddie whispered.

"Relax, we got this," Julia answered quietly.

Julia placed a hand on Maddie's waist and brought their joined hands up between them. Maddie rested her free hand on Julia's shoulder, her fingers reaching out to caress her bare neck. Julia started to sway to the beat of the song and Maddie rested her cheek against Julia's and followed her lead, conscious of her thigh brushing Julia's as they danced.

"I knew we would be good at this," Julia whispered as they moved and swayed in sync.

"How did you know?" Maddie pulled her head back to meet Julia's gaze.

"We already know how to move together." Julia smiled. "And we do it so well, don't we?"

Maddie laughed lightly. "Yes, we do."

Maddie inhaled deeply and glanced around her, realizing that the looks they were getting had smiles attached and she relaxed. Maddie pulled Julia closer as they danced together, their bodies moving together easily and pressing deliciously. Even being in a very public setting did little to ease Maddie's desire for Julia and she rubbed her hand up and down the length of Julia's bare neck.

The music changed to something with a decidedly Latin beat and Maddie felt a little more in her element. Maddie's brother, Enzo, hated to dance so whenever there was a family wedding, she and Maria would hit the dance floor and Maria loved to dance to Latin music.

"Will you let me lead for this one?" Maddie asked.

Julia nodded. "Just be gentle."

"That's not what you usually say," Maddie whispered into her ear and Julia laughed, the deep and raspy sound of it making Maddie shiver.

Maddie moved her hips a bit more and quickened her step. To her surprise, Julia laughed as she followed her movements easily and Maddie stepped back, keeping their hands attached before she pulled Julia back in. They clung to each other as Maddie moved her entire body to the music, but she kept her steps uncomplicated so Julia could easily follow her and she did. Maddie laughed as they danced, feeling as happy and as free as she could ever remember feeling, with Julia in her arms.

Maddie woke, warm and satiated and reached a hand out, smiling when she felt Julia sleeping beside her. Maddie opened her eyes and saw Julia cradling a pillow, only partially covered by the sheet, a tantalizing glimpse of her hip and the side of her breast visible. Her skin looked soft and pale in the morning light and Maddie sighed at the beautiful sight.

The previous night seemed like a dream to Maddie, dancing with Julia, laughing with her and Steven over drinks and then bringing Julia home with her. Maddie thought about how beautiful Julia had looked in her gorgeous dress and how she had looked even more beautiful out of it. They had made love slowly and passionately with Julia professing her love for Maddie until they had curled up together and slept.

Maddie shivered at the memory and then inhaled sharply when she realized that she could have lost this, this woman, this feeling of love and acceptance, this happiness that was unlike anything she had ever known. Her eyes filled with tears and spilled onto her cheeks. She was feeling a combination of joy over being with Julia, and regret over how much they had hurt each other getting here.

Maddie vowed to do everything in her power to hang onto this woman and this feeling, to live the life she had always wanted. She wiped her face with the corner of the sheet and sniffled, trying to pull herself together when Julia's eyes slowly opened, the crystal blue color beautiful in the morning light.

"Good morning," Maddie whispered.

Julia reached for Maddie, caressing her face. "Hey, baby, what's wrong?"

Maddie smiled, overwhelmed by the obvious concern, as well as Julia's sexy, raspy voice and she shivered slightly at her strong and ever-present physical attraction to Julia. "Nothing, Jule, I promise. I just love you so damn much and I love waking up with you."

Julia smiled at that and pulled Maddie in, embracing her with her entire body, the way that Maddie loved, with her arms and her legs, rocking her slightly as she placed kisses over her face and neck and shoulder. "I love waking up with you, more than I can say."

Maddie kissed her back, lightly on the lips. "Don't move."

Maddie untangled herself and strolled out of her bedroom naked, down the hall and into her kitchen, pouring a mug from the coffee maker. She added Julia's preferred amounts of cream and sweetener and brought it back into the bedroom. Julia was sitting up against the headboard smiling.

"I could get used to this," Julia said in a raspy whisper as Maddie handed her the mug. "No one's ever brought me coffee in bed."

Maddie ran her gaze over Julia's naked form, enjoying the view and the effect her gaze seemed to be having on Julia, her nipples hardening as she squirmed slightly. "I could get used to this," Maddie said as she stared at Julia. "Waking up to you naked and looking so beautiful." She took the mug from Julia and sipped from it before handing it back.

Julia took a generous sip of coffee and then placed the mug on the bedside table. "C'mere," she whispered.

Maddie climbed back into the bed, moving up to straddle Julia as Julia guided her closer, taking Maddie's nearest nipple into her mouth, sucking gently as Maddie responded with a soft moan and her hips rolling gently into Julia. Julia slowed her oral caress and stopped, resting her forehead against Maddie's chest.

"I can't believe how much I want you, baby, especially after last night. Is it okay that I want you all the time?"

Maddie inhaled a surprised breath at Julia's question. "It's more than okay. I want you all the time, too."

"You want me now?" Julia's voice was quiet and tentative.

Maddie brought one of Julia's hands to her center and Julia gasped as Maddie jerked at the contact. Maddie could feel how incredibly wet she was as Julia's fingers gently explored. Maddie brought her lips close to Julia's ear.

"I love you," Maddie whispered. "I want you. Fuck me."

Maddie grabbed the headboard and moaned loudly as Julia gave her exactly what she had asked for.

Chapter 19

Julia smiled as Maddie held her hand firmly as she led her into the somewhat busy neighborhood restaurant. She expected Maddie to release her hand at any moment, especially when several patrons turned to stare as they strolled in, but she held on tightly. Julia saw someone she assumed was Maria waving from a booth in the back as they made their way through the gauntlet of closely arranged tables. Several members of a group involved in a lively discussion at one table smiled and nodded at Maddie and she smiled and nodded back.

"Olá, Layna," someone called from another nearby table and Maddie turned, smiling and waving at an acquaintance with her free hand. It was obvious that Maddie was well known in this place.

Maria was already sliding out of the booth to kiss Maddie on each cheek in the European manner before hugging her closely, talking softly to her in a combination of English and Portuguese. Maddie nodded and smiled as she pulled away and turned.

"Julia, this is my sister-in-law, Maria. Maria, this is Julia."

Julia smiled at Maria as she reached a hand out, but Maria pulled her in to kiss her on both cheeks. "The famous Julia," she said as she ran her sharp eyes over every inch of Julia, taking her in.

Julia raised her eyebrows. Maddie had told her that Maria supported their relationship, but Julia also knew that Maria was probably a little wary of her, as was Vivienne of this new and sudden change in her life. Julia knew that Maria was concerned because of Julia's potential to hurt Maddie, but Julia would not back down from Maria or from anyone else for that matter. Julia wanted Maddie and she would do anything to keep her.

"The famous Maria," Julia returned easily with an intentional bit of snark in her tone.

Maria smiled at that and Maddie laughed, pushing Julia into the booth and sliding in beside her. Julia took a moment to look around the crowded restaurant.

"You two come in here a lot?" Julia asked.

Maddie smiled. "Can you tell? A lot of the customers are from the same island in the Azores our parents are from, or go to the same church or went to school with us. It's the old neighborhood, for both Maria and me."

Julia nodded, suddenly facing the stark realization that Maddie had a life here, a full and rich life of family, friends and a neighborhood that Julia was not a part of, and that Maddie would be reluctant to leave. The insight gave Julia pause and she tried to push back the kernel of worry that settled in her gut.

After they ordered breakfast, Maria sat back and looked at Julia. "How was Layna's work thing last night?"

"It was fun, more than fun actually." Julia looked at Maddie and smiled. "I had a great time."

"What are you two going to do today?" Maria asked.

Julia shrugged. "It's up to Maddie. I don't care what we do as long as I'm with her."

Maria snorted. "That's because you don't know what she does on Saturdays instead of going shopping with me."

"I could probably guess," Julia said.

"You think so?" Maddie asked with a smile and a bit of a challenge in her voice.

"An art museum?" Julia asked. "An obscure foreign film or curling up with a good book? Maybe a Buddhist class or yoga? Am I close?"

Maddie blushed as she smiled widely at Julia. "You are close. So...you'd come with me to meditation class...or to an art gallery?"

"Either or both, if you like," Julia said.

Maria laughed. "You better hang onto this one, Layna, I won't even do that shit with you."

Julia heard Maddie's delighted laughter and turned to look at her. Her eyes were warm and her dimples were out and Julia thought that she would do almost anything to keep seeing Maddie look this happy.

Meditation at the small Buddhist Center that Maddie frequented was more enjoyable than Julia would have guessed. It was a guided meditation so Julia just followed along while sitting beside Maddie on a padded mat. She spent a good amount of her meditation time looking at Maddie, who looked serene and beautiful with her eyes closed. Looking at Maddie made Julia feel warm and centered so she assumed that it would count as meditation. When Maddie finally opened her eyes and saw Julia,

247

she smiled as widely as Julia had ever seen her smile and that was more than worth it.

The art gallery was more Julia's speed and she wandered the space with Maddie, getting distracted by a section of black and white photographs while Maddie perused a series of small watercolors of the ocean nearby. Julia walked over and noticed the painting that Maddie was staring at, an ocean scene that reminded Julia of home.

"You like this one?" Julia asked.

"Yes," Maddie said nodding. "It makes me feel calm and happy."

Julia nodded. "Yes, I can see why. I like it, too."

Julia made a note of the artist and title before Maddie reached her hand out, taking Julia's arm and pulling her close. Every positive gesture from Maddie settled Julia's heart a bit more, but she knew that a relationship involving any kind of distance would not be easy. Julia realized that the more time she spent with Maddie, the more she wanted to be with her. She looked at Maddie and smiled, leaning in to kiss her but she suddenly stopped and pulled away, not wanting to make Maddie uncomfortable. She saw the surprise on Maddie's face.

"What was that?" Maddie asked.

Julia shook her head. "I don't know how comfortable you are with PDA's, especially...well, from me and especially here, so close to home."

Maddie's eyes searched her face for a moment. "If you want to kiss me, kiss me," she whispered.

248

Julia leaned in and brushed her lips across Maddie's once and then again before pressing gently for a few seconds while Maddie returned the kiss, pursing her lips to move against Julia's.

When Julia pulled away, Maddie blinked her eyes open and smiled. "I don't care where we are, Julia, I can't hide the way I feel about you...and I won't."

Julia was nearly overcome with a combination of joy and relief. "God, Maddie, I love you." Julia pulled her close. "Is Gabe working today?"

Maddie nodded. "Yeah, until six o'clock."

Julia licked her lips. "Can we go back to your place for a while?"

"Of course we can." Maddie looked at her closely. "Are you okay?"

Julia nodded. "I just need to be alone with you."

Maddie smiled. "Let's go."

Julia panted heavily, sprawled on her stomach with Maddie draped across her back. She felt Maddie rub her leg and kiss her ass cheek and she smiled, having no idea how Maddie had ended up in that position across her body. Julia was hot, sweaty and breathless, and as sexually satisfied as she could ever remember being. She also realized that she'd had a really nice day with Maddie, getting to know her a little better, becoming friends with her. Julia mulled this over for a few moments, comparing this to her failed relationships with men. She and Maddie had been becoming friends since their very first meeting, and had become lovers, as well. Her sex-addled brain could come to no conclusion other than she was continuing to fall more deeply in love with Maddie.

Julia sighed deeply, realizing that she would dread having to leave Maddie the next morning. She missed her daughters certainly, but she would miss Maddie terribly after spending such a lovely time with her. Each good-bye and subsequent separation was becoming increasingly more difficult, but things were still a little fragile between them and she did not want to verbalize these feelings and make Maddie feel pressured in any way.

Julia felt Maddie's finger run along the crease between the bottom of her ass and the top of her thigh, and she inhaled deeply as her nipples tightened beneath her and she felt the warmth of fresh arousal gush between her legs. She did not have the energy to move quite yet, but her body was already alert and wanting Maddie again. Maddie kissed her ass wetly and Julia shuddered.

Maddie slowly moved off her and rolled over to lie beside Julia, pulling a loose pillow under her head to look at her. Julia could not help but reach over with a soft hand and tugged gently on Maddie's pubic hair. Maddie closed her eyes and bucked her hips toward her.

Julia smiled. "Something you want, beautiful?"

"Can you even move?" Maddie asked with a smile, her eyes still closed.

Julia could move and she did, sliding over Maddie and gently spreading Maddie's thighs open, making Maddie's eyes pop open. Julia slid down and lowered her head near Maddie's center, making her buck lightly in anticipation. Julia ran the flat of her tongue up through her warm folds, holding Maddie's hips down firmly as Maddie's eyes once again closed. Julia lifted her head and waited until Maddie opened her eyes and looked down at her, meeting her gaze. Julia slowly licked Maddie's essence from her lips.

"I love you," Julia managed to whisper.

Julia watched Maddie swallow. "God, Jule, I love you."

Julia smiled as Maddie reached up over her head, gripping the edge of the mattress and digging her heels into the sheet as Julia's tongue licked every fold, every bit of impossibly soft, wet skin. Julia patiently and meticulously worshipped her with her mouth, savoring every scent, taste and sound attached to the experience. Julia never slowed or faltered in her attention, slowly building her arousal until Maddie was moaning and bucking. Julia pulled her closer, loving her until she was close to orgasm, and then loving her a little harder.

It was loud and violent and beautiful and Maddie screamed as she peaked, one hand clinging to Julia's head and the other pulling the sheet from the mattress. Julia held her closely and tenderly, absorbing the moment, the beauty, and the emotion as Maddie shuddered beneath her. Julia realized that she would do anything for this woman and anything to keep her.

"It's going to kill me to let you go home tomorrow," Maddie whispered.

"I know," Julia whispered back. "It's going to kill me to leave."

They both moved and shifted so that they could embrace and they intertwined themselves together, as closely as possible. Julia willed herself not to cry, but she felt Maddie stifle a sob against her shoulder and she let her own tears come. She pulled at a corner of the sheet to dry her eyes and they pulled apart to look at each other.

"No matter how hard this gets, I'm not going to let you go," Julia said.

Maddie smiled through her tears before she placed a firm kiss to Julia's mouth. "Do you promise?"

Julia nodded. "Cross my heart."

"Okay, so, maybe we should agree, right here and now, that there will be no letting go of each other."

"Agreed," Julia said. She wiped tears from Maddie's face. "Okay, enough of that. Let's make dinner plans. Should we go out? What does Gabe like?"

"He can spend another night at Enzo and Maria's."

Julia shook her head. "No. We're here, let's do something with him."

"You don't mind?"

"Of course not. Do you mind having Viv and Norie around?"

Maddie smiled. "No, not at all." Maddie kissed her softly. "I love you."

Julia sighed, her heart feeling as though it was slowly settling into place. "I love that you tell me that all the time." Julia pulled her close and held on for dear life.

The knock on the door while they were dressing seemed to startle Maddie and she hurriedly finished buttoning her oversized shirt as she walked toward the front of the apartment. Julia simply smiled as she followed behind at a leisurely pace. She saw Maddie shaking her head at a young man standing in the hallway with a package wrapped in brown paper.

"I didn't buy anything at the gallery," Maddie was saying.

"I did," Julia said.

"Oh, sorry." Maddie took the package. "Well then, thank you."

The young man left and Maddie turned to Julia. "I didn't realize you bought something." Maddie held the package to Julia. "Here."

Julia shook her head. "It's for you."

Maddie looked at the package in her hands. "For me? You bought me something?" Julia nodded. "When?"

"I didn't actually go to the ladies' room," Julia said quietly. Maddie looked stunned, staring at the object in her hand so Julia moved closer. "You can unwrap it."

Maddie looked at Julia and smiled. "You didn't have to...why did you...no one has ever..."

Maddie slowly moved to the sofa and sat down, pulling the string on the package and beginning to gently pull the brown paper and bubble wrap away. Julia sat beside her to watch, the look of wonder on Maddie's face as she slowly revealed the painting filling Julia with a quiet joy.

The remainder of the packaging fell away at her feet as she stared at the framed painting in her hands, looking awed as her gaze moved from the painting to Julia and back again before resting on Julia.

Julia smiled. "Do you like it?"

Maddie smiled back, her eyes filling with tears. "Like it? I love it. It's beautiful. I've never had anything like this. Why did you do this?"

"I know you love art, but I noticed you didn't have any. Why don't you have any?"

Maddie inhaled deeply and slowly. "I was raised to believe that spending money on things like art, music, film and theater were an unnecessary extravagance."

"But you don't believe that."

"No, of course not."

"Your mother?" Julia asked.

"Yes. She got angry with me when she stopped by once and noticed that I had fresh flowers in here. I lied and told her they were going to throw them out at work. It was easier to hide my love of so many things than to have to listen to her go on and on about it." Maddie looked at the painting and smiled. "But not anymore."

Julia smiled. "I want you to have beautiful things around you."

"I have you," Maddie whispered.

Julia stared at Maddie, thinking how sweet and loving she was, despite the misguided influences of her mother. "I want you to know what it can be to have all the art, music and dancing, and weird little art house films that you want."

"You remember I like those?"

"I remember everything you've told me including that love shouldn't be conditional."

Maddie wiped away a stray tear. "It shouldn't and it has never felt that way with you."

Julia smiled. "Because it never was and it never will be."

Maddie placed one call on hold while she answered another, the Excel worksheet on her computer screen left unattended once again. She tried to handle the phone request as someone handed her a folder that apparently needed her immediate attention. She dropped it in front of her and rubbed her forehead. The only good thing about this Monday morning was that she didn't have a lot of time to dwell on how much she missed Julia.

Having to say good-bye to Julia the previous afternoon had been as difficult as she had been afraid it was going to be. They had both cried and then laughed as they told each other there was nothing to cry about. They had spoken twice since then, but Maddie still missed her, knowing that she would not see Julia again until Friday at the earliest.

Maddie took care of the calls and leaned back in her chair, recalling their weekend, starting with the dancing, meeting Maria for lunch, the art gallery and hanging the painting that Julia had bought her in Maddie's bedroom. Maddie wanted it to be the last thing she saw at night and the first thing she saw in the morning.

Julia had insisted on letting Gabriel pick the dinner venue that evening and his favorite spot was a hipster taqueria with loud eclectic music. Dinner had been a meal of guacamole, chips, tacos and beer and the three of them had talked and laughed throughout the simple but delicious meal. Maddie had caught herself imagining that this was what her life could be all the time. She had been toying with a plan for some time now, too afraid to take the final steps to put it into motion. Watching Julia drink beer from a bottle as she and Gabriel laughed together was the moment that Maddie found the last bit of courage that she needed.

She picked up the folder still needing her attention and opened it, but she could not concentrate so she closed it. She looked at the spreadsheet on her computer screen and then looked up at the ceiling. Her mind whirled with a thousand different thoughts concerning the tasks in front of her, as well as her son, her family and what was best for her. Maddie was not accustomed to putting herself first or simply doing what she wanted to do. One thought rose to the top of all the turmoil of thoughts in her head and settled gently over the rest, quieting her mind and making her smile. That thought was Julia.

Julia paced slowly in the conference room she used as an office, gazing out the windows at the harbor with one of her own business cards in her hand. One of her realtors was at a desk up front talking quietly on the phone and she heard the bell of the front door jingle. She looked up to see Vivienne walk in and stop short.

"Are you alright?" Vivienne asked.

"Yeah, why?" Julia asked.

"You've not checked your e-mail or answered your phone," Vivienne said to her with an impatient tone.

Julia had been lost in thought for a good part of the morning and hadn't thought to check either. "Oh, I'm sorry. Really sorry, Vivie. Is there a problem?"

Vivienne smiled at her mother. "No. We got an offer on the Maple Street property."

"Oh, good, that's great. Can you take care of the follow-up on that?" Julia couldn't seem to concentrate on business and knew that Vivie could handle it.

"Sure, but I thought you'd be thrilled. We haven't had a bite on that listing."

"I am," Julia said, looking again at the business card in her hand. "Do you think we need a new logo? Maybe a slightly more modern look for us?"

Vivienne cocked her head. "Is there something wrong with the logo we have now?"

"I don't know. I was thinking about asking Maddie to take a look at it. She does graphic design and I saw some work she did for a friend of her brother's and it was good, really good. Maybe she could just give ours a slight update, if she'd be willing."

Vivienne laughed lightly. "Oh, I'm pretty sure Maddie would be willing to do absolutely anything for you."

Julia looked at her daughter. "You think so?"

"Don't you?"

Julia inhaled deeply and shrugged. "I'd really like to think so, but I don't know."

"Did something happen over the weekend?"

Julia shook her head. "Not really, except me realizing that I would like to be with Maddie...all the time and to the end of time." Julia turned away from her daughter, suddenly feeling ridiculous for saying something that foolishly romantic. Julia liked to think of herself as practical and pragmatic, and was never overly dramatic or emotional. When she turned back around she saw Vivienne staring at her, her eyebrows high and her mouth open.

"Are you serious?" Vivienne asked as she walked around the table to her mother and pushed her down into a chair, sitting beside her. "You've really lost your head over Maddie, haven't you?"

Julia shook her head and snorted. "Or maybe I've lost my mind."

Vivienne smiled widely. "Maybe you've lost your heart?"

"Maybe I have," Julia said quietly.

"Have you told Maddie how you feel?"

Julia looked at her daughter and blinked rapidly, trying to stave off the tears quickly forming. "She knows I'm in love with her but that's all I've said. I don't want to freak her out and I'm afraid to get my hopes up. You saw what it did to me after we stopped seeing each other."

Vivienne sighed. "Are you doing that thing you always tell me…about keeping expectations within reason?" Julia nodded as Vivienne rolled her eyes. "Well, stop it because it's stupid and it sucks."

"Vivienne!" Julia looked at her daughter in surprise.

"Sorry, but that's not an awfully positive way to look at life, Mom. I would much rather expect the best and so should you. You should expect that Maddie feels the same way you do and that everything will work out the way you want it to."

"Easier said than done."

"I know it is, but open your heart, Mom. I know it's been stomped on in the past. Whose hasn't? Just please stop expecting the worst. The worst has already happened to you…and you came out on the other side just fine."

Julia nodded. "I'm scared, Vivie."

"Of what?"

Julia sighed. "Deb said something to me after the first time Maddie and I were together and I hadn't heard from her. Deb said that it may have meant something to Maddie, but that it meant

258

everything to me. I don't want to be just something to her, Vivie, I want to be everything to her."

"Then be everything to her, Mom. Be here, be willing, be open. Let things happen, but expect the best. Try to relax and play it cool."

Julia decided that maybe Vivienne was right and that her attitude or maybe her outlook did need some improving. Julia would try to take a lesson from Maddie and start to look at things differently. Maddie always seemed to be positive and upbeat, even after being raised by a woman as rigid and controlling as her mother. Julia remembered what Maddie had told her about hesitating to have fresh flowers around her to avoid her mother's criticism.

Julia picked up her phone and smiled at her daughter. "I'm going to send Maddie some flowers."

Vivienne laughed softly. "Way to play it cool, Mom."

Julia laughed with her. "Shut up. I love you, Vivie. Thanks."

Maddie sat at the busy deli, waiting for Steven to join her for lunch. She stared at a list of pros and cons she had meticulously typed up and had been studying all morning. She was not staring at it to make a decision, but she was still surprised at how much longer the pros list was than the cons list. She put it down when Steven slid into the booth on the other side of her. He smiled widely as he noticed his favorite sandwich was waiting for him.

"Thank you, you're a doll. So, what's going on?"

"I need to talk to you about something," she said quietly.

"Are you going to tell me about the rest of your Friday night?" He lifted an eyebrow.

Maddie smiled. "Sure. After we left the Marriott we went to my place and had mind-blowing sex all night," Maddie said.

He choked on the sip of water he had just taken and stared at her, wide-eyed. Maddie was never this blunt or honest and he was obviously taken aback. "Holy shit, Mads. Okay. How was the rest of the weekend?"

"Life altering."

"How?"

"We had breakfast with Maria, so they could meet and I held her hand as we walked in, in front of a ton of people who know me and my family. It was such a little thing but..."

He smiled. "I understand."

"We went to an art gallery and she hesitated to kiss me. I told her if she wanted to kiss me she should."

"And did she?" He asked smiling.

Maddie could feel herself blushing. "Yes."

"You blush about the kiss, but not about the mind-blowing sex?" He teased.

Maddie shrugged. "Julia bought me a painting I admired at the art gallery. Just like that, I liked it and she bought it for me. Then we went home in the middle of the afternoon for more...mind-blowing sex." She smiled at Steven. "Gabe was supposed to stay at Maria and Enzo's, but she insisted that Gabe spend the evening with us. She took us out to that little Mexican place Gabe likes. We had tacos and beer for dinner and they were like two peas in a pod. That night there was more..."

"Mind-blowing sex?" He asked smiling.

"No. Slow, hot romantic sex. I cried when she left yesterday."

Steven's eyebrows had climbed high on his forehead and his mouth was open. "Mads, what's gotten into you?"

"I'm completely in love with Julia."

"Yes, I suspected as much."

"And I want to be with her all the time."

He smiled. "I'm happy for you. What are you going to do?"

"I've already done it, Steven, but I need you to tell me that I'm not completely crazy."

He leaned forward and took one of her hands in his. "What did you do?" he whispered.

She looked around nervously and leaned forward as she whispered quietly to him for a moment. When she finished he leaned back and smiled widely.

"Oh, Mads, you're not crazy at all."

After lunch, Steven walked Maddie back to her office, but he stopped short outside of the glass doors leading to the VP's reception area where her desk was located. He smiled widely.

"Well, I think you're not the only one getting serious."

Maddie turned to see what he was talking about and gasped. There was a large vase of red roses sitting on her desk. She walked through the doors and simply stared at the roses for a long moment, slightly overwhelmed by the romantic gesture. Steven nudged her gently.

"The card, Mads, read the card."

Maddie reached for the envelope and realized that her hands were shaking as she tore it open. The card was a depiction of a Georgia O'Keefe painting. She opened the card and gasped.

"Jesus, tell me what it says," Steven prodded.

"It's a quote by Georgia O'Keefe. 'I feel there is something unexplored about women that only a woman can explore.' Maddie, I could spend my life in the pleasure of exploring you."

"Holy shit, Mads, that woman is gone over you."

Maddie smiled. "Yeah, well I'm pretty gone over her, too."

Chapter 20

Maddie smiled as she watched Julia take a cleansing breath and slightly move away from her in the kitchen while she drank deeply from a glass of water. Maddie had only just arrived at Julia's and the sexual tension between them was almost overwhelming. Julia hadn't even waited for Maddie to come into the house, but had simply run out the front door to meet Maddie in the driveway. They had held each other in a close embrace, both of them hanging on to each other tightly.

"God, I've missed you," Maddie had finally whispered after long moments.

"Not as much as I've missed you," Julia had whispered back.

They had gone into the house and spent long minutes kissing and groping each other in the foyer, but Eleanor was due off the bus in a few minutes so they had gone into the kitchen for water as she and Maddie tried to cool their raging libidos.

Maddie noticed that Julia was smiling. "Why are you smiling?"

Julia's smile widened. "I'm so happy you're here and...and I like knowing that you want me as badly as I want you."

Maddie smiled as she rubbed her forehead, trying not to think of how good Julia felt in her arms. "Trust me, I want you more."

"I do...trust you." Julia cleared her throat. "And you won't have to wait as long as you think to have me."

"Waiting has never been the problem as long as you're the reward."

Julia nodded. "Good to know."

The front door opened. "Maddie, where are you?" Maddie heard Norie's excited voice and she smiled as she rushed into the hallway to greet Julia's daughter. Maddie picked her up and Norie giggled as she was swung around in Maddie's arms.

Maddie watched Julia pretend to pout and cross her arms. "Hi, Mom, I've missed you so much, too. My day at school was really interesting," Julia teased in a singsong voice.

Norie smiled at Maddie and then rolled her eyes at her mother as she headed straight for her, hugging her. "Hi Mom, I did miss you, but not as much as I missed Maddie because I've seen you every day. Is that okay?"

Julia smiled and nodded. "I can live with that."

"And the most interesting thing at school today was Kepler's laws of planetary motion."

Julia kissed the top of her daughter's head. "Thank you for sharing, although I have no idea what that is."

Eleanor turned to Maddie. "And we talked about *To Kill a Mockingbird* today and after class Ms. Vaz said she was impressed by my grasp of the adult perspective juxtaposed with Scout's childish ignorance. That was thanks to you, Maddie. So, thanks."

Maddie smiled as she looked at Julia. "I have never said the word juxtaposed in my entire life." She turned to Eleanor. "You're welcome."

Maddie and Eleanor were Facebook friends and they chatted online often. What Maddie had not admitted to anyone is that she had done some research on the Harper Lee novel so she could keep up with the bright girl. Maddie loved that she and Norie had their own relationship, that Julia allowed her that kind of access to her daughter.

"Go get your stuff together, sweetie, so you won't be late," Julia said to her daughter.

Maddie looked at Julia as Eleanor ran upstairs. "Where is she going?"

Julia moved close to Maddie, not touching her but leaning in, her lips close to Maddie's ear. "She's going to her father's in about an hour. I would never have let things get that far in the foyer if I had to wait the rest of the day to have you." Julia softly licked Maddie's earlobe.

Maddie groaned softly at Julia's teasing. "You will pay for that, Julia Sinclair."

Julia laughed softly. "I'm counting on it."

Julia crawled slowly over Maddie's naked form and nestled herself between Maddie's legs, Maddie's warm wetness spreading against her ribs and stomach. Julia inhaled a sharp breath as her mouth returned to the now stiff nipples as her hand brushed the inside of her thigh.

"How did you get this wet?" Julia whispered.

"That is a ridiculous question," Maddie panted out.

Julia stilled both her mouth and her hand. "It may be, but I want to hear your answer."

Maddie caressed Julia's jaw as their gazes met. "You may not know this, but simply being near you can make me wet. I'm this wet right now because you're sweet and sexy and all I can think about is you coming in my mouth."

Julia closed her eyes as her hips unconsciously arched against Maddie and she let out a small moan. "Oh?"

"Yes." Maddie pulled Julia up. "Put your breasts in my mouth."

Julia did not respond, but simply complied, moving slowly up over Maddie until her breasts were hanging within reach of Maddie's mouth. Julia watched as Maddie pulled one of her nipples into her mouth, sucking it firmly until she ran her teeth against it the way that made Julia a little bit crazy. Julia heard her own loud moan.

Julia had thought she had the upper hand with Maddie beneath her, wet and ready, but in just a few short moments, Julia was a panting, undulating, quivering mess and Maddie was firmly in control. She felt Maddie reach between her legs and tug playfully on the thin strip of curly hair covering her folds. Julia moaned again and Maddie tugged again and again, setting a purposeful rhythm. Julia bucked, seeking friction and Maddie released the nipple in her mouth with a playful pop.

"Come up here, baby."

Julia reached for the headboard and pulled herself up onto her knees and Maddie guided her directly over her mouth before she slowly pulled her down by the hips. They both moaned in pleasure as Julia's dripping center met Maddie's waiting mouth. Julia felt Maddie's grip tighten on her thighs as Maddie's tongue lapped through her folds ravenously, as if she was savoring the feel and the flavor of Julia against her tongue. Maddie suddenly started to lash at her clit firmly and steadily with her tongue and Julia tightened her grip on the headboard.

Julia shuddered and moaned, her nipples impossibly stiff, a light sheen of sweat forming on her lower back as Maddie made love to her with her mouth. Simply being loved and cared for by Maddie had always felt different, somehow better than being loved by anyone that had come before her, but Julia had never imagined, and still found it difficult to believe, that sex with Maddie would always be this good. It was sometimes prolonged and gentle, sometimes hurried and rough, but it was always glorious and wildly intense, and always beautifully loving.

Julia gripped the headboard with her left hand and placed her right against the wall behind the bed for leverage as Maddie's tongue lashed a perfect rhythm against her clit and the sensations became more intense with each passing second. Julia knew she would soon lose all control, but she did not care. Julia was no longer embarrassed at how loudly Maddie could make her moan, how quickly she could get her off and how easily she could make her cry when the orgasms were so intense that no other response would do. Julia shuddered deeply as she surrendered to the inevitable, as everything clenched beautifully as Maddie brought her to a screaming, blinding orgasm.

Maddie gently but firmly guided her down, cradling Julia against her as she tenderly soothed her, drying her tears as her breathing slowed almost to normal. Julia lay against Maddie's warm and naked form, feeling as loved as she had ever felt. She slid herself slightly to the side and slowly opened her eyes, finding Maddie watching her closely. Julia smiled as she looked down at the woman she loved.

She leaned over, placed a light kiss to Maddie's lips, and moaned as the unmistakable scent of her own sex on Maddie's mouth ignited the passion that was always lingering between them. Maddie's tongue filled her mouth and she pulled Maddie closer, their hips arching against each other. Julia kissed her deeply as she brought her hand to Maddie's center, her fingers slipping through the warm river that seemed to be pouring from her. Maddie's legs fell open in invitation and Julia slid two fingers easily inside her, pumping gently.

"Baby, please, don't be gentle...I need you," Maddie whispered.

The request filled Julia with equal parts of overwhelming love, desire and pure lust. Julia suddenly had to give Maddie exactly what she asked for. She moved over Maddie, pushing into her firmly as Maddie bent her legs back to accept the forceful thrusting. Julia caressed Maddie's cheek.

"Okay, love?"

Maddie moaned as she bucked harder. "Don't stop."

Julia smiled as Maddie threw her arms over her head and pushed against the headboard as Julia fucked her deeply and relentlessly. The sight of Maddie, open and wanting, the sounds of her fingers pushing inside her again and again, Maddie's deep panting, and the glorious scent of Maddie's arousal mixed with her own, all spurred her on. Julia increased her efforts as Maddie started to come, shouting out as her hips jerked wildly. Julia watched as Maddie fell over the edge, wondering if she had ever seen anything as beautiful as this woman in the throes of passion.

Maddie woke slowly, feeling the soft, warm and familiar feeling of Julia against her own naked skin. She could smell the lingering and now familiar scent of Julia's arousal blended with her own. She felt like she was home. Surprised at that unexpected thought, she opened her eyes and focused on Julia, sleeping nestled beside her. Maddie smiled as she watched her, still amazed at what simply looking at this woman could make her feel. It made no sense when she tried to articulate it in her head. Julia made her feel both serene and excited, both assured and uncertain, both in love and well loved. Maddie was certain she had never before experienced anything like being with Julia. Julia rubbed her nose against Maddie's shoulder in her sleep and Maddie smiled widely, any lingering doubts about her plans for the future erased by that sweet little gesture.

Maddie took a quick shower and dressed in the clothing that Julia had impatiently pulled from her body only hours before. She looked at Julia, still sleeping peacefully and left her sandals behind, heading downstairs in her bare feet. She peeked in Julia's refrigerator and found some avocados, deciding to make some guacamole to stave off her hunger before they decided on dinner. Maddie felt comfortable in Julia's home and that made her smile.

She was in the pantry, looking for tortilla chips when she heard water running upstairs. A few minutes later, Julia wandered into the kitchen, smiling as she walked toward Maddie and pulled her in close. Maddie loved that Julia was demonstrative and affectionate. She decided she loved everything about her and pulled her closer.

"You keep making all these fantasies come true," Julia whispered to her.

Maddie pulled away to look at her. "Oh? Which part was the fantasy? I'm pretty sure we've already done everything we just did upstairs."

Julia smiled widely. "Not that, although that was...holy shit wow. I was talking about finding you in my kitchen, cooking."

Maddie laughed. "It's nice to have someone else do the cooking, isn't it?"

"More than nice, so thank you."

"I've only had time to mix up some guacamole, but I think I could manage some quesadillas, too, if you're interested."

"That sounds great. I'm going to have some tequila. Can I pour you one?"

"Plain tequila?"

Julia laughed at the look on Maddie's face and then placed a soft kiss to her lips. "It's very good tequila, trust me."

Maddie returned the favor, this kiss lingering. "I do trust you."

They moved around in the kitchen together with Julia pointing out where Maddie could find spices as she helped by chopping fresh red peppers. Maddie found that she liked fine tequila after Julia had shaken it with ice and added some fresh orange slices, squeezing the juice from a couple into it.

When Julia stopped to hug Maddie for no apparent reason, it gave her the little boost of confidence and she inhaled deeply. "Jule?"

"Yeah?"

"Do you remember when I told you I needed to take care of some things, get Gabe situated?"

Julia became very still for a moment and then looked at her. "Of course I remember."

"And you asked if there was anything you could help me with?"

Julia nodded. "Yes. Is there something I can help you with?"

Maddie inhaled deeply. "Yes. I need help to find an apartment."

Julia blinked, looking confused. "In Boston?"

Maddie smiled. "No, here, in Fairhaven."

Julia just stared at her. "Here? You...I..." Julia simply stopped speaking, her mouth partially open in apparent surprise.

The reveal did not get the reaction that Maddie had expected from Julia. She quickly started to backtrack. "Do you do that? Rentals, I mean...if you don't...I can...go...."

Julia shook her head slightly. "Sorry, wait, I don't do that actually...not usually, but for you I will do anything. Let me make some calls and see which properties use a broker." Julia inhaled deeply and looked at Maddie. "You need an apartment? Here?" Maddie nodded slowly. "You're moving here?" Julia asked, seeming to need confirmation or assurance.

"Yes. Is that alright?" Maddie asked tentatively.

Julia's answering smile was wide and blinding as she moved toward Maddie, taking her in her arms. "Oh my God, more than alright. Are you kidding? When did this happen? How?"

Maddie pulled away to look at Julia. "I've been trying to make this happen for a while, even before we...got back together. I started looking for a job in the area, just to see what was available."

"That's why you were in New Bedford that first time?"

"Yes. I didn't want to say anything, in case I couldn't find anything and because you and I, well, I didn't think it really mattered to you at that time."

"You're wrong. It would have mattered because you have always mattered. So, you found something?"

Maddie thought about the numerous positions she had submitted her resume for, the four job interviews she had eventually gone on, how she had felt almost no nerves during the process, just confidence in her abilities. She knew that was due, in large part, to believing the things that Julia regularly told her.

"Yes, I turned down the first offer because I thought I was worth more money than they were offering. The entire time, I kept thinking about something someone once told me about confidence, that it's simply having enough of an attitude to go after what you want," Maddie said, repeating Julia's words back to her. "And I started to believe it because you kept telling me I was impressive...and accomplished and smart."

"You are all that and so much more." Julia kissed her lightly. "So, Gabe must be pretty excited that you're moving here to be closer to him."

Maddie smiled. "Let me be clear. I'm not moving here for Gabe. I'm moving here to be with you."

Chapter 21

Julia sipped her lemon drop, as happy as she could ever remember being. "Guess who's moving to Fairhaven?" She threw out to Vivienne and Deb.

"Gloria Steinem?" Vivienne guessed one of her mother's idols, as she sipped her own wine.

"No. Better than that."

"Who's better than Gloria Steinem to you? Oh, oh, I know, Ashley Judd."

"Vivienne, please get serious."

Deb had been watching her carefully, ignoring the draft beer in front of her. "Holy shit, Julia. Get out? She's moving here? For you?" Deb's voice was unusually high, her eyebrows higher.

Julia smiled wider and nodded. "Yes, she wanted to be clear it was for me, not for her son."

"Maddie? Is moving here?" If possible, Vivienne's voice was even higher. "This is serious. Deb, isn't this serious?"

Deb nodded. "More than serious. She's leaving her job, where she's worked for years, she's leaving the home where she's raised her son, she's leaving her friends, her support system. Think about it. She was completely in the closet when she met you. She came out, for you. She told her son, her family, for you. Even after the rift this caused with her mother, she's never faltered in her commitment to you."

Julia nodded, the truth of that statement washing over her. "I know Deb, I do."

"What are your thoughts about all this?"

Julia ran her fingers through her hair. "All over the place, truth be told, but if you had asked me before I met Maddie, what would make me happy I would've said 'having my health and my girls with me.' After the divorce and getting sick, I was content to just have those things." Vivienne reached for her mother's hand and they smiled at each other.

"And now?" Deb asked.

"Now? All I want is those things and Maddie. And you know I wasn't looking for anyone or anything, but Maddie hit me like a ton of bricks, in a good way and then in a bad way. I was so hurt, but I missed her so much...every minute. I've never been so hurt."

Deb nodded. "We know that, hon, we were here, but do you think you're holding back, just a little, because you're afraid to get hurt again? It's perfectly understandable if you are."

Julia nodded. "Sure, maybe a little." Julia rubbed her face. "Shit, I am. When she told me she was moving here, I froze. I realized later that I just didn't want to get my hopes up."

"Well, get your hopes up," Deb said with a snort. "She's changing her entire life for you."

"Mom, honestly, stop with the 'glass half-empty' attitude."

Julia mock glared at her daughter. "I thought you'd tell me I was being prickly."

"Okay, you're being prickly with a 'glass half-empty' attitude."

"Well, it's scary," Julia said, not liking how whiny she actually sounded to her own ears.

Vivienne smiled at her mother. "If you're scared, how do you think Maddie feels? She's taking a big chance here, Mom."

Deb nodded. "She's right. This is a grand gesture, Julia."

"I know."

"Does the gesture simply mean something to you, Julia, or does it mean...?" Deb paused.

"Everything. It means everything." Julia smiled at Deb, the friend who had seen her through the worst scare of her life and the friend who still supported her, pushed her and made her think. "It means everything and Maddie means everything."

"Does Maddie know how much this means to you?"

"No, and I need to find a way to tell her...my own grand gesture. Maddie is taking a giant leap of faith here and I need to take one, too."

Vivienne raised her glass to her mother. "Glass half-full, Mom."

Deb and Julia matched her gesture. "Glass half-full," Deb agreed.

Julia smiled widely. "Glass half-full." Julia sipped her cocktail then looked at Vivienne and Deb. "I'm going to run something by the both of you and then you can tell me if you think I'm crazy."

277

Julia wanted to be as professional as possible so she brought Maddie into the office to show her the three rentals she had deemed good enough for Maddie that fell into her price range and met her needs. Julia explained her choices as they perused the photos on Julia's laptop.

"The first two are located in New Bedford. One is in a private home on a quiet street with off-street parking and the second one is in a complex converted from an old mill into apartments. The converted mill is larger, but more expensive. The third one is in Fairhaven in a historic home that's been converted into apartments. We can look at all of them or none of them. I thought you'd like these best."

Maddie simply nodded as she scrolled through photos as Julia looked on, trying not to smell Maddie's hair or snuggle into her neck. Maddie had surprised her by arriving earlier than she had planned, enabling them to spend the previous night together and Julia could not stop thinking about how nice it had been to hold Maddie all night after they had made love sweetly.

"What are you thinking about?" Maddie's whispered and Julia realized that Maddie was watching her carefully.

Julia slid her arm onto the conference room table and rested her head against her hand. "How much I love you. How wonderful last night was. How happy I am right now."

Maddie smiled widely. "Wow, that's really nice to hear."

"So...which apartment would you like to see first?"

"The one closest to you."

Julia smiled. "As you wish."

Maddie decided she wanted to see two out of three apartments that Julia had picked out and after looking at both, it was obvious that Maddie appreciated the choices Julia had made, each place having oversized windows, old-fashioned woodwork and hardwood floors.

Julia cleared her throat. "So there is another place that wasn't on the list that I think maybe we should take a look at."

Maddie smiled. "Okay. Sure."

Julia drove back to her own home and pulled into the driveway.

"Did you forget something?" Maddie asked.

Julia simply smiled. "Not exactly. Come in with me." Julia waited for Maddie to exit the car and took her hand as she escorted her inside the house. "This is the place not on the list and I wanted to show you this house because the property is a little unique."

Maddie smiled. "Julia, this is your house."

"Yes. Yes, it is," Julia said.

"Why are you showing me your house?"

"Because I think you should seriously consider it as a housing option as it offers amenities the other properties we just looked at do not, including me...and my daughters."

"Julia..." Maddie's expression was a combination of a frown and a smile and Julia stepped forward to take her hands.

"Sweetie, when you told me you were moving to Fairhaven, I was stunned, but so incredibly happy and it took me a few days to realize that I hadn't told you that, so I want you to know that it means the world to me that you're moving here...for us and I really want you to consider living here."

Maddie smiled. "You're asking me to move in with you?"

"I'm asking you...and Gabe, as well because he'll have his own room, whenever he wants to stay here, so, yes, I'm asking you to move in with me and with Norie, well and Viv, too, really."

"This is a lot to think about."

Julia shook her head. "It isn't, not really."

"How can you say that?"

"Would you...hear me out?"

Maddie nodded. "Always."

"Thank you." Julia inhaled deeply. "After the first time we were together and I hadn't heard from you, I didn't know what to think or do. So, I called Deb and told her about you. How taken I was with you, how incredible it had been to be with you...and how I'd not heard from you. Deb pointed out that our encounter, as incredible as it was, may not have meant to you what it meant to me. She said it probably meant something to you, but it was obvious that it meant...everything to me...and it did." Julia cupped her face gently. "Maddie, I want you to know that you mean everything to me. Absolutely everything...and you have from the beginning."

Maddie inhaled so deeply she shuddered, but her gaze stayed on Julia's. "You mean everything to me."

"You already have my heart and...already share my life. Come and live with me and share my home, too."

Maddie's smile was wide. "God, Julia, I love you...beyond anything I have imagined."

"I love you the same way. That's a yes, right?" Julia asked tentatively, hoping beyond hope that Maddie wanted to throw her lot in with Julia because that was exactly what Julia wanted to do with Maddie.

Maddie's smile got impossibly wider. "That's a yes."

Chapter 22

Julia had not told her anything about her anniversary surprise and she had not asked. Maddie knew by now that Julia would plan something that she would enjoy so Maddie had simply smiled when they had pulled into the parking garage of the elegant Boston hotel where they had first met and where they had spent their first night together. Maddie had discovered that Julia was as romantic as she was loving and generous.

When Julia led them to the same suite she had stayed in well over a year ago now, Maddie's face was beginning to hurt because she was smiling so widely. They quickly shed their bags and purses and stood facing each other in the small seating area of the suite. A bottle of white wine was already chilling and two glasses sat on the table in front of the same love seat. Maddie slowly unbuttoned the buttons of the blouse she wore, remembering that's what she did that night, to let Julia know that she wanted her, that she was going to spend the night with her.

Maddie raised one eyebrow as Julia slowly walked toward her, holding a cuff toward Maddie so she could remove the feminine cuff link there. Maddie smiled, as she realized how perfectly Julia had recreated the scene for them. "Feeling nostalgic?"

Julia smiled. "Yes. The first time we made love was right here, like this, and I want you as badly now as I did then."

Maddie laughed lightly as she removed the cufflinks and continued to unbutton her blouse as Julia opened her own, the warm meeting of skin on skin making them both shiver. "Oh, I think you wanted me a little more desperately that night."

Julia laughed lightly as she embraced Maddie before she bent her head to pull down the cup of her bra and take one of her nipples into her mouth, sucking gently. She pulled away with a pop and brought her hand between Maddie's legs. "Don't be too sure about that. I'm pretty desperate for you right now."

Maddie moaned at that exquisite sensation. "God, baby, you feel so good."

Julia inhaled deeply and stepped back, cupping Maddie's face before reaching to open the wine. "I'm going to pour us some wine. Could you keep going...?" Julia pointed at Maddie's blouse, "and wait for me...in bed?"

Maddie swallowed. Julia's raspy voice, hot blue gaze and the anticipation of what was to come making her heart race. "Hurry, baby."

Julia smiled at her. "Oh, I will."

Maddie inhaled deeply, letting all the feelings and emotions she had for this woman to wash over her in a warm wave of love as she went into the bedroom.

Julia poured two generous glasses of wine, her hands trembling slightly, and she smiled, surprised that the thought of Maddie waiting for her could still make her hands shake. She quickly stripped down to her bra and the garter and stockings she had specifically worn for this occasion. She had been wearing some that first night and they still drove Maddie wild every time she donned them for her.

Julia walked into the bedroom and stopped at the beautiful sight before her. Maddie was lying across the bed, pillows stacked behind her, as naked as the day she was born. She was gently writing in obvious arousal as her feet slid up and down the bedspread restlessly. When she saw Julia, she stopped for a moment to run her gaze over every inch of her before she started to move again.

Julia thanked God, fate, the universe and whatever other deity came to mind for this gorgeous creature who loved her as she placed the wine glasses down carefully on the bedside table. There was no need for words as she slid onto the bed and covered Maddie's gorgeous form with her own, the first contact of warm skin both familiar and exciting. She sucked on one of Maddie's nipples for a moment before she moved her hand slowly down Maddie's abdomen.

She pulled her mouth away to be able to watch her own fingers slide into Maddie gently, making Maddie gasp and Julia paused, simply reveling in the moment. As much as Julia wanted to recreate their first time together, she quickly realized that this wasn't anything like their first time together. Julia was no longer hesitant to state her desires or to simply take what she wanted. She was secure in the knowledge that Maddie not only wanted her as much as she wanted Maddie, but that she loved her as much, as well.

Julia was no longer uncertain that she could satisfy Maddie's every need, but was just as certain that Maddie knew exactly what she needed, even when she didn't know it herself. This time, when Maddie groaned and moved her hips to meet every loving thrust, there wasn't that completely overwhelming excitement, but there was the deep exciting pleasure in knowing what was coming, a lovely familiar anticipation.

Julia moved to kiss Maddie, their hot wet mouths fusing, their tongues dueling as she slid inside of Maddie again and again. The exquisite feeling of power and love was still there, but this time, she knew exactly what to do and what Maddie needed. Maddie moaned into Julia's mouth, her hips jerking sharply onto Julia's fingers as Julia pushed into her. This time, when she felt and heard the unmistakable signs of Maddie's impending orgasm, it wasn't relief that she felt, but love and joy that she could make Maddie always feel this good and this loved. Watching Maddie orgasm never got old and she enjoyed it now as much as she had enjoyed it the very first time, still watching with a sense of wonder as Maddie shook and shuddered and moaned.

After long moments, when Maddie had recovered enough to roll her over slowly, her thigh pressed deliciously and teasingly against Julia's clit. She had admitted to Julia that during that first night, she had reveled in the feel of Julia's wetness leaking all over her thigh and she still loved to feel it. When Julia felt Maddie snake her hand down to her center, she slowed her movements and spread her legs wide, allowing Maddie easier access to where she desperately needed her, as she always had, since that very first time.

Julia inhaled sharply as Maddie slowly glided her fingers through her hot wet folds, finding her hard and swollen clit unerringly. Julia could not believe how good it felt, Maddie's fingers circling her clit gently, then firmly, as if she knew exactly what Julia needed, as she had always known.

Unlike their first time together, Julia wasn't the least bit nervous about her body or Maddie's reaction to it. Maddie leaned forward, rubbing her breasts and stomach against Julia and taking a nipple into her mouth. Julia felt good and secure about how much Maddie wanted to touch her, how much she adored her body, how much Maddie loved her.

When Maddie's mouth moved down her torso to take over for her fingers and started to do exquisite, magical things to her, she relaxed and gave herself over to the sensations, to the love, to the woman in command of her.

"So delicious," she heard Maddie murmur.

Maddie's mouth was already creating an exquisite stirring when her fingers pushed into her firmly, and Julia felt the inevitable climb to heaven, to nirvana, to the pleasant oblivion that being with Maddie always provided.

The first time together, it had been so good, so exciting and so overwhelming in its newness and its intensity. This time, it was so good, so exciting and so overwhelming in its familiarity, its deep security and in its incredible depth of love. It was both familiar and exciting, both soothing and erotic. It was more than something. It was absolutely everything.

If you enjoyed the story, please consider taking a moment to leave a review. Thank you kindly.
Lily

Made in the USA
Middletown, DE
10 January 2020